CONTENTS

BOOK ONE OF
DARKNESS RISES

darkness come alive

PAUL STEPHENSON

HOLLOW STONE

For Dad, who I miss every day.

I

Blood Roses

The city passed by in a blur, bathed in stabs of blue light that overwhelmed the lamplight, pulses that came round every two seconds. Her seat jostled with every patch of cobbled road. Outside, faces stared up as they passed, all with the same look. *Thank God that's not for me,* their faces said, but there was something underneath that, something new. In the years since the world returned to some kind of normal, she saw a new expression on the faces of the people they passed. *Why? Aren't we done with your kind?*

Beside her, Adrian blathered on. She wasn't listening. Too busy thinking about the note. Folded. Pressed to her breast in the pocket of her green uniform. The same place it had been for the last five shifts. Would tonight finally be the night she got the courage to take it out, to hand it over?

The blathering stopped with an abrupt silence that meant she'd missed some kind of required interaction.

'Hmm?' she asked, turning her gaze from the passing streets.

'Earth to Lucy,' Adrian said, smiling. 'Come in, Lucy.'

Lucy's cheeks flushed. 'Sorry,' she said. 'I'm being rude, aren't I?'

'Little bit,' Adrian said, but with enough of a smile in his voice that she knew he wasn't angry. 'What's up, Luce? You've been weird all week.'

'Sorry,' she said again, but offered nothing more.

The truth was, she couldn't articulate the chaos in her mind in the five minutes before they got to their next job. How do you tell the partner you've worked with for the past five years that you've given up on the only thing you've ever wanted to be? After everything they'd been through in the past few years?

'Well, if you need to talk,' Adrian said, but any smile in his voice was ebbing away.

'What have we got?' she asked, leaning forward to peer at the knackered screen to see where they were going.

'Stumbling Juggler pub on Micklegate. Two males, one head wound from a possible stabbing, one with minor injuries.'

She sighed. 'Great. First call and we're already on the Micklegate run. This is going to be a shit shift.'

'That's the spirit,' Adrian said with a chuckle.

'Sorry,' she said again. 'I'll try to cheer up.'

'Oh, yeah, you're usually such a positive person.'

'Shut up,' she said, punching him on the arm.

She went back to looking at the streets of York as they buzzed through them. The city had not long replaced its old yellow bulbs with ugly LED lights; Lucy still couldn't adjust to the way this once beautiful city looked under them — as though the warmth and history of the place had been stretched out on a gurney.

Not that York was a picture-postcard; it wore the bustle and chaos that lived at its heart for centuries like a tattered old cardigan. As they wound through the tight streets, their blues illuminated ancient walls with homeless sleeping against them, pubs with heritage going back hundreds of years with young drunks arguing outside, and ornate bridges clogged with traffic too heavy for roads built by Romans.

Adrian weaved them through the busy centre of town, ignoring the honks of irate drivers too wrapped up in their own problems to care about their flashing lights, making sure to avoid crashing into the drunken revellers wandering like dazed creatures into traffic.

Home to at least a dozen out-of-town stag and hen do's every weekend of the year, the Micklegate run was as close to hell as you'd likely find in this otherwise charming city. Women in dresses two sizes too small stumbled in and out of the road while men in identikit shirts leered after them, pint in hand. She eased through the traffic. The Stumbling Juggler public house sat halfway up the hill, with two police cars in attendance outside its doors already. Whatever violence had flared was gone, save for one woman wailing and trying to pull away from the police officer trying to calm her down. Two men sat metres apart on the kerb, each covered in blood. One held something red to his head, while the other looked woozy, swaying to some unheard rhythm.

Parking up, Lucy and Adrian grabbed their go bags and stepped out.

'Evening,' Lucy said to one officer, a tall man with the thousand-yard-stare of someone done with everyone else's bullshit. The howls of the woman arguing with his colleague a few feet behind him explained that one. 'What's happened here?'

'Drunks,' the officer replied, as though that encapsulated everything Lucy needed to know.

'These two gentlemen our injured?' Lucy asked, pulling on a pair of green disposable gloves. Neither man had looked up from the ground at their arrival.

'One broken nose, where the other gentleman punched him. He returned the favour with a glass to the side of head.' If there'd been compassion in the officer's voice, it left a long time before she got there.

She took the one holding his head, while Adrian crouched down in front of the broken nose.

'Hi there,' Lucy said, and the man gave a start. He looked up. His eyes were bloodshot, and tears rolled down his face. She gave him her widest smile, working extra hard to summon it from within herself. 'I'm Lucy. What's your name?'

'Nigel.'

'Okay, Nigel, can you tell me what's happened here?'

'I'm getting married tomorrow. Abigail is gonna kill me.'

Lucy was crap with accents, but there was no mistaking thick Geordie. He had a balled up bar towel held to his head, grimy and brown. Blood dripped underneath it, and Lucy wondered how hygienic it was to hold a city-centre bar towel to an open wound.

'Let's take a look, shall we?'

He pulled the towel away, revealing a large gash in his bald head.

'Okay, well, that's going to need stitches.'

'Fuck's sake, Gary,' he said, glancing over to where the other man still swayed back and forth while Adrian examined him.

'You know him?' Lucy asked, pulling wipes and a fresh gauze from her bag, pulling the bar towel away and cleaning the wound.

Nigel winced. 'He's the best man.'

'Well, it'll give him something for the speech, eh?'

Nigel gave a hollow little laugh. 'Is he going to be okay? I hit him bloody hard.'

'Let's worry about you for the moment. My friend is going to look after yours. It's up to you. I can patch this up for you here, and you won't need to go to hospital. But it won't be the prettiest. If we take you in, they can do a much better job, and hopefully have you looking alright for the wedding photos, okay?'

He nodded.

She put the stitches back in her bag.

Adrian's swaying patient stood abruptly, revealing blood smeared over his face and covering his salmon shirt. 'I'm alright,' he barked at Adrian. 'Just fuck off, mate.'

'Unit fifteen,' Lucy's radio squawked once more. 'Come in.'

'Unit fifteen,' Lucy replied.

'What's your status?'

'Two males with minor wounds. One head wound could do with coming in.'

'Scratch that,' the woman at dispatch replied. 'You've got a divert.'

Adrian heard it at the same time as Lucy — divert meant a serious call, life-threatening. Something more in need of attention than this man's suitability for his bride.

'Go ahead,' Lucy said.

'Serious neck trauma. Ongoing situation.'

Lucy looked back at the two men. They weren't in danger, but she hated to leave a job unfinished. 'Can you send anyone else?'

'Negative. We're swamped.'

'Received.' She turned to Adrian. 'We've got to go.'

'What about my head?' Nigel asked.

'I've given you a temporary fix. I advise you and your friend to get a taxi to A&E.' She turned her attention to his swaying friend. 'Oi!'

The friend swayed in her direction. 'What, man?'

'You're best man, yeah?'

'Yeah.'

'Best man duties are to get him to hospital without hitting him again. You hear?'

'Aye, marra.'

Lucy packed her equipment away. One of the pub's security guards ambled over. 'You're not leaving them here, are you?'

'Another call, sorry. Any issues, take it up with the officers over there.'

Even as Lucy pointed toward the police car, the two police officers climbed back in and pulled away without so much as a word.

'Great,' the security guard said sarcastically. 'So helpful.'

Even as Lucy climbed back into the driver's seat, the security guard busied himself trying to convince the two bloodied men they couldn't reenter the pub.

'What a pair of dicks,' Adrian said, putting his own seatbelt on. 'Where are we going?'

Lucy flicked the blue lights on, peeled off her disposable gloves, and checked her screen. 'Holgate.'

They pulled away, committing an illegal u-turn on the busy street, then moving through one junction after another until pubs gave way to new-build apartment blocks jostling alongside hardy Victorian townhouses. The foot traffic fell away to nothing.

Lucy switched off the blues as she pulled up to the address. Nobody rushed from the doorway, which wasn't the best of signs. The door stood open to darkness within.

'Grab a defibrillator and a suture kit,' she said, opening her door. She picked up her own bag and stepped down onto the street. Adrian ran round the back and rummaged around as she stared up at the austere building. It was old, with an anonymous dusty emptiness that somehow made the eye glaze over it.

Adrian joined her, weighed down with two heavy shoulder bags. She scrabbled around in her own bag and fished out a tiny pen light before heading inside.

'Hello,' she called out. 'Paramedics, coming in.'

The smell hit the back of her throat first, acrid and coppery. Blood. Lots of it, and not all of it fresh. Her stomach churned. Her hand went instinctively to her radio to summon police back-up, but she stopped herself. The whole place looked rotten, like the drug dens you saw in American crime movies. The walls were yellow, almost moist. No point in calling the police. The chances were more than even they were about to disturb a lot of high addicts, a scenario not usually improved by the presence of their brethren in blue.

'Christ,' Adrian said, 'stinks like an abattoir.'

The pen light barely helped; she turned it off, giving herself a moment to adjust to the light. The murk resolved into four walls. They were in a hallway, stairs leading up ahead. Two doors, one ahead, one to their left. The doors were warped and diseased looking, like they were holding back oceans of fetid rank and might burst their seams at any moment. Dark wooden floor — mahogany, perhaps — but as warped and spoiled as everything else.

'Hello?' she called again, her voice sounding a lot smaller.

'Did we get a flat number?' Adrian asked.

'No.'

'Up here,' a voice called, deep, flat, and calm. It did nothing to calm the voice of instinct in her head, yelling at her to turn tail. She again considered calling the police, but knew there was no way they could wait for the police before checking on their patient.

They started up the stairs. At the top, they saw their patient — a body laid out in a room off the landing. Lucy's nerves evaporated as she clicked into crisis mode. She ran up the last few stairs, Adrian behind, puffing under the weight of heavy bags.

'In here,' the voice said, more urgent than before, but not much more. Lucy entered the room, pausing as the carnage inside revealed itself.

The room was empty, save for the two bodies laid out inside. One dead, one almost. Splashes of red adorned the walls. A man kneeled by the head of the dying man, hand pressed to the other's neck.

'Please,' the man said, teeth gleaming white against the blood smeared across his mouth. 'Help him.'

2

GOUGE AWAY

Willing herself to block everything else out, Lucy knelt by the dying man. He stared up at her with eyes full of panic at the surety of his own imminent death. The other man, the huge one, the... other... he stayed by the dying man's head, holding a cloth to the wound.

As Lucy looked into the dying man's eyes, she felt a pull of recognition, but batted it away. It didn't matter, and she'd seen too many faces in this job to go through the catalogue.

Adrian went to the third body, kneeling down into a pool of blood leaking from its chest.

'Not that one,' the man by Lucy said.

Adrian ignored him, checking for a pulse on the man on the ground.

Lucy smiled at her patient, trying not to think about the blood soaking through the green of her uniform at the knees. 'Can you hear me?' she asked.

The patient nodded; the movement set off a cough of bloody foam.

'Okay, don't move.' She looked up at the kneeling man. 'I need you to take it away for a second, alright?'

The patient stared up in blank-eyed horror at the prospect. The kneeling man eased his bloody palm away, revealing a wound which pooled red within seconds. She tried to ignore the fact the laceration had two distinct entry points.

'I've got a laceration of the jugular here, Adrian. It's a nick. Can you get me a suture?'

'Sure. This one's dead,' Adrian said of the third body, the one whose gaping chest wound made that fairly apparent. He crossed back to Lucy and rummaged in his bag. He looked warily at the kneeling man. 'What can you tell us about what happened?'

The man kneeling over the patient ignored the question. 'Save him,' he commanded Lucy.

'I'm going to do my best. It would help if you answered my colleague's question.'

The man paused.

Lucy placed a pad against the wound to stop the flow and looked up, waiting for him to answer.

He looked tired. 'A bite,' he said, looking at the floor. 'The other man, he bit him, drained him. Made him drink... he will need a transfusion. He cannot die.'

'Not my call,' Lucy said, fixing Adrian with wide eyes as he settled opposite her, taking the pad from the other man, easing him out of the way.

'He will need a transfusion,' the man said again. 'O neg.'

'Friend of yours?' Lucy asked.

'Yes.'

'What's your friend's name?'

'Cain.'

The twinge of recognition from a moment earlier resolved itself, and she looked back at the man staring up at her with blind panic. 'Cain?'

'Lucy,' the dying man whispered back.

She offered him a weak smile and got to work. Her hands worked quickly, trying to stem the flow. The nick wasn't too severe, but a slight movement could tear the artery, spilling what blood remained in his body so fast the heart would shut down. Better he die here because she tried to save him than he died halfway down the stairs.

'I need to call this in,' Adrian said in a low voice.

'I know,' Lucy replied. Adrian was talking about the police.

The kneeling man stood, moving backward.

Adrian leaned in, his voice little more than a whisper. 'You should see the other guy. Chest wound, looks like…'

Neither of them said it, but the look between them said it all. They'd walked into a horror movie, and there was a decent chance they'd not make it to the end credits.

Adrian looked up and got to his feet. 'What the fuck?' he said. 'Where did he go?'

'What's happening?' Lucy asked. She couldn't look up from what she was doing for more than a second, holding a man's life in her fingers as she applied a lateral suture to the tattered artery of her patient.

'He's gone.'

'The big guy?'

'Both of them. Dead one, too.'

She chanced a look up. They were alone in the room with the dying patient.

'You know him?' Adrian asked, motioning to the patient as he joined Lucy once more.

'Long time ago,' she replied, her brain too full of the task at hand to dredge up old memories. She placed the gauze back over the wound. A quick patch job — it needed a surgeon. He at least had a hope of getting to the hospital.

'One thing at a time,' she said. 'Call it in from the road. Help me get him up.'

'He needs a stretcher,' Adrian said. Lucy's stomach lurched at the thought of being left alone in this place while Adrian ran for the stretcher.

'I can walk,' Cain said, his voice a burble of blood.

They helped him to his feet and walked him slowly back to the ambulance. The walk down the fetid staircase seemed to stretch into forever; drawn-out seconds in which Lucy expected to be launched upon by some fresh horror with each tentative step.

She took a deep breath of fresh air as soon as they were outside, wanting to purge her lungs of the spoiled air of that place. Slowly, they walked Cain to the ambulance.

Adrian pulled open the back doors. Their patient stepped up gingerly before laying down on a stretcher with a wince. Lucy lifted the back up so his neck was elevated and looked at him. Tall, middle-aged, vaguely handsome if you ignored his pallid skin and the bandage attached to his neck. His cotton shirt was tacky with blood.

'Cain?' she said.

He looked at her and tried a smile. She smiled back. His was a face she'd never thought she'd see again, but it wasn't altogether unpleasant to find before her. At the same time, he looked an entirely different person than the one she'd known. She imagined she looked as different to him. All those years of distance had forged them into entirely new people.

'We're going to take you to the hospital, okay?' she said.

'What?' he said, sitting up. 'No. No hospital. I can't...'

Whatever he couldn't do was unclear. He fell back onto the gurney like a cut puppet.

'Shit,' Lucy said. 'Blue lights.'

Adrian closed the doors and ran round to the front, gunning the engine and pulling away from the house with a squeal of overworked tyres.

Lucy checked Cain's pulse. Weak, but still there. He'd better hang on, she thought, because she had a hell of a lot of questions.

3

FADE INTO YOU

Lucy felt useless as she checked Cain's vitals. There wasn't much more she could do, save ripping away all her previous work and starting again, but she didn't think it was the neck that was the problem — the bandage was in place, not reddening, and his pulse was steady.

She listened from the back to Adrian on the radio to central dispatch to call in the events back at the house.

'Understood, unit fifteen,' the voice on the other end said. 'But we have a backlog of incidents. We'll send a car as soon as we can.'

Adrian pushed the button. 'Just get someone over there,' he said, meeting kind with kind on the sarcasm front, 'or explain to the DCI why you thought they might not be interested in someone being murdered and the body removed, or that a second victim is dying in my bus as we speak.' He threw his receiver on the empty seat next to him. 'Fucking cretin,' he added.

A sharp turn signalled that they'd turned into the A&E ambulance bay. Lucy realised her hand had gone into Cain's, was gripping onto it.

'We're here,' she said to his unconscious body.

Adrian turned off the engine and jumped down from the driver's seat to open the back doors. Two doctors walked out from the hospital to greet them with insufficient urgency for Lucy's liking. Adrian already had the ramp activated, so Lucy wheeled the bed with Cain's still body on it into place and jumped down.

She started as soon as they were in earshot.

'Male, late forties, laceration to the throat. Torn artery. I patched as much as I can,' she said, trusting the doctors were taking it in. 'He was lucid for a moment, but he lost consciousness. BP is eighty over forty, temperature one oh three and climbing. I…' she paused, trying to form the words. 'I don't know, guys. It's a fucking weird one.'

'This all his blood?' the doctor asked, looking over the state of his patient.

'Unknown. Possibly not. His name's Cain.'

'You know him?'

The man on the stretcher's eyes opened in a wild stare, and his body convulsed.

'Intubate,' the doctor said. 'Get me 10 cc's…' but Lucy didn't hear what they were going to give the man. He was already being wheeled away toward the ER, leaving Lucy and Adrian standing in the entrance.

A little man appeared out of nowhere with paperwork to sign releasing the patient. Adrian checked it over while Lucy stared down the corridor.

'We should change before we head back out,' Adrian said, as the little man scuttled off with the forms.

Lucy looked down at herself. Red stains mottled most of her uniform, covering her trousers. Patients tended not to react well to paramedics looking like they'd come straight from the abattoir. Both kept spare uniforms in the ambulance, and they wordlessly trudged inside and pulled the doors closed behind them. She stripped off to her underwear, thankful Adrian wouldn't be remotely interested in sneaking a peek, trying not to laugh at the Pokemon underwear it turned out he wore under his greens.

'Never took you for a Pokemaniac,' she said, turning her back on him to allow him a moment of shame.

'Dan got them for me as a joke when I got obsessed with Pokemon Go for about three weeks,' Adrian said. 'They're the nicest pants I have.'

'I'm not judging.'

'You're completely judging, I can tell by the smugness in your voice.'

She laughed. The sound rang hollow across the tiny ambulance. She buttoned up her top and turned back to face her partner.

'Are we going to talk about what happened?' he asked.

She'd been running on adrenaline this whole time, but as it ebbed away to nothing, it left creeping dread in its wake. She knew what she thought it was, but it was too crazy to say out loud. 'I know it scared the shit out of me.'

'Who was that guy?'

'Which one?'

'Either. Both.'

She sighed. 'Cain, I knew a long time ago. Old boss. Friend. Could have been something more, for about five minutes. I haven't seen him in years.'

'You didn't know the other one?'

She shook her head. They stood in silence for a moment, each wanting the other to say it first, neither of them willing to make a move toward discussing neck wounds and staked hearts.

Thankfully, the squawk of their radio broke the tension for them.

'Unit fifteen, come in,' Cathy said.

'Unit fifteen,' Lucy replied.

'You clear of your last job?'

'We are.'

'We've got an elderly gentleman with shooting leg pains, unable to move.'

'We'll take it,' Lucy said.

Neither said anything more as she and Adrian placed their soiled clothes in a plastic sack, took the covering off the gurney, and wiped down the surfaces. She carefully removed the note from one front pocket and put it into the new one, checking to see if Adrian had noticed.

They climbed down from the back of the van and got in the front in silence, the whole undertaking lasting less than two minutes. Adrian took the driver's seat, so Lucy strapped herself into the passenger seat and stared out of the window as they pulled away from the entrance to A&E, back out of the hospital and onto the main road.

Adrian's focus was on the road, but as Lucy watched through the side window, a shiver worked slowly up her spine.

A man stood in the shadows of the main entrance.

Impossibly tall, with shoulders like carved granite. Head down, but as they moved past him, he looked up, his eyes locking with Lucy.

The man from the flat.

The vampire.

'You okay?' Adrian asked.

'Fine,' she said, tearing her eyes away from the figure in the shadows of the night. It couldn't be. She was imagining it. She thought about saying something to Adrian, of turning them round. But it was just her mind playing tricks on her, surely? 'Hit the lights,' she said.

They bathed the streets in blue as Adrian stepped on the accelerator, easing them away from the hospital and into the night.

4

DIM THE LIGHTS

The rest of their ten-hour shift was punishingly busy; enough to push the events in that house out of Lucy's thoughts. She drifted home from the depot on autopilot, her brain unable to process much more than the prospect of shit food and a warm duvet.

It wasn't until she opened the door to her second-floor flat that the memory of the hell house crept back into her mind, sending a shiver down her spine and across her whole body; someone not so much walking over her grave as much as dancing a two-step on it.

She half expected the tall man to be there waiting for her, ready to punish her for seeing the horrors he'd made her see. But her apartment was empty save for Jones, her ginger ball of fluff and disdain. He marked her arrival with his customary flounce in the opposite direction. She breathed a sigh of relief to see him, an omen of normality to fend off the shiver still working its way down her spine.

Slipping her trainers off, she put down her bag. She closed the door behind her, locking the double bolt and putting the chain across for good measure. The shiver was still there. It didn't leave until she'd checked each room, leaving the lights on in each just to be sure. To hell with the planet; she needed to feel safe. The light from four bulbs in three rooms was hardly going to tip the balance for the ice caps.

Her flat comprised a decent-sized bedroom, a bathroom, and an open plan lounge and kitchen. A singleton's palace. She closed the curtains on the dawning day, pulled a pizza from the freezer, and turned the oven on. There was a bottle of white wine chilling in the fridge so she pulled that out, too, resisting the urge to down it straight from the bottle. On a normal work night, she'd allow herself only two glasses of wine and half the pizza, but tonight would see no such restrictions.

Leaning against the counter as she waited for the oven to warm, she thought back over everything. The call. Arriving at the house. The doorway. The hall. The stairs. Dread. Blood.

Cain.

The other body.

Her rational brain threw all manner of explanations and justifications at her. Cosplay gone wrong. A prank. An accident. Sexual deviancy gone awry. Every one a possibility, but none held water with the reality of what she'd faced in that room.

But that couldn't be right, could it? Cain was no deviant. Or was he? They went for drinks together a handful of times. She really had no idea who he was.

If that man in the shadows was what she thought he was, why call an ambulance? She'd seen a lot of horror films in her life, and she didn't remember Christopher Lee ever ringing 999.

This was ridiculous. She didn't know what was going on in that room, and likely never would. She should chalk it up as one more marvellous memory of life as a paramedic, to be filed alongside such highlights as 'drunk man holds own severed arm like a baby' or 'man with replica Eiffel Tower stuck far enough up his backside to give the people on the viewing platform an uncomfortable view'.

That was why the folded slip of paper was in her pocket, after all. She should have taken it out and slammed it on the desk on her way out the door tonight, and headed straight into town to get hammered.

She took a sip of wine. It was as tart as her darkening mood.

Whatever had happened in that room, they'd stumbled into the end of a dark chapter at the end of someone's story.

Picking the phone out of its cradle, she thought about calling the A&E reception to see what happened to Cain, but stopped herself. It wasn't like they were close. There was a thread of deeply unpleasant something there, and no good could come from pulling at it.

Her hand went to her pocket, fishing out the small square envelope that had spent the evening pressed to her breast, then transferred to her jeans pocket. She stared at it, its corner tinged now with the blood of a man she knew. She should walk straight into the office tomorrow, hand it over. Be done with this life.

The pizza went in the oven, came back out, got eaten. She drank a second glass, and a third. She sat in front of an episode of some Netflix show no doubt bound for cancellation and took nothing in, while the day kept swimming around in her head, the pull of the waves increasing with each sip of wine.

'Fuck it,' she declared to the empty flat, and took herself to bed. The ceiling span as she got under the covers. She pulled her phone out to check Twitter and Facebook for mention of the night's grisly events, but the battery was dead. She let it drop to her bedside table.

Despite fearing endless wakefulness or vivid nightmares, the tug of sleep came quickly, her heavy eyes closing on a room well-lit by lamplight and sunlight eking through her curtains.

When her alarm went off, the lamp was still on, but the light from the curtains was on its way out. Her head pounded and her mouth felt like someone had filled it with soil.

'Ugh,' was all she managed to say, an utterance which didn't raise so much as an interested flick of the ear from Jones, who'd curled up in the crook of her knees.

Wine was an awful choice. The remembrance of that came back first, followed by the memory that drove her to it. That room seemed more remote with the distance of sleep and the fog of alcohol between her and it. The portentous reality of a new day turned the thought of the supernatural into the ridiculous. It was impossible, the product of a tired mind working overtime, making connections which weren't there.

She laughed at her own ridiculousness, and this at least roused Jones from his slumber. He showed her his arse and wandered out of the room, stopping for a second for the briefest pet from his owner.

She brushed her teeth, sank two paracetamol and rubbed at her temples for a bit. She made toast and coffee and felt vaguely more human. What remained of her post-wine fog would dissipate on the walk to work. She got dressed, her hand hovering over the envelope on the side for a second. She grabbed it. Maybe today.

Adrian beat her to the depot, and was busy readying the van in the day's last's light.

'Hey,' she said, the word coming out in a cracked croak.

'Hey.' He looked like shit. He'd skipped his usual careful grooming regimen this morning; a shade of stubble dirtied his face and his eyes looked red. She'd always thought he looked like the living embodiment of a Coldplay song, but this morning he looked like something more ragged. A Paul Weller song, perhaps. Still cardigan rock, but with holes in the sleeves.

'You alright?' she asked.

'Didn't sleep well. You?'

She shrugged. 'Wine helped. Weird day yesterday, huh?'

'You could say that.' He looked like he wanted to say more, but didn't at the same time. She wanted to say that if it helped, she didn't want to talk about it either, but that would involve talking about it. She guessed there'd be an enormous elephant travelling around with them all day in their tiny ambulance.

'You want to talk about it?' she asked, squinting at him as she grabbed a kit bag.

He said nothing for a moment, long enough for her to wonder if she shouldn't just climb in the cab and move on from it, but he finally broke the silence.

'That house. It couldn't have been....'

She thought the response out of her mouth would be a resounding no, but nothing came out. She searched for the right response. 'I don't know. We've seen some weird shit over the years, but that's just....'

'I can't wrap my head around it. It's like my brain won't let me,' he said, his brow even more furrowed than usual. 'I know it scared the shit out of me. Couldn't sleep last night.'

They stood in awkward silence.

'Look,' Adrian said, 'the guy was a friend of yours, right?'

'Kind of,' she mumbled.

'Let's go pick up some jobs, and when we find ourselves back at A&E we can find out what happened to him, yeah? Maybe he'll be on the mend. We called the scene in. That's about as much as we can do, right?'

She nodded. Maybe finding out what happened to Cain, either way, would settle the unsettle at the pit of her stomach.

As if to underline the plan, the radio squawked at them from the front of the cab.

'Unit fifteen, you on the clock yet?'

5

Lie Down in the Light

Their first call was to the city centre, an unresponsive homeless man. Lucy grimaced — if anything could distract her from the imaginary grimness of her flights of fancy, it was the grim reality of the homelessness issue in her hometown.

They pulled up to the kerb outside a boutique clothing shop with a name that made no sense, its shutters down for the night. What looked like nothing more than a heap of dirty clothes lay across its doorway. An overweight man in a blue uniform waited for them with his hands indignantly placed across his wide chest.

They parked up, and Lucy climbed down. 'What have we got?' she asked.

The guard shrugged. He was in his thirties, his rent-a-cop uniform bulging under the stress of a body earned sitting at a desk and eating too much junk food. A scraggly black beard did just as poor a job hiding the man's double chin as his shirt did of holding in his gut. 'Dunno,' he said. 'I tried to move him. He told me to fuck off.'

'And that meant you had to call 999?' Lucy asked, her voice showing none of her frustration. She'd learned long ago sounding antagonistic got you nowhere.

'I wanted the police to come and move him,' he replied sulkily.

'You said he was non-responsive?' Adrian asked, joining them from the cab.

'Well, he's not moving.'

Lucy left the guard for Adrian to deal with and crouched over the homeless man within the bundle of clothes facing into the doorway. 'Hey,' she said. 'You okay?'

The man turned, the smell of cider and old sweat wafting off him as he turned. 'What do you want?' he asked through a mouth of broken teeth. Long-term homeless, for sure, but not anyone she recognised. She was familiar with the usual faces.

'Just wanted to check you were okay, mate,' she said. 'I'm Lucy. What's your name?'

He shrugged. 'I'm fine. Just tired.'

'You want us to take you in, find you a bed for the night?'

'No,' he said, turning back away from her to face the wall. She expected nothing less — a trip to A&E wouldn't fix anything for this guy, just keep him from his next bottle of White Lightning.

'How about a fresh blanket?' she asked.

He turned back to her and gave a hesitant nod.

She stood back up, her knees popping as she went. Adrian stared forward, ignoring the continued rambling of the security guard.

'...taxes do you think get wasted on people like him, eh? How many times do you and the police get called out to move them along, eh?'

'Depends on how many people call us out instead of leaving them alone,' Adrian growled in response. He never seemed to get the hang of Lucy's sunnier approach to dealing with the public.

'Can you grab a fresh blanket from the rig?' Lucy asked.

Adrian turned away from the guard to get it, which was a shame, as it meant he missed the indignant look on the guard's face.

She fished around in the pockets of her trousers and pulled out her wallet. Best thing about these trousers, the pockets. Only a few quid in change, but it would do. 'Two secs,' she said to the guard. She walked a few metres down the road to the Cornish Pasty Bakery, about to close up for the evening. She queued behind a couple of kids looking to line their stomachs before hitting the town and bought a vegetarian pasty and a cup of tea.

Back outside, Adrian gave the homeless man a couple of fresh blankets, as well as a neck support that could double as a pillow. He took the old stained blanket in return, handling it as carefully as he could with green latex gloves.

'Here you go, mate,' she said, offering the food and drink to the homeless man.

He sat up and took both. 'Cheers, love,' he replied, fishing around in his pocket, presumably for tobacco and skins.

'You sure we can't do anything for you?' she asked, getting a better look as he sat up. 'That rash on your neck looks painful.'

'No, love, cheers.'

She hated to leave him there, but there was nothing more she could do. The city's shelters were full to bursting point.

'You can't leave him there,' the guard said, his voice raising several pitches as he gestured uselessly toward the man biting into his steaming pasty.

'What do you want us to do?' Adrian asked, not even trying to hide his weary frustration.

'Take him away,' the man squealed, as though this was the most obvious thing in the world.

Lucy flashed him a smile. 'Thanks for your concern, sir, but you'll be pleased to know, given your obvious concern for this gentleman's well-being, that there's nothing medically wrong with him.' She turned her back on him before he could respond. Not that he seemed to have a ready comeback waiting for her — too busy turning a particular shade of ham. No doubt in a few hours he'd lose his rag again and phone for the police, and the whole charade would start again. On the plus side, by the time Lucy pulled the wagon back onto the road to their next call, they'd both forgotten the hangover of dread from the night before.

'What a prick,' Adrian chuckled as he hit the lights.

6

SHELTER

The second job of the night was an elderly lady who'd taken a fall. She was so frail they called for backup from a second crew to lift her as gently and supportively as they could. The second crew took her in, so Lucy and Adrian kept going from job to job, each one keeping them from returning to the hospital.

When they finally had a patient to take in — a young boy with a broken arm who'd trapped it somehow in his bed and snapped it trying to take it back out — she'd forgotten all about Cain. That lasted right up to the moment the admitting nurse took the boy off their hands and they stood in silence together on the threshold of the busman's entrance to A&E, staring down the empty corridor.

'Do you want to check?' Adrian asked, sounding like someone who didn't want to check himself.

'Sure. You prep the van.'

She took a deep breath. There was an itch she had to scratch. She had to know — Cain was her... well... she was the one with the connection, after all. It made sense she be the one to go in.

Winding her way through the backstage area of A&E, the part the public only ever saw strapped to a gurney, was a strip-lit nightmare after the night outside.

'Morning, love,' a voice called out. Lucy turned and found Brian, the counter clerk, his stick-thin body barely filling his scrubs as he walked back to his desk with a pot of unnecessarily low-calorie yogurt in his hand and a smile on his face.

'Hey, Brian,' she replied, falling in step with him. 'How's it going?'

He waved his yoghurt in the air. 'Oh, you know this place. The fun never starts,' he said with a wide smile. 'What brings you back here behind the veil, and where's that lovely partner of yours?'

She laughed. 'He's setting up for the next job. I swung by to check up on a friend of mine who I brought in yesterday.'

'Sure,' he said, getting to his desk and slumping into his chair with a flourish. 'What's the name?'

'Cain. Daniel.'

'Cain, Daniel Cain,' Brian replied in a terrible mock-Scottish accent. 'I think I know who you mean. Strange case. Neck wound, right?'

'Yes.'

'They patched the wound fine, but he went tachycardic. They induced a coma. He's still in intensive care,' he said, calling up the record. 'Doesn't look like the specialist has been round yet. You can go see him, if you like?'

'No, it's fine,' she replied, but it wasn't. She had to go see for herself. 'Actually, I might.'

He gave her an understanding smile, and she headed to the lift. Paramedics rarely ventured this far in, but nobody gave her a second glance. When she was first on the job, she'd come back to check on her patients all the time. After a few months, it got to be too exhausting, mentally and physically.

The sad fact was she'd lost too many patients to get emotionally invested in them, even the ones she saved. She stopped checking in on them altogether. Occasionally, she ran into a patient in a shop or on a night out, or working the concession stand at the cinema. At least she never had to pay for popcorn. Often she couldn't remember the person she'd saved.

She found Cain in a darkened room, tucked under a tight sheet, only his head and shoulders visible. A tube ran from his throat, where it met with the several other tubes giving him drugs and sustenance. A large white bandage wound round his neck like a grotesque polo neck. With the blood washed off, he looked halfway toward the man she'd known, though there were still traces of it on his hairline, a hairline receded somewhat since the time she'd known him.

She moved over to the bed, looking down at the man she'd been on two dates with. She slipped her hand into his and found it warmer than she'd expected.

He'd been her boss, at least nominally. Both worked in the local evil call centre, selling unnecessary insurance products to people who didn't need them. The place was more zoo than business, with the bosses doing lines of coke in the bathrooms at break time and televisions off the back of a dodgy truck given as sales incentives. In a place like that, who the hell cared if a team leader asked out a girl from the team next to him? In the grand scheme of things, it probably counted as the least egregious crime committed under that roof.

Like most of the staff there, Lucy fell into working there out of a strange mix of desperation and the ease of finding work there. Cain was no different. His marriage had spun apart, and he'd lost a career as a university lecturer in some kind of unspecified scandal, so the only place that would hire him was a place that considered ethics as an optional extra to its core business.

He was a nice guy, one of the few team leaders not to lose their shit when sales slipped. One Friday, when the office decamped to The Fox for post-hell drinks, Lucy chatted to him all evening. She found a quiet intellect, a quick sense of humour, and a pleasant smile. It was enough to give an instinctive yes when he asked her out, even though he was a good ten years older than her.

Their first date was the definition of awkwardness. He was a decent enough guy, but there was no spark, and he was nowhere near getting his shit together after the collapse of his marriage, something that became apparent ten minutes into their date.

Still, she agreed to a second. That went better, but not enough to warrant as much as a peck on the cheek at the end, let alone a third date. He was interesting, though she'd never understood how he went from university lecturer to sales agent for the devil's own credit card company.

As something of a reformed goth, it had impressed Lucy when Cain told her of his research into the legend of Countess Bathory, allegedly the most prolific female serial killer in history. She was better known to Lucy as Countess Dracula from the old Hammer horror movies she'd watched with her dad, and figured this knowledge would stand her in good stead, but it turned out he hated the Hammer films, and what he called 'the nonsense' around her legend. This was a pretty big red flag to someone raised on Christopher Lee movies. Whatever had happened in the intervening years, he was obviously taking the Bathory thing to a whole new level.

He looked peaceful, at least. Despite the receding hairline and the fact he was in a coma, he looked better than he had when they'd dated — he'd worn the dishevelled look of a man who'd divorced the woman who'd kept him tidy. Here in the bed he was clean shaven, and halfway toward handsome.

'Thank you,' a voice said from the doorway behind her, making her jump. She whirled round and found herself face to face with the man from the flat.

'I...' she said, but nothing more came out.

'I'm not going to hurt you,' the man replied, moving out of the shadows. He was huge, his broad shoulders blocking out the light from the corridor beyond. He dressed in dark tones, his jacket fitting well over what looked a well-built frame. His close-cut brown hair matched his eyes. A crooked nose, as though broken at some distant point in the past. Almost impossibly pale skin, even in the warm glow of Cain's bedside lamp. The whole thing coalesced into an almost unfeasible level of handsomeness that Lucy cursed herself for noticing, under the circumstances.

'Who are you?' she asked, her voice full of the fear creeping up her neck.

'A friend,' was all he offered as he moved toward the bed. For a moment Lucy thought he was crossing toward her, but he moved to the other side, giving her a clear path to the door if she needed it; a subtle but deliberate act.

'Friend to who?' she asked.

'To him,' he replied, gesturing to Cain, but not looking down at him. He held Lucy's gaze; she found it hard to break free of it.

'What happened to him?' she asked, picking up the chart at the end of the bed to give herself something else to look at.

'I'm sure you've worked it out for yourself,' he replied, the tiniest hint of a smirk crossing his face.

Of course she had. As he stood there before her, she had no question as to what he was, even if she couldn't bring herself to admit it.

'Right,' she said sarcastically. 'That would make you...'

He smirked, shifting his weight from one foot to the other and leaning against the wall. 'We're not overly fond of the term, but we never have settled on another.'

'What should I call you, then?'

'Adam.'

She didn't know what to say to that. This was too surreal. 'Okay, say you are what you say, and last night was what I think. What's going to happen to him?'

His smirk disappeared. 'That depends,' he offered.

'On what?'

'On whether he can fight off the infection. They've given him a transfusion and pumped his stomach. It may be enough.'

She stared at him for a moment. His eyes were on Cain. He looked sadder than she thought possible to look. 'And if not?'

He looked back down at Cain again. 'If it takes him, it will not be a good way to die. Those left for the infection to kill them rather than receiving a quick death suffer fevers, convulsions, and worse. Four days.'

They stood in silence for a moment, staring at the man in the bed. He looked perfectly healthy, aside from the coma. There were no signs he was about to die and become a...

No. This man spoke of infection, and infections could be cured. If she spoke to the attending doctors, she might help them fight this.

'Is there a cure?' she asked.

'No.'

She felt his eyes burrowing into her, imagined them trained on her neck, right up to the moment she no longer felt them.

She looked up and found him gone. The room felt diminished by his absence, somehow.

Staring at Cain for a moment, her stomach swirled — anger, frustration, fear, all mixed with a little bile.

She left, mumbling a goodbye to Brian the receptionist, weaving numbly through the corridors until she found herself back outside in the frosty night air. She climbed back into the cab.

'No calls for an hour,' Adrian said cheerily. 'This carries on much longer, we could go grab an ice cream from Tesco.'

She offered him a weak smile in response. He looked as though he wanted to ask after their patient, but something held him back. 'How was he?' he asked.

'Unit fifteen, come in,' the radio squawked, sparing Lucy from having to answer.

He sighed. 'No ice cream for us.'

7

Quiet as a Rat

By the time she'd reached the end of her shift, bone-weary exhaustion made the climb up the stairs to her apartment all but impossible. She entered through her front door considerably less fearful than the night before, and collapsed straight onto the sofa, much to the annoyance of Jones. He skulked away and curled up at the far end, but not before giving her the stink-eye for making him move.

Tomorrow was Wednesday. No, wait, it was already Wednesday. Most of the town would be waking, heading off for the midpoint of their working weeks. Lucy, on the other hand, had two glorious days off ahead of her. Although, being on nights, it never quite felt that way. Still, two days off and no plans was all anyone could ever ask for.

She thought about Cain, wondering what the next few days might herald for him. Death, life, or something else? Would anyone be there for him as he went through it? Would that ex-wife who'd so spectacularly binned him come sit by his bedside?

No, there was no point thinking about that. Getting off the sofa, she crossed to her bookcase and ran her finger across the rows of Blu Rays and DVDs, pulling out every one featuring vampires. There were a fair few. She did the same for her bookcase, finding fewer printed monsters, but a few nonetheless. Taking the haul, she spread it out across her kitchen table, having to double stack in places — an indictment of both the table and the collection. She stared at it all and felt silly.

As someone who'd spent most of her drunken twenties at rock and goth nights in a city which didn't have many of either, she'd known plenty of guys — and girls — over the years who'd fancied themselves creatures of the night. At least, they'd had a propensity for black clothes and bleak music, as though being aloof made them more attractive. To be fair, it had, sometimes.

Hell, she'd known at least two blokes who bleached their hair, wore black leather trench coats and called themselves Spike. Whatever happened to them? Did they ever run into each other, or did they phone each other at the start of the night to divvy up the turf? She had to hand it to them; it seemed to work for both of them — she rarely saw either leaving a dodgy night club alone, but then she rarely saw either with an abundance of friends.

She put away the films and books, phoned for a takeaway, and opened another bottle of wine. She was already halfway to sleep when the man knocked on her door with dinner and lasted little longer past that.

When she woke the next morning, Jones had finished her dinner and thrown it back up for her, but she'd slept long enough on the sofa that she could deal with such grimness despite the crick in her neck. Hell, she'd barely touched her wine.

Most of the day was gone, which, as always, felt a bit of a waste. If you get to live free two days of your week, it felt weird to spend half that time unconscious. But there was nothing for her to do. Her normal friends had boring weekday jobs. Maybe she'd go to the cinema, or the library, or the park. Luxuriate in the opulence of free time.

Or....

An hour later, she walked into the hospital, flashing a smile and her ID card at the confused receptionist in intensive care, a woman Lucy had met a few times but never gotten to know. 'Just going to check on a patient,' she said, without waiting for a reply.

The room was as dark as before, and as still. She let her eyes adjust and checked the chart. No change by the looks of it. He was still comatose, and his blood pressure and temperature were both off the chart.

'It's quite interesting,' a voice said from the chair next to the bed.

Lucy let out a startled cry and leapt into the air. 'For fuck's sake,' she hissed at Adam, sat in his chair, the same wry smile as before on his face. It was both maddening and reassuring. After all, it definitely didn't make him look like a killer. He looked more like a male model, all high cheekbones and pale skin.

'Sorry,' he said, without sounding it. 'You look nice,' he added, sounding half surprised.

She was dressed in jeans and a flannel shirt like it was the nineties. Hardly glamourous. She wondered how old he was. Maybe he was in his nineties.

'You're back.'

She paused. 'I know him. Or knew him.'

'I see.'

An awkward silence fell between them.

'How is he?' she said, going to check his charts, which hadn't changed since the last time she looked.

'He's definitely going through the change,' he said. 'He will be dead before long, I'm afraid.'

'I see.'

Adam got to his feet, dwarfing her instantly. He leaned over Cain. 'I've never observed it like this. Usually it's a hideous process, but the sleep your people put him in...'

'Coma.'

'It's made the process easier. I suspect it won't make the next bit easier, though.'

'Death?'

'The bit after.'

'Oh.'

He looked up at her, and for the first time, she noticed his eyes. An ocean of melancholy swirling in dark hazel.

'I'll see him through it,' he said sadly. 'It was not what I wanted for him, but it is what is.'

She looked back at Cain, wondering desperately what was happening inside that body of his. She was no biologist — she'd been known to joke over a pub table she was more butcher than doctor — but the possibility of there being vampires in the world and one transforming on a hospital bed before her was... intriguing. Also, completely impossible. Some part of her brain kept insisting on that. The man in the chair was just a man, and anything Cain was going through was a result of extreme trauma, not folklore.

And yet. None of that was true.

Already she could feel the part of her brain that allowed her to kneel over a child with a broken limb and not want to scream taking over. Here before her was a medical marvel; but nobody knew that except the people in this room. Or it was just another patient.

She looked back at Adam, and a shiver ran down her spine. She was sharing a room with a myth (or just a man), albeit one in a distinctly pleasant form, and she had the chance to walk away — probably the safest course, whether all of this was real or not. If this was all just some show, the man opposite her was a fraud. If it wasn't, he was a monster.

'Well,' she said, patting her hands against her thighs as though to emphasise the point, 'I had better be going.'

'Wait,' Adam said, crossing the gap between them at speed. Lucy stepped back involuntarily, almost crashing into Cain's IV.

'I don't feel like this is the best introduction.'

'Introduction to what?'

'To us. To me.'

She laughed. 'In terms of possible interactions with a... whatever you are... this has probably gone about as well as expected, what with me not being eaten.'

'Sure.' He frowned. 'I'll let you go,' he said, and returned to his seat.

This was it. Her last chance to turn her back on all this, to walk back to her normal life. There are few times in our lives when we can consciously choose between two wildly different paths, Lucy knew, and one was right there before her. On one — safety, security. On the other — who the hell knew?

She knew in an instant which path she *should* take, and which she would.

'What did you want to say?' she asked.

'I wondered if you wanted to get a drink with me. A coffee. I could explain better.'

'You're asking me out?' she asked, with a half laugh.

The smirk returned. 'I guess I am, yes.'

Lucy's cheeks reddened, and she found that despite of everything, of every instinct, she was deeply drawn to him.

But before she could answer, something crossed Adam's face. He turned to the door as it opened with a crash. Lucy turned to it, too, expecting a harassed nurse, but four new people walked in. Two men, two women, each looking as though they'd walked straight out of a music video.

She could sense Adam's hackles go up from across the room, though there was no discernible shift in his being.

She should have walked out the door a moment earlier.

'Adam,' one woman said. She had flawless skin, her features arranged in an impossibly porcelain doll way, offset by heavy makeup around her eyes and a crop of bleached blonde hair. If Adam didn't look like her mental image of a vampire, this woman tried a bit too hard to fit it. 'New pet?'

'Go fuck yourself, Autumn,' Adam snarled, revealing his teeth to show extended laterals, sharp and gleaming white.

'Easy,' one of the other newcomers said, a man who looked a lot like Adam, except he had blond curtains. The last time Lucy had seen him, he'd been on the floor with a gaping wound in his chest. Dead.

It was real. All of it.

Adam noticed the man, too. 'You,' he hissed, his voice deepening into a growl. 'What's he doing here?'

'We're here to claim our newest recruit,' Autumn replied. 'What are you doing here?'

'He was mine,' Adam hissed back.

This seemed to take the woman aback. She cocked her head slightly toward the blonde. 'You took from our own?'

'That became clear later,' the blonde man said. 'I had instruction. He tried to kill me.'

The woman sighed. 'For fuck's... Adam, whatever transgression has occurred here, on either side, I was unaware. You have the right to tribunal, if you so desire.'

'I waive it,' Adam replied, his voice still full of menace. 'So long as your new friend here explains what he means by instruction. Who gave you this name, boy?'

The blonde made no move to answer Adam's question, but bristled at being called boy.

They seemed to have forgotten about Lucy, but she didn't dare move a muscle, on the off chance that continued. She had to assume all four new arrivals were monsters, which made her position as the only potential food source in the room somewhat precarious.

The vampires faced each other down, the group of four waiting for some movement clearly not forthcoming from Adam. The silence stretched into uncomfortable, on to weird, and kept going. Lucy was terrified to even breathe, especially once she realised she was the sole one in the room doing so.

'What about *my* right to tribunal?' the blonde one asked. He had an accent, Lucy realised, Eastern European or Russian.

Autumn hissed at him and stood down from her staring contest. It was as though air had been allowed back in the room for the first time. Without a word, she and her three companions turned back toward the door.

'Autumn,' Adam said, stopping her in her tracks. 'What about the convention?'

'Prichádza tma,' she replied with a smile, and left.

Adam looked bereft — whatever those words meant, they were not good news.

He turned to Lucy, his fangs away once more. 'You should leave,' he said, his eyes not catching hers. Was he... afraid?

'I work here,' she said. 'Are you saying I'm in danger?'

He paused. 'No,' he said, but the pause was too long for it to be truth.

'What the hell is going on?' she asked. 'What is this?'

He stared in silence for a moment. 'I can't...'

A scream pierced the air from the corridor outside. Lucy moved to the door but Adam got there first, bursting through the door in full attack mode, his movements beyond anything her brain could process.

Autumn and the other four vamps were in the hallway, by the nurse's station. The blonde one had a nurse by the neck, holding her up with no effort as her legs flailed around and her face turned redder and redder.

'Put her down,' Adam growled. He squinted under the harsh strip lighting. All four of the vamps squared up against him had sunglasses on and showed no such issue.

'Make me,' the blonde growled back.

'Let's take a breath here,' Autumn said. 'Give us the turn, and we'll leave quietly. I know you, Adam, you don't want us to have to take him.'

'I don't want him becoming part of your toxic crusade, either,' Adam replied.

'He'll have the same choice we all have,' one of the other vamps said. The other woman. Jet black skin, dark hair, and clothes sleek enough for a runway. 'You're the first one to say no. What makes you think he will?'

'He's a good person.'

Autumn laughed. 'This is becoming tiresome. You can be the dissenting voice as much as you like, but you know what happens in the end. You know where this ends.'

'You only think you do.'

'This is pointless,' the blonde said. 'Give him to us or I kill this woman, and every human in this damn hospital.'

Adam sneered. 'You wouldn't dare.'

Lucy wasn't so sure. The finality in the vampire's tone suggested he'd be happy to carry out the threat.

'Please,' the nurse said, her voice choked by the grip of the taller woman. 'Help me.'

Autumn returned her own sneer. 'Hand him over, Adam. I know you don't want this much blood on those clean hands of yours.'

Lucy watched as Adam cooly surveyed his options, his gaze looking from door to door. Lucy did the same, though her options depended entirely on his choices. He could grab his friend and run, leaving Lucy and a hospital full of people at the mercy of the vampires. Perhaps they'd get lucky, and he'd draw them away.

'Take him,' Adam said, sullenly.

The briefest hint of surprise flickered across Autumn's face before she motioned for the two vamps behind her to move forward, leaving her and the blonde male vampire holding his hostage before them. The two other vamps walked past Lucy as though she weren't there, into the darkened room where Cain lay oblivious to the arguments over his stricken body.

'Wait,' a doctor said, hovering near the back of the room, unnoticed. 'If you move him, you'll kill him.'

'He's already dead,' Autumn said, motioning to the two vamps inside the room. Lucy turned her head just enough to see the tubes being yanked out of Cain, before one vampire slung the dying body over their shoulder.

'This isn't over,' Adam said.

Autumn's look said otherwise. Lucy didn't much care, as long as everyone got out alive, including the nurse still held aloft by the blonde one. Cain wouldn't, but she'd already understood he wouldn't be walking out of here. The nurse flopped lifelessly back and forth with every movement of her captor's arm, eyes open but lolling about her skull. Passed out, Lucy hoped. All alternatives were worse.

'Put her down,' Lucy said, to the blonde one.

The attention of five vampires who'd barely noticed her existence moved slowly to her.

'Your pet is talking,' Autumn said.

'Not a pet,' Lucy said, the anger creeping up her neck overwhelming the part of her brain telling her to shut up. 'Put her down.'

'Or you'll do what?' the blonde male said.

Lucy didn't have an answer.

'We got what we came for,' Autumn said, letting Lucy's big mouth off the hook. The vampires regrouped, Cain's limp body held between them. The blonde one set down the unconscious nurse on the counter, and they marched out of the ward, down the corridor.

Lucy rushed over to the nurse, checking her pulse first. Strong. Good. The doctor joined her, standing uselessly beside her. 'Go get a nurse,' Lucy shouted at him, a little harshly. He disappeared. Lucy grabbed the hands of the nurse and rubbed them, trying to rouse her.

Adam stood staring down the corridor, shoulders tense and fists balled.

'Are you going to stand there being useless, or are you going to tell me what's going on?' Lucy asked him.

He shook his head. 'I have to go,' he said, and turned to follow them.

'Hey, wait,' she said, but he ignored her. She couldn't leave the nurse unattended, so she had to wait for the doctor to return.

By the time he brought a nurse back, the vampire was nowhere to be seen.

'We have to call security, and the police,' the doctor said, trying to take charge now there was no danger.

Lucy ran to the window and opened the blinds, spilling the dying daylight from outside. That meant he wouldn't go out that way, right? She didn't know, but if it was true, it narrowed his options somewhat. And the other four vampires, for that matter.

She ran to the lift, ignoring the protestations of the doctor, who was busy calling the cops already. Both lifts had gone to the basement already. She hit the button, but neither made its way back up.

Security barged through the wide fire doors, ignoring her on their way back up the ward. She ducked through the door and rushed down the stairs. Only a few stories, she may even catch them.

Bursting through the door, she entered the brightly lit but somewhat dank car park. This was staff parking — the public had to use the one across the road which charged in increments akin to mortgage statements. This one was full of the shitty old bangers of the nurses and ancillary staff, next to the Audi's and Beamers of the surgeons and doctors. There was no sign of Adam or the other vampires. Part of Lucy was relieved, the majority still angered.

As the cloud of anger cleared, staring out at the concrete walls, she realised she should head back inside, wait for the police. Abducting a patient was a serious business, especially when the patient was likely killed in the effort, and she would need to recount what she'd seen, as well as why she'd been there. She wasn't sure she could do either without either lying or sounding certifiable. Neither sounded appealing.

Even if she spoke to the police, it wouldn't help the fact she'd put herself on the radar of immortal beings capable of immense violence. Not quite how she'd hoped her day off would go.

'They're gone,' a voice said from behind her. She whirled round to find Adam leaning against the wall. 'So, what do you want to know?'

8

WILDBLOOD

As a signal as to the left turn her life had taken in the last forty-eight hours, the fact Lucy now sat in a restaurant well outside her price range opposite a vampire dressed in a suit, hours after being confronted by cyber goth monsters at her place of work was pretty striking.

The suit made Adam a good deal more dashing than he'd already been, which was quite dashing indeed. She'd tried quite hard not to notice that element to him before, but there was no hiding it now. Where his bulky coat had made him seem huge, broad like a mountain, the suit jacket he wore revealed a toned, well-kept physique.

He sipped from his glass of red wine, barely taking any in, if at all. Lucy shifted in her seat and took a hearty glug from her own glass.

Since the car park, the rest of the day had been a blur. She'd spoken to the police at length, and had stuck to the facts as she could verify them. They didn't seem like they were overly concerned, and she didn't get the sense that they'd be mounting a city-wide manhunt.

When Adam suggested they talk somewhere more neutral, more public, somewhere she wouldn't feel under threat, she agreed. When he suggested Le Cochon Aveugle, one of the priciest and swankiest restaurants in town, and she said yes without thinking about just how weird a suggestion it was. She wasn't much of a foodie, but she knew about this place. How the hell he got a table was beyond her, but she supposed she knew little about the ways of a creature of the night.

Now here she was, trying not to think about the fact the most expensive dress in her wardrobe cost less than a starter, or the fact it didn't fit as well as it had when she'd last worn it, nearly five years earlier.

'Not that I don't appreciate the free meal,' she said. 'But why are we here? Shouldn't we be out there looking for Cain?'

He frowned. 'There is nothing more we can do for Cain,' he said.

She wasn't sure how true that was, but perhaps this wasn't the time or the place to press the point. Besides, her curiosity was almost bursting at this point.

'Okay,' she said, taking a sip of wine herself. It tasted a lot better than the six-pound supermarket wine she'd had the night before, but perhaps not fifteen times better, as the price would suggest.

'I like it here,' he said with a wry smile. 'And they know me. They bring me a wine, and they leave me alone.'

'You don't eat?'

'Not in the way you mean, no.'

'Right. Blood?'

'When I have to.'

'And how often do you have to?'

'It's not a daily requirement.'

She looked into his eyes. They looked normal enough. She wondered if he could control her mind with his thoughts. That would at least explain how she could sit here so calmly with a man she knew to be so dangerous. What the hell was she doing here? All gussied up like this was a first date. 'I don't even know where to start,' she said, taking a mouthful of fattened guinea fowl in.

'I understand. It's hard. Like walking in on The Archers for the first time and not understanding who anyone is or what's going on.'

She swallowed. 'The Archers? That's a cultural touchstone for you?'

'Me and five million others.'

'There are five million vampires?'

'Archers fans.'

She took another sip and straightened her napkin. 'Right. But you are?'

'A vampire?' He shrugged. 'Sure, by the term you know. Yes.'

'How old are you?'

'Two hundred and thirty-two.'

'Wow. You still keep count?'

'We attach a certain amount of status based on age. Our society is small, but it thrives on the rules it sets for itself.'

'Why?'

'Because that's what allows us to stay hidden.'

She finished her plate. There were eight courses; a tasting menu. Two courses in, she already felt full. She pushed the empty plate forward.

'You want to continue?'

'This conversation?'

'Your meal.'

'Sure.'

A slight gesture of his head brought a waiter over. 'Can we have a pause before the next course?' he said.

'Of course,' the waiter said, whisking the empty plate away. Lucy noted the man never made eye contact with her.

'Thank you,' she said. 'I couldn't possibly have made that decision for myself.'

He smiled a vaguely smug smile, the first thing he'd done so far to take himself down a notch in her estimations. Well, outside of the whole creature of the night thing. 'This is where you tell me how women are much different today than before?' she asked.

'Not so much,' he said. 'You remind me of a friend of mine.'

'Autumn?'

The smile left. 'She's no friend. Not for a long time.'

He stared at the edge of his glass in contemplation.

'Come on,' she said, finally. 'You need to clue me in here a little.'

He looked back up at her with those dark eyes. 'Our people have been around for a long time, living in the shadows. The oldest among us are older than me by about a hundred years, but there were others before them.'

'Who... turned you?' she asked.

'I no longer recall,' he replied. There was sadness there. 'Turning a human... it is not pleasant. What comes back is not the same person, but it is not the demon of folklore, either. There is no mystical element to this. What we become... is more animal. At first.' He took a sip of wine. 'Hungry. Over time, one claws back the person one used to be. Learns to control the thirst.'

'And this is about to happen to your friend?'

'What they have done to him is a thing rarely done. A newly turned vampire is a mess of noise and attention, which risks our ability to stay hidden. When we turn, it is usually after a committee agrees it, and done under circumstances we can control.'

'But not this time?'

'No.'

'Why? And why Cain?'

'I do not know. But I fear it is no accident. Because there are so few of us, we often have friendships with humans. The nature of these friendships differs from each of us to the other, and depends also on the humans. Some take a slave, willing and subservient. Some take a partner. Some have deep friendships. It is often from these that our numbers swell, but only after agreement. It can be a political game. There are factions, power levels. Being granted the ability to turn someone grants you an eternal ally.'

'Upsets the balance of power.'

'Exactly.'

'But you weren't trying to change Cain?'

He shook his head. 'Cain had no desire to become one of us. No. This was done as an act of violence.'

She frowned. 'I find it hard to think of the Cain I knew being a part of this world. He was, well, an ordinary man.'

'I take it you knew him after his marriage?'

'He was my boss.'

'Ah,' Adam said. 'The call centre?'

'Yes.'

'That was when I was away. I travelled for several years, and when I came back, I found a man lost. It was a shame.'

'You knew him before?'

'Cain's interests brought him before me when he was a much younger man. He had an obsessive compulsion toward certain folklores; wished to find the truth at the heart of them.' The memory summoned a slight smile to his lips. 'When I first met him, he had pretensions of a hunter of our kind.'

Lucy contemplated this as the waiter brought over another plate. Apparently, the time between courses had been deemed sufficient. She had to admit; she could face the food again. Or maybe she wanted something to do with her hands. She wanted to move on from Cain, too. 'One question. You say your kind have... stuck to the shadows. But you've not exactly been successful, have you?'

He smirked. 'The Stoker book.'

'And everything after. The world is primed for your existence. So one thing I don't get. If vampires are real, and they are immortal — why not go public?'

'A dozen reasons. There are limits to our power. And limits to our numbers. Also, we are not monsters. Mostly. As I said before, we are not demons. We may be different to the people we once were, but we're also the same, if you follow?'

'But this Autumn, she has other ideas, right?'

'The fragile peace between us wears thin.' He flashed her a weak smile and took a deeper sip of his wine, wincing as he did so. 'The balance we have struck is worn by age and complacency. There are those of us who feel the time has come to follow our impulses. Reveal ourselves, take control. Take power, by force.'

'You don't agree?' she asked, looking deep into his eyes. She enjoyed his company, but the future of that depended entirely on his next answer.

'No.' He stared back, but when that didn't seem to satisfy her, he continued. 'We have watched the world of men for centuries, watching as you fall deeper into folly. The earth we share is dying, and there are those amongst our number who think the way to deal with the problem is to... deal with the problem.'

She laughed. 'Vampires against climate change?'

'Yes.'

She stopped laughing. 'Seriously?'

'If humanity does not stop its current course, Earth will not remain habitable for long. This current generation are... we have little faith in humanity's ability to salvage the situation.'

'Right. But you're not monsters?'

'I mean, in the literal sense, yes.'

She pushed another empty plate away and took another sip of wine.

'You have more questions?' he said, leaning back in his chair and straightening the entirely superfluous napkin on his lap.

'Lots.'

'Ask away.'

She looked around at the restaurant. Nobody else seemed to be listening in to them, all wrapped up in their own worlds, their own meals, their own company. 'You don't eat. Do you drink blood?'

'Yes.'

'Human?'

'Yes.'

'Do you kill people?'

'Not for a long time. That was the first time I've tried to take a life in decades. I thought I had killed him.'

'Staking. So the legends are true?'

He paused, evidently trying to weigh up whether he should trust Lucy with knowledge that could be his undoing. Or perhaps he risked breaking some kind of vampire covenant.

'Partly. The risks to us centre on our heart and head. Pierce the heart or the brain, sever the head, or burn us, and we are as fragile as you are.'

'What about garlic, crosses?'

He gave a little chuckle. 'Superstitions ingrained in folklore and passed through literature into spurious fact. The first tales of us came out of Eastern Europe at a time of religious superstition and crusading fervour. Naturally, priests and doctors and writers believed us to be demonic creatures, and built in religious ways to deal with us.'

She nodded, and the two of them sat silently as the small waiter brought over a tiny dessert and refilled Lucy's glass.

'Sunlight?' she asked.

'We suffer an extreme reaction to it. Our skin cells regenerate at an extreme rate to counter the decay of our bodies, but sunlight interrupts the process. It is extremely fast. We are not fond of bright lights, as a rule.'

An awkward silence fell between them as she took a small forkful of delicious chocolate torte.

'May I ask you a few questions?' he asked.

'I can't imagine I have anything interesting to tell you,' she said, her mouth glued together by chocolate divinity.

'Tell me about yourself,' Adam said.

She swallowed the mouthful as quick as she could, which seemed a waste. 'I appreciate the effort, but you don't need to ask me about my life. This isn't a date.'

He took another sip and smiled. 'Isn't it?'

The question sparked a tiny flutter in her stomach, but before she could ponder the answer, the reality of what she'd seen in the past twenty-four hours crashed around her. She frowned at him. 'Your friend's body has been kidnapped, probably killed, and about to be resurrected in what sounds like a pretty unpleasant manner, and you don't seem to have much of a handle on why. You're taking this calmly. Or maybe you don't care about him as much as you claim?'

The smile disappeared. 'Of course I do. Do not presume to know my feelings. He is gone, and he will be back. There's nothing I can do to help. Turning can take days. We have lost one already. I fully intend to find him and guide him through the turn. And you are right. I do not know what Autumn is up to. But I plan to find out. And I would like you to help me.'

Lucy finished the mouthful of chocolate pudding and washed it down with the last of her wine. 'I guess this isn't a date, then.'

'Will you help me?' he asked, and for the first time, she saw something approaching helplessness cross his expression.

'Why me?' she asked. She had the sneaking suspicion the genuine answer was that he didn't know anyone else, but she was curious to hear what reason he'd give. 'I can't imagine for one second how I could help you, except to maybe pop down the shops for you when the sun's out.'

'You didn't back down,' he said. 'With Autumn. You knew what she was, and you've seen what we can do first hand, yet you didn't back down to save that woman. And you have not run from me.'

'That's it?' she asked, leaning back in her chair and taking another sip of the excellent wine.

'I like your company. And you're the last human I know.'

She considered it for a moment. Here it was, another one of those moments where she had the chance to walk away. Signposted and everything. She thought back to the disgusting house where she'd first encountered Adam. That was what he was. A monster in filth. But that didn't seem to tally with the man before her.

Then there was Cain. She still didn't believe it was too late to save him, and as Adam had said, this was not a choice he made. Perhaps she could still save him, and wasn't that what she spent her life doing; saving people?

'Okay. I'll help you. On one condition.'

He arched his eyebrow, clearly amused by the prospect of her making demands on him. 'What's that?'

'No meeting at your house.'

He smiled. 'I can live with that.'

9

LEAD BALLOONS

She regretted that last stipulation the moment she got home — somehow it'd been turned round to her inviting Adam to her home the next night. If a vampire was coming to visit, she should probably tidy the place up. So she spent most of her second day off cleaning her flat, a job that needed doing, in fairness, but which didn't seem the most auspicious start to her career as, what, a vampire detective?

Adam had one counter demand — that she lock Jones away. He wasn't allergic to cats, but they tended not to like his kind, and he didn't want to be attacked by a tabby ball of fur. It seemed fair, but made her extra conscious of cat hair, especially when he seemed to know already she had a cat from her general odour — that part of the myth about vampire senses was true, at least. Now she was terrified she smelled of cat piss to him, and even more worried about her flat doing so. Given the state of his house, he was one to talk. It struck her at one point, as she got the vacuum out, that perhaps housework was the least of her problems — she'd invited a vampire to her house, something she knew from every movie and book she'd ever seen rarely ended well.

Jones watched with his usual quiet disdain as she cleaned the toilet, the sinks, dusted the room, changed the bedding, cleaned the television and million other tiny jobs that seemed to thrust themselves into her eye-line whenever she thought she was about done. It allowed her plenty of time to order her thoughts. At least, it offered her plenty of time to think of a million questions she had about Adam and his kind. Did he use the toilet? Would he sweat? Did his hair grow? His fingernails? Did he brush his teeth? Could he perform in bed?

She tried not to think about Adam in that last way, what with him being a blood-drinking monster of myth and legend, but he was almost tailor made to make her slightly weak at the knees. Plus, there was the whole thing where she'd been conditioned by almost every vampire portrayal in popular culture to think of him as a romantic figure.

She had to stop thinking like that.

After the previous night's abortive 'date' vibe, she dressed a lot more casually this time around. Black jeans with a simple black top and a jumper. She pulled on her battered old Converse with the thought that wherever the night took her, it'd be better in comfortable shoes, and sat on the edge of the sofa. The light of the day faded, and she wondered if she should try to eat before he got there — there was something decidedly weird about eating opposite someone who wasn't. She'd have to avoid that in the future.

In future. God.

Jones leapt from the sofa and stalked toward the door, his hackles raised. He hissed and looked at Lucy. She checked the clock. Christ, he was early.

'Come here, you little shithead,' she said, picking up the ball of angry fur. He mewled back at her with whatever was cat for aghast. 'Don't give me that look,' she added. She opened the door to the bedroom and placed him on the floor of the dark room, pulling the door closed behind her. At the very least, that would stop her taking Adam in there.

Get a fucking grip, she told herself.

She checked herself in the mirror, fussing over a few strands of red hair, putting a little effort into making them look effortlessly tousled.

Her visitor rapped on the door.

She gave it a few seconds so as not to seem too eager and tried to swallow whatever the hell was fluttering in her stomach. She wondered if the thing about having to invite a vampire in was going to be another myth. Maybe she could tease him about it, put a few little cracks in the conversational ice.

She put her hand on the lock.

The door burst open in a shower of wood splinters and noise, knocking Lucy backward. A blur of violence erupted through the doorway a second later. Lucy screamed in panic, but before the sound could even make its way through her oesophagus, there was a hand around her throat, cutting off the sound to a garbled squawk. The force by which the intruder grabbed her slammed both of them to the floor, cracking the linoleum and possibly a few of her ribs.

'Don't make a fucking sound,' the vampire hissed. For a second Lucy thought it might be Adam, but as her eyes adjusted to the man crouched over him, she realised it was the blonde, the one with the bad curtains. He leaned over her as he spoke, pressing down on her throat, his rancid breath close enough to fill her nostrils with decay.

She coughed, spraying blood over her assailant's face. He licked his lips with a horrid grin.

'Thank you,' he said. 'But you shouldn't tempt me.'

'Not my intention,' she tried to reply, but the words came out squashed, compressed into nothing but garbled noise.

Lifting her by the throat as he had the nurse back at the hospital, he yanked her to her feet so hard she thought he might tear her head clean from her body. Panic gripped Lucy as she tried to breathe.

The vampire cocked his arm back and threw her into her lounge. His strength was unlike anything Lucy had ever encountered; as she clattered into the rear of her sofa, pain ripped through her hip. She fell to the carpet, scrambling desperately to get away from her assailant.

He moved toward her like a boxer crossing a ring, half on his toes.

'What do you want?' she howled at him, grasping at anything to pull herself up. She hooked her hands over the back of her sofa and pulled, but the sofa broke apart, sending her back to the floor.

'Darkness,' he replied, the rancid stench of his breath even stronger when he spoke. Trying to remember what Adam had told her about his weaknesses, her hands cast about wildly, looking for a weapon, but there was nothing.

He reached down and dragged her back to her feet. She brought her hand up to his face, clawing desperately at his face, to no avail. She kept her nails too short, a habit formed over long years in an ambulance.

She stared into his eyes. Dark pits of empty rage; he barely looked human. His lateral incisors protruded like razors. His hair may be blonde, but his eyebrows were thick, coarse brown, wild and unkempt and sat atop a permanent scowl.

Whipping her hand round once more, she drove her thumb into the socket directly below those thick eyebrows and pushed.

Howling, he dropped Lucy, stumbling back toward her kitchen before losing his footing on the divider between her carpet and the linoleum. He crashed into her mirror, smashing it into pieces.

The door.

She sprinted forward, thinking that if she could somehow make it through the splintered remains of her doorframe, that somehow, she might find a way out of this. But even before she was halfway to the threshold, he was in front of her once more, sneering, his right eye bloodied but intact.

'I'm going to enjoy this,' he sneered, but even as he readied himself to launch at her, he was whisked backward, back through the doorway and into the corridor behind. Stood in his place, his fangs out and a look of pure rage on his face, was Adam. 'Stay there,' he growled at Lucy.

Adam turned his attention back to the vampire on his arse in the corridor outside. Adam moved in a blur, scooping the blonde up into a fight so immediately brutal that Lucy's first instinct was to shut her door on it, but it lay in splintered pieces inside her flat.

The two vampires pummelled each other with ferocious power and speed, each blow drawing blood. The white walls of the corridor splashed with sprays of muddy red.

The blonde laid a headbutt on Adam's nose and tried to follow it up with the same move Lucy tried on him, but Adam was too quick for him. He pulled the roving hands back, snapping the other vampire's wrists in a crunch of bones met with a feral howl of rage.

This was the opening Adam needed. He whirled round in a flash, grabbing the howling head of his opponent under his arm and dropping to the floor. They fell together in a grind of breaking bones, the howl cutting off abruptly.

Adam looked up from the ground at Lucy, his face bloodied to a pulp. 'Knife,' he said, his tone calm and even. 'Big one.'

She ran back inside and grabbed the biggest chopping knife from the top of her knife block. By the time she got it back into the corridor, Adam's victim writhed and buckled under him, albeit with limited success. It looked like someone trying to wrestle their way free from a tree root, so steadfast was Adam's grip.

'Heart,' Adam said. 'I cannot let go. You will have to do it.'

'No,' she said, affronted. 'I can't.'

'He died a long time ago,' Adam replied, his even tone struggling with the effort of keeping the other vampire in place. 'Do it.'

Lucy hesitated. She'd been around death so much, but never taken a life. Had watched it slip away, held hands as it went, locked eye contact and seen the dying light, but never been the cause. Adam's words hardly helped — it was impossible not to watch the panic in the blonde vampire's eyes and see anything but life.

She slid the knife under the vampire's ribcage, breaking the skin effortlessly and pushing the knife upward. It amazed her; the ease with which it travelled — for all his apparent strength, he seemed almost comically delicate.

Angling the knife, she pushed it through the diaphragm into the heart. Immediately, the squirming stopped, and the body went limp. She stopped, her breath ragged from the effort. 'No,' Adam said. 'We have to be sure.' When she looked at him, pleading, he shrugged. 'He came back once. I killed him.'

Pulling the knife out slightly, she pushed it back in at an angle. Blood poured from the wound, coating her arms and hands with thick black. She'd spent enough time with her arms in blood to know this was different — the blood was cooler, not quite cold but not body temperature, either, and thicker, darker. It hardened at the edges if it had the chance to sit for more than a few seconds, pulling at her arm's hairs as soon as it dried.

'Has it stopped?' he asked. 'You need to check.'

The knife slipped out of her hands and she pushed a hand into the wound, searching inside his torso. Her hand touched the heart, which felt different from the rest of this creature, and for the first time she sensed how different, how completely alien it was compared to the bodies she knew.

'It's done,' she said, out of breath from the effort, pulling her hand out from inside the blonde vampire's ribcage, dripping blood over her hallway. It made little difference; the place looked like the inside of an abattoir.

'We need to get you out of here,' Adam said. 'You've killed one of us. They'll be hunting you.'

She looked up into his eyes, seeing his concern. It was the first time he'd looked scared.

'Why did he come after me?' she asked.

He shook his head. 'I don't know, but we don't have time to find out. Autumn and the others may be outside.'

She got to her feet slowly, unsteadily. Her top was caked in blood, her ribs ached, along with most of her limbs. The corridor looked like a Jackson Pollock painted in a single colour; the scene capped off by the destroyed door to her flat and the chaos beyond. She imagined Mrs Phatak from down the hall coming out of her flat and finding this scene. God, was she in there, terrified for her life? 'What the hell am I going to do?' she asked. 'You're going to have to help me clean this up.'

'There's no time,' Adam said, standing up and brushing himself down. She realised why he always wore dark clothes — the blood didn't show up. Still, he looked in a bad way, his face covered in cuts and bruises, his nose broken and out of joint.

'Like hell, there's no time,' she replied. 'I'm not having my neighbours finding a dead vampire in the hallway. What the hell am I going to do about my door? If I leave it like that, my stuff will be stolen.'

'If we don't go, you'll die.'

'What about Jones? I can't leave him trapped in my room. There's no food in there.'

Adam grabbed her shoulders, firmly enough she thought the bones might shatter. That would be a logical next step for the evening. 'They will be here soon,' he growled, 'and if we're here when they are, I won't be able to protect you. You will die. Your neighbours will die. These are not people. They have no mercy. They see humanity as a plague.'

Tears welled in her eyes. 'The fuck have you gotten me into?'

'I don't know. But I will get you out of it.'

Composing herself, she wiped the tears welling in her eyes, careful not to get vampire blood in them. 'I'll have to leave Jones some food, at least.'

He sighed. 'Let him out. He can come with us.'

'I thought cats hate vampires.'

'Believe me, the feeling is mutual. But you might never be back here.' He frowned, and Lucy tried not to let the weight of that statement weigh on her in the moment.

'Okay,' she said.

'Though,' Adam said, frowning. 'At least tell me you have a cat box.'

IO

WIDOWER

A fear gripped her as she stepped into the chill of the evening; that Adam would have no choice but to take her back to the slaughterhouse where he lived. She thought back to the stench of decay in her nostrils as she and Adrian stepped over the threshold — her stomach couldn't take that, too busy lurching at the thought of the decimated body in her hallway. She'd seen worse on the job, but death had never been at her hands before.

Jones hissing in the box at her side, she marched with as much purpose as she could muster down the pavement, Adam's striding gait a few steps ahead of her. The rucksack on her back had gone mouldy after too many festival treks, the stench no doubt invading every item she'd hurriedly stuffed inside. A problem for tomorrow. She added it to the mental list she was busy compiling, right after the fact she seemed to be homeless, and the fact the police would almost certainly be after her within hours.

She realised after a few minutes they were headed the opposite direction to Adam's house, and a wave of relief washed over her. She would ask where they were going, but she was too busy fighting for breath.

They headed out of town, along the river Ouse, past endless reams of student buildings. They turned onto a quiet cul-de-sac, its more-affluent houses sat atop up a steep rise on the road, overlooking the river and the main road below. A fog had settled over the evening, bathing everything in cool white light from the street-lamps, diffused across grey mist.

They stopped at a tall house, old like Adam's home, but far less decrepit. Grander, even. A detached house, tall and austere, the kind of house she looked at with longing whenever she was busy contemplating her life's direction. Lights were visible through the curtains. Adam marched up to the door and knocked out a strange rhythm of taps.

There was a rustling of locks and keys and the door opened, revealing a woman so breathtakingly beautiful that Lucy almost dropped her cat. She seemed to have the same effect on Jones, too — he stopped hissing at the vampire and stared at the woman. Tall, thin, tousled brown hair shining so brightly in the hallway light it seemed like a halo, framing a face that held oval brown eyes and luscious red lips in a configuration almost impossible in its symmetry.

'Adam,' she said, in a voice that possessed no surprise, but not much welcome, either. 'How may we help you?'

'I request sanctuary,' he said.

'You cannot ask that of us,' she said, surprise in her voice.

'Not for me,' he said. 'For her. And her cat.'

The woman looked round Adam to Lucy, who felt like the least glamorous person in the world, sweating and frumpy, her top covered in vampire blood, and carrying a cat.

'I'm Lucy.'

'Pleasure to meet you,' the woman replied, sounding the opposite and offering neither welcome nor her own name in response.

'Lucy, this is Elle.'

'She's human?' Elle asked.

'She is.'

'She's right here,' Lucy said.

Elle cracked a half smile for the first time. She looked Lucy over once more. 'Come in.'

Lucy stepped forward, past Adam, into the house, which issued warmth and welcome as soon as she crossed its threshold.

'You'll be safe here,' he said, and she believed him. He looked as though he could not physically get closer to the house. So much for his claim there was nothing magical about his... kind. Clearly, something kept him from the threshold.

'You have trouble?' Elle asked, her nose wrinkling slightly.

'I wouldn't be here if I didn't,' Adam said. 'It is between my people.'

'I thought you needed my help,' Lucy said, feeling stupid the minute she said it, like an infant asking if they can help with dinner and peeling a single potato while their parent makes a full meal.

'I will. Tomorrow. First, I need to understand a bit more. I will go to Autumn, try to understand.'

'Won't she kill you?'

'We don't kill each other,' he said.

'Okay,' Lucy replied, too numb to say anything else. She stepped inside. A wave of exhaustion washed over her. She wanted nothing more than to curl up on her sofa with a book and a glass of wine.

'No work tomorrow. Call in,' Adam said.

'Fine,' she replied wearily.

He offered a terse smile and turned away, blending into the darkness immediately. Elle gave a quick look around the street before closing the heavy door and turning to Lucy.

'Welcome to my home,' she said, breaking out into a wide smile. 'You can let your cat out.'

Lucy set the box on the ground, opening the hatch. Jones sprang out, tail up. He headed straight for Elle, dancing in and out of her legs, purring wildly. The tall woman laughed with an exaggerated delight, reaching down to pick the ginger cat up. 'Ah, he's a delight. What's he called?'

'Jones.'

'Well, nice to meet you, Jones. It's been a while since we had an animal in the house, but we have milk.' She wandered off into the house, leaving Lucy to trail behind with her bags, wondering how best to start a conversation that might fill in some blanks for her.

'How long have you known Adam?' Elle said, taking care of the problem for Lucy.

She shrugged, the action feeling again too childish in front of this woman. 'Not sure I do. I'm a paramedic. I was called to an incident at Adam's house. His friend, Cain.'

Elle stopped. 'Cain? Is he alright?'

She shrugged again, a hard thing to do laden down with bags. 'I don't know. Autumn and her people took him.'

Elle stared at her for a moment. 'You must tell me everything,' she said. 'Let's get you settled and find something to eat.'

Lucy's temporary room was like a museum, albeit warm, with a lived-in feel. There didn't seem to be anyone else at the house but Elle, despite her referring to herself in the plural sense. But if the guest bedrooms were this plush, she'd love to know what Elle's looked like. The blanket covering her duvet looked more expensive than everything Lucy owned combined. Elle told Lucy to have a shower, and when she came out there were fresh pyjamas and a dressing gown laid on the bed, and slippers beside it. Jones had already taken up residency on her new bed, and watched her with half an eye open as she got dressed. She dried her hair, glad there were no longer flecks of vampire blood congealing within its strands.

Downstairs, Elle was in the kitchen, fixing a meal of vegetable stew and fresh bread, the smell of which drew Lucy forward. She hadn't realised how hungry she was until that smell, but now she could think of nothing else.

'Come, sit,' Elle said, putting a bowl down on the breakfast nook of the kitchen. 'I won't grill you until you've eaten.'

'Okay,' Lucy said, pulling up her chair, letting the smell of fresh bread fill her head. 'Maybe you could tell me how you know Adam.'

Elle let out a long laugh. 'Oh, I'm not sure we'd have time if we sat up all night. We go way back. He is... unique to his kind. As, I suppose, am I.'

'Your kind?' Lucy was desperate to know, but reticent to ask.

Elle smiled. 'You might think of it as witch. It's the closest approximation. But it's also completely wrong. As most things are, when it comes to it.'

'No broomstick?' This came through a mouth full of bread and broth, which Lucy couldn't help but shovel in so fast she was more inhaling than eating.

Elle laughed, but there was no mirth in it. 'No. I use a cordless vac, but only for cleaning.'

'You know,' Lucy replied, regaining her composure enough to speak properly between mouthfuls, 'two days ago I didn't believe in the existence of anything more exciting than Wi-Fi, now someone tells me they're a witch and it makes perfect sense.'

Elle smiled. 'It must have been a strange few days for you. Why don't you tell me about it?'

Lucy wasn't sure whether it was the way the woman asked, the warmth of the broth hitting her stomach, or some kind of devilry, but it felt good to unburden everything. And unburden herself, she did. She recounted everything that had happened since she and Adrian got the call, right up to the moment they came to Elle's house. Lucy supposed it was fine. Adam led her here. He must trust this strange woman. He didn't warn her to be on guard, he just said she was safe. And that was exactly how she felt.

So safe that after dinner she went straight to her room, climbed into bed, and fell into a deep and peaceful sleep, so deep and peaceful she slept through her alarm the next morning, waking when the incessant trill of a phone call woke her up.

The phone was jammed into her bag, stuffed under her clothes, all cleaned and folded, showing none of the signs of yesterday's struggle. Elle had restored even the mouldering inside of the rucksack to its pre-festival glory.

By the time she fished the phone out, she had missed the call, but saw it was not the first of the day, nor even the tenth. It was work, phoning about a shift she was already two hours late for. The warm, serene glow she awoke with turned to a hard, sinking feeling in her stomach. Next came the memory of why she was not at work; the memory of killing a man, and realisation the police were probably — no, *definitely* — going to be looking for her.

She turned the phone off, which seemed the most elegant solution for the moment. In the same spirit, she sank onto what looked to be an antique chaise lounge, which was more comfortable than it looked. In the light of day, what had looked like an elaborate, if slightly stuffy, museum bedroom transformed into a place of total serenity, punctured solely by Lucy's own lack of it.

What the hell was she going to do?

Maybe Elle might accept her as some kind of live-in servant? She'd never have to go outside again, because there were monsters out there, and even worse, consequences.

Although, none of those consequences seemed entirely fair to Lucy, who had done nothing more than try to help save a dying man.

There was a knock on the door. Lucy stood up, wishing she'd at least changed out of her pyjamas, especially since the time on the face of her phone had shown closer to teatime than breakfast before she'd shut it off.

'Come in,' she said.

The door opened and in walked Elle, looking as beautiful as ever, her sheer presence masking for a second the fact she seemed to have a young girl with her. The girl looked to be about thirteen and dressed in strangely old-fashioned clothes for her age, like her grandmother had dressed her. Her gaze seemed to follow Elle's feet, but when she looked up and met Lucy's gaze, a wide smile followed it.

'Good afternoon,' Elle said. 'You must have needed the sleep.'

'It's been a long few days,' Lucy replied, as the memories of opening up to Elle so thoroughly flooded back, adding to the gnawing feeling at the pit of her stomach. She couldn't shake the feeling Elle had coerced her somehow.

'You'll be pleased to know the situation with your apartment has been resolved,' Elle added, moving to the curtains and pulling them wide. Lucy thought Elle was probably the kind of woman who'd pull open the curtains to any room she entered.

'Resolved?'

'Yes. We have disposed of the body, repaired your door, and cleansed the place. We also ran into your neighbour...'

'Mrs Phatak?'

'Yes. Lovely woman. Missed it all, thankfully. Memory charms are tricky to do correctly, and they're a real problem when they go wrong. Do you remember the one up in Glasgow, Missy?'

The young girl gave an embarrassed laugh but stifled it immediately.

'Oh, Lucy, my apologies. This is my friend, Missy. She works with me.'

'Hi,' Lucy replied.

Missy gave another giggling response and looked down at the floor.

Lucy composed herself. 'Have you heard from Adam?'

'The sun's still up. I doubt we will until tonight,' Elle replied breezily. 'You're quite safe from the others, too.' She sighed and crossed to the bed, picking up Lucy's discarded towel and fussing with it. 'I don't know what Adam thinks he's gotten himself into,' she said. 'No doubt he's got the wrong end of the stick, as per usual.'

'What do you mean?' Lucy asked, resisting the urge to grab the wet towel from her host and fold it herself.

'Your friend has a habit of this,' she said with a wry smile. 'Do you remember Paris, Missy?'

Missy giggled.

'What happened in Paris?' Lucy asked.

'Adam always had a soft spot for the people,' she said, but wouldn't elaborate further.

'I need to contact work,' Lucy said. 'I should get dressed.'

'Of course. We've prepared lunch for you downstairs.'

'That's kind of you,' Lucy said. 'But I think I need to get out there and start fixing things.'

'Oh, I'm not sure that's wise,' Elle said.

'People are going to be worrying about me,' Lucy replied, noting how Missy had moved to block the door.

Elle raised her hands in front of her, cupping them to make a bowl. A spark of red kindled in the centre, growing into a ball of red fire. 'I'm sorry,' she said without the vaguest hint of remorse, 'but I can't let you leave.'

II

EVEN DEEPER

Being at the whim of powerful eternal beings was more tedious than Lucy would have imagined. For someone used to the hustle and action of a paramedic's life, a few hours cooped up in the world's lushest cell had her ready to try shimmying out of the window. Even Jones was tired of this place, the adulation he had for Elle when he met her wearing off quickly. He paced around the room, failing to find anywhere he wanted to settle.

Vampires. Witches. Dead bodies. Lucy wanted to go home.

No, she didn't just want to go home, she wanted to go back. To undo the last seventy-two hours, preferably without the magic wand of the woman who had her trapped here.

Her anger dissipated into fear quickly enough, a knot building in the pit of her being that tightened with every pace of her room. There wasn't even a television here to distract her, and they'd taken her mobile phone. Christ knew how work was taking her sudden absence. Or Adrian. All that remained was running through the mental tape of the last days. Adam. Cain. The hospital. Her apartment. She wanted to walk out into the street, pull a hoodie up over her hair and disappear. She wanted, even, to pull on her uniform and be useful again.

What the hell was Elle's agenda? Was she with Autumn and the others in whatever their nefarious plans were? Was Adam simply as naïve as Elle seemed to think he was in dropping her off, or was this his way of trying to get some dirt on the other side?

If the latter, she needed to have a conversation with him about keeping her in the loop, because she could have done a lot more if she'd have known. But would she have walked into the home of a powerful witch willingly if she'd known she was playing for the other team?

God, listen to her, thinking of this in terms of teams. Why was she so convinced Adam was the good guy? Because he was the first supernatural being she'd had the misfortune to run across, or because he filled out a jacket well?

There was a knock on the door. Missy came in, carefully carrying a tray of tea and sandwiches, a look of total determination on her face. She set down the tray with what seemed like a herculean effort and stood, looking satisfied.

Lucy considered the girl. There was a simpleness to her, or so it seemed. Maybe Lucy could use that to her advantage. She didn't much like the idea of taking advantage of a young girl's simpleness, but then she didn't like being held hostage, either. 'Thanks, Missy,' she said. 'These look nice. Did you make them?'

'I saw your fridge, so I know you like it.'

'Thanks. You sorted my flat out?'

Missy nodded enthusiastically. 'You have nice things.'

'Thanks. That's nice to say. It's not as glamorous as this.'

'Oh, this is nice, but I don't see it anymore. It's been so long.'

'How old are you, if you don't mind me asking?'

Checking the door was closed before she answered, Missy broke out into a smile. 'I'm going to be a hundred years old. Elle is throwing me a party.'

'That's nice of her. Wow. A hundred years old. You don't look much older than thirteen.'

Another wide smile. 'That's how old I was when...' She checked behind her again. The door stayed shut, but she seemed to think this was a step too far, because she said nothing more.

'Well, thank you for the sandwiches,' Lucy said, and the wide smile came back. Missy backed out of the room, pulling the door behind her. Lucy waited for the turn of the lock, which came soon after. Okay, not quite the fierce interrogation she should have attempted, but she knew a little more than she had before.

A hundred-year-old child. Missy didn't seem like a vampire. The ones Lucy had met so far glowed with a physical intensity marking them out as other, somehow. Neither did she seem like whatever Elle was.

She picked up a sandwich. It was straight after Elle's stew the night before Lucy had spilled her guts. She could still feel the hazy after effects of whatever spell had been cast over her. Or maybe it was something more prosaic. Either way, she wasn't sure how much she could trust the egg mayo in her hands.

Had she put Adam at risk last night, telling Elle everything? She didn't think so, but without knowing Elle's intentions, how could she be sure? Lucy felt like she was drowning in this new craziness.

Adam hadn't made his intentions clear, though. He may have known what she was likely to do. But what did it make her, exactly? A pawn?

God, it was confusing. To top it off, she was starving, and the sandwiches looked amazing.

Elle could make fireballs with her hands, she remembered. If there was something she wanted to take from Lucy, she could bloody well reach out and take it from her, of that she had no doubt. The sandwiches were probably the least of her problems. And if she wanted to get out of here, she was going to need her strength.

She ate the sandwiches, paced around the room for a bit, picked up a few books and put them back again, thought briefly about rearranging them as some kind of rogue rebellious act, but decided it didn't quite carry the weight of her anger. She went to the window. Her room stood at the back of the house, overlooking a long strip of green, overgrown and wild looking, but somehow still coherent; a magical wonderland like the Secret Garden that entranced Lucy from its pages as a child. Huge green fences surrounded the garden, effectively blocking out views from the other houses. Witches needed privacy, she guessed.

Maybe she could climb down. She tried the window first. It opened, more or less. The frame was old, wooden, its mechanism a mix of brass and rope, both of which had long seen better days. She inched it up six inches, enough to let the cold of the day in, but not to squirm out of. Lucy wasn't big, but she wasn't thin like Elle.

Two bronze blocks had been screwed into the wooden frame, stopping the window from opening fully. No way to unscrew them, nor dig them out. Still, she tried until her nails ached, to no avail, so engrossed in her escape she entirely missed Elle setting up a position in the garden below, watching her toil away. At the moment Lucy gave up, slumping down on the cushioned window seat, she saw the witch. Elle flashed her smile, waved her hands, and the two bronze clasps fell from the frame. The window inched up slowly, giving Lucy the room she might need to escape.

'You can climb down, if you like,' Elle called up. 'Or I can let you out and you can come down and talk to me?'

Lucy didn't much fancy either at this point. But she supposed being down there was better than being stuck up here.

Anticipating her response, the latch to her bedroom door turned on its own.

Lucy grabbed her bag and eyed Jones, who stayed curled up on the bed.

Lucy half ran down the stairs. It occurred to her she might try the front door instead, but she found Missy there, if not guarding then watching. Lucy reckoned she might be able to take a little girl, but also suspected Missy was nothing of the kind. Beside Missy stood a table with dozens of perfectly identical pottery urns, which Missy moved vaguely in front of when Lucy's eye fell on it. Missy fixed Lucy with a wide smile, and Lucy smiled back, though she doubted it would pass many sincerity tests.

The garden was even more beautiful at ground level, with butterflies and bees wandering in and out of the flora and fauna. Amidst them, lounging in a high-backed wicker chair, was Elle.

Jones darted through the door after Lucy, rushing to settle at Elle's feet after dancing around her ankles for a moment. The little traitor.

He seemed utterly oblivious to the other creatures buzzing around the witch.

'It's amazing,' Elle said, 'the extents to which humans will trust someone based on the reaction their animals have to them.'

'Are you saying I shouldn't trust you?' Lucy asked, standing before her, arms crossed across her front.

'No. Making an observation. But I'd be interested to know whether you feel I should be trusted.'

'Honestly, I'm tired of trying to work out who, or what, to trust.'

Elle smiled. 'I like you. You've got something...'

'If you say spirit, I'm going to find out if I can hit a witch.'

'Fair enough.'

They considered each other in silence for a moment, Elle looking at her enforced houseguest as a bird of prey might consider a tasty morsel.

'Why are you keeping me here?' Lucy asked.

'For your safety.'

'It's daylight, so I call bullshit. You would have let me go, but you changed your mind.'

'What makes you say that?'

'You had Missy deal with the dead body in my hallway, and repair the mess. Not an inconsiderable task. But this morning, you won't let me leave. Why go to the trouble of sorting out the flat if I'm not going back to it?'

'You don't think I'll let you out?'

'Not seeing a lot of evidence to the contrary.'

Lucy wanted to push further, to dig in to Elle's allegiances, but she also didn't want to tip her off to her suspicions.

'You'll be free to go this evening once Adam returns.'

'I see. I don't belong to him, you know.'

'Don't you?'

'I really don't. But since we're on the subject, how do you think he'll react when he hears you kept me against my will?'

'I imagine he'll be pleased we've not allowed harm to come to you.'

Lucy shook her head. She wouldn't get anywhere with this woman, nor get anywhere close to her intentions. 'Fine. I'll be in my room. When he comes, please let me know.'

'Of course.' She sat back and closed her eyes, clearly comfortable she'd put Lucy in her place, which made Lucy want to get out even more.

She should get back to Adrian and work, let them know what was going on, she thought.

'I need my phone,' she said.

'Why?'

'I need to contact work.'

Elle shrugged and pulled Lucy's phone out of a small bag tucked beside her. 'Go ahead,' she said.

Lucy headed back inside expecting to be called back to make her call, walking past Missy's still silent sentry duty by the front door and back up to her room. She closed the door, and went back to the chaise lounge, sitting down on the edge, rubbing her temples.

She turned the phone back on, waiting for the fruit icon to turn into her lock screen, sure the Witches would burst through the door and rip it from her hands. But she was dealing with supernatural beings with over a century apiece in their rear view; perhaps they didn't realise the power of the gadget they'd returned to her. There were no signs of other technology in the house — no televisions, no computers.

She waited for the phone to reboot, thinking about her best move. Waiting here for Adam for the next few hours didn't seem like it. Adam had brought her here, which called his judgement into question.

The police may well be looking to question her. Elle said they'd cleaned up her apartment, but there was still the abduction from the hospital. As the screen came to life, it filled with notifications. Mostly from Adrian, reaching out across every fathomable social media platform to reach her. Bless him. She went to dial his number, but paused. Sweet Adrian — she couldn't get him mixed up in all this.

There were no good options. She needed to get out of this house, that much seemed clear, but the witches were not about to let her out, and she couldn't exactly force them. And whatever exit she could engineer, it needed to happen before the sun went down.

She needed a distraction.

A really stupid idea entered her mind, and she decided to act on it before her rational mind could talk herself out of it.

Punching in the number for the main work switchboard, she was about to hit dial when she realised there might be ears at the door. She went into the en-suite bathroom, locked the door, and sat on the edge of the old tub, a glorious Victorian affair with burnished brass taps and trimmings.

She hit call and waited.

'Switchboard.'

'Hey,' Lucy said. 'Cathy?'

'Lucy?' Cathy replied, any pretence toward professionalism transformed into a gossipy whisper. 'Holy shit, everyone's looking for you. Is it true you abducted someone from the hospital?'

'Not exactly. Listen. Me and Adrian were on a call a few nights back, and there was a patient. I came into the hospital yesterday to visit him, and there were some... people... there. I've been trying to work out what they've done with the patient. But I've gotten mixed up in some stuff.'

Cathy paused. 'There's a bulletin out for you. Adrian was really worried.'

Lucy smiled. 'I hope you've already called it in.'

A pause. 'Yes, sorry Lucy.'

'It's what I wanted you to do. Listen, I'm in an old house off the river. New Walk Terrace. I'm not sure about the number. I'm being held hostage. What's the name of the investigating officer?'

'Let me find out,' Cathy said, unable to hide the excitement from her voice.

'I'll stay on the line.'

12

WHEN THE WALLS CLOSE IN

'This is DI Turner,' a gruff voice cut through. 'Is this Lucy Barker?'

'It is.'

'We've been looking for you, Lucy. What can you tell me?'

'The incident at the hospital. I went to see a patient I'd attended the previous night. The same man was there who'd been at the scene. I spoke to him a little. Others came and took the patient, threatening one of the nurses.'

'Putting her in Intensive Care,' Groom interjected.

'Is she okay?'

'She will be. But she said you were there. Recognised you from the paramedic crews. And we got you on CCTV.'

'Then you know I didn't steal the patient.'

'No, and I have the notes from the scene officer who said you told her everything that had happened. But then you didn't show for work today, and your colleague seemed to think you were in some kind of trouble.'

She took a deep breath. 'I might be.'

'So where are you, Lucy?'

'It's a street off Fishergate. New Walk Terrace. If you follow it about halfway down, there's a house on the right that, well, I guess it looks... different.'

'Cathy tells me you're being held hostage.'

She winced. That sounded much worse than it had sounded in her head when she said it to Cathy. But there was no turning back now. 'That's right.'

'But they let you keep your phone?'

'I think they forgot about it.'

The DI paused on the other end of the line, as though he was mulling something over. 'You know, we went to your apartment this morning.'

Her heart sank. 'And?'

'Forensics haven't been able to find a single fingerprint. Nor DNA. They swear it's the cleanest place they've ever been. All the way out to the corridor.'

'I'm not sure where you're going with this, Detective Inspector.'

Silence.

'Teams are en route as we speak. Are you safe?'

'I'm locked in a bathroom on the first floor.'

'How many in the house with you?'

'Two I know of. Both women. One looks like a child.'

He paused. 'And you cannot get away?'

She bit her lip. This needed to go quicker. If Elle came in here... 'I'm afraid so,' she replied. She didn't know how to explain any of this when the police got there, but she wasn't planning on having to, at least not in the short term. She just knew she had to get out of there while the sun was still up. 'Both are dangerous.'

She could practically hear the Detective Inspector's frown down the other end of the line. Thankfully, she wasn't familiar with him, because she was about to make him look a right idiot, and she'd hate to do that to someone she knew.

'Okay. Well, sit tight. We'll come and get you out of there.'

'Thank you.'

The call hung up. She flushed the toilet, in case anyone was listening, and went back out to the bedroom, where Missy waited for her.

'What were you doing in there?' she asked, her head cocked to one side.

'Um, toilet?'

'I heard voices.'

Lucy shrugged. 'I don't think so.'

Missy sighed, and her head rolled over to one side. Her eyes fixed right ahead and rolled up into her skull, while her eyelids flattered like a trapped moth. For a second, Lucy thought she was having a seizure, but her head came back up and her eyes came back to normal.

Elle appeared at the door, out of breath. 'What is it?' she asked Missy.

'She's up to something.'

'I was going to the toilet,' Lucy sighed. 'Honestly, I don't know who the fuck you people are, but...'

Before she could finish, Elle brought her hand up, and Lucy flew backward, crashing into the far wall, the edge of a picture digging into her back. It was as sudden as it was violent. Invisible hands pinned Lucy like buffeting winds holding her inches off the ground.

Elle walked slowly toward her. 'What have you done?' she asked, as her eyes flamed with a blue spark, lighting up her face.

'Wait,' Lucy said, heart pounding. Pain covered every inch of her body, as though the force holding her against the wall drilled into her, a thousand tiny needles at a time. She struggled for breath.

'I will not. What did you do?'

'Police. I called the police.'

The two women looked at each other, panic crossing between them.

Lucy crashed to the floor, landing awkwardly on her knee, which seemed to bend backward. She let out a howl of pain.

'We should go,' Missy said, her voice different from before, more assured, less childlike.

Elle looked at Lucy, crumpled on the floor, hatred in her eyes. 'Humans,' she hissed. The two women turned and left the room, leaving Lucy panting for breath on the floor.

Lucy half expected them to lock the door behind them, but they left it wide open. Lucy tried to stand, but went straight back over on her knee.

Damn.

Hobbling over to the chaise lounge, she sat and took her jeans down to examine the knee. Already swollen, she worked the muscles with her fingers. Nothing too bad, a sprain perhaps. She should be able to walk on it in a few hours. Except she didn't have a few hours. The police would be here soon, and she didn't know what she was going to tell them if they found her in an empty house.

At least she'd gotten rid of the other two.

If she had a crutch, she could get out.

Sirens blared in the distance. She forced herself to her feet and hobbled to the window. No sign of Elle or Missy down there. Day was already threatening its turn to night; the threat to her life was about to expand exponentially.

Hobbling to the door, she hopped over to the ornate staircase, worried for a second she might crash through it and tumble to her death. She caught herself, using the thick bannister as a support as she worked herself down the long, curved stairs. The flashing blue lights spilling through the small window atop the door were the only thing stopping her from hobbling through it. The police were here.

By the door was a round wooden tub, out of which stood two umbrellas and one ornate walking stick. She grabbed the latter. She had to hunch over to use it, but it was better than nothing.

The cane clacked over the wooden floor as she set off through the house.

The side entrance door stood open. That must have been Missy and Elle's escape, if that was indeed what they'd done. Fishing her phone out of her pocket, she stopped and dialled Adrian.

'Lucy, Jesus, where have you been?' he answered.

'I'm having a few issues,' she replied. 'Are you working?'

'Yeah.'

'Who are you with?'

'Nobody. Just finished. I'm taking the bus back.'

She gave a sigh of relief. 'Can you come pick me up?'

Adrian paused. She could hear his brain working overtime at the other end of the line.

'Where are you?'

She gave him the address, and he hung up.

Edging round the building, she could hear armed police taking up position by the front door. No doubt they'd come through the rear gate, too. Heading into the garden, she tried to find somewhere she could hide. The lush greenery offered plenty of opportunities. She hobbled over to an old stone planter and crouched behind the thick fronds streaming out of it, half expecting to find two witches cowering there before her. It hid her from the rest of the garden pretty well. A second later, the rear gate opened and four armed police swept through, guns sweeping the garden for movement before focusing on the rear patio doors.

'In position,' one of them said.

She held her own position, waiting for them to move. She wondered what had happened to Elle and Missy. With their power, they could take down every man and woman the North Yorkshire Police could throw at them, yet they turned tail and fled instead.

Of course. It wasn't violence they feared; it was exposure. Exposure to a human world they existed in the shadows of. They were probably really pissed at Lucy for bringing the police to her door. She'd like to feel like they deserved it, but was more worried about having yet more supernatural beings enraged by her.

Still, there were more immediate concerns. She'd have to pick her moment.

More armed police arrived on the scene.

'Breach, breach.'

An officer smashed the door, and the armed officers stormed the building in force. Lucy crawled out from behind the box, climbing to her feet hesitantly. Taking her stick, she walked as calmly as she could to the side entrance. Holding her breath, she walked through it, onto the house's main driveway.

The garden entrance was far enough away from the main door that nobody noticed her, and she walked to the road without interruption. Parked a hundred metres up the road from where the police were busy breaching the witch's house was an ambulance, perfectly in place in a street filled with police cars and flashing lights.

Adrian stood beside it, looking at his phone. He saw Lucy hobbling over, and made to start toward her, but she waved him away. Slowly she made her way toward him, expecting with every breath the shout from behind her, the cry for her to stop. But it never came. Adrian helped her into the back of the ambulance without a word, their eyes meeting just once as he closed the doors on her. As she put her weight onto the bad knee, she winced, and Adrian caught her.

'You alright?'

'Let's get out of here,' she said, strapping herself into the family seat, intended for those unable to leave their loved ones on the way to the hospital. The panic chair, they called it, the chair in which everyone got their first chance to contemplate life without the loved one on the stretched next to them as they tore through the streets to the hospital. He nodded and jumped back down before climbing back into the cab. 'One getting out of

here, coming up,' he said, putting the ambulance into gear and
pulling away.

13

AGAINST THE GRAIN

Lucy had given little thought to a destination beyond '*anywhere but here*' back at the witch's house. She'd assumed that they might head to Adrian's house, but her friend pulled up outside a crumbling terraced house with an overgrown clump of weeds acting as a front garden. He said nothing as he parked the ambulance outside and ran to the front door.

A surprised looking man answered, and after a few words Lucy didn't hear, Adrian motioned her out of the cab, and disappeared inside. Lucy followed, her curiosity feeling like a lump in her throat — she'd had enough curiosity for one day. Hell, for one lifetime.

'How do you like your tea?' the man from the front door asked her, guiding her through the hallway. He was a big man, but stocky rather than fat, and he had a strong accent, eastern European. He was familiar to Lucy, but not in any way that married up his face to his name.

'Milk, one sugar, please,' she replied.

The man disappeared into the kitchen to make the teas, leaving Lucy and Adrian alone in an extremely messy lounge filled with the detritus of obviously committed weed smokers, which didn't exactly chime with Lucy's vision of her erstwhile paramedic partner. Smoke had tinged the walls yellow, and the table piled high with clutter had three ashtrays full of roaches stacked atop DVD cases and records.

'Let me take a look at your knee,' Adrian said, trying not to look embarrassed by the place, and failing somewhat.

Lucy peeled off her jeans, revealing a bruised mess where her knee used to be, twice its usual size. 'Where the hell are we?'

Adrian knelt beside her and touched the darkened, puffy skin. Pain shot up her leg, and she winced. 'Do you remember when our holidays didn't align?'

'What?'

'Pawel was the relief they brought in. And over the last six months I've been picking up a few extra shifts to....'

Lucy tried to parse the meaning of that from her partner's eyes, but he wouldn't meet hers. 'To?'

'Look, I couldn't take you home,' Adrian with a finality.

'Woah,' Pawel said, bringing through three mugs in his large hands, cutting off any further explanation. 'Looks nasty.' He went to set down the mugs on the table, realised he didn't have anywhere to do so and took them back to the kitchen, coming back through to clear some space amongst the mess. 'Apologies for the mess,' he added with a chortle. 'Four men sharing a house, you know?' He didn't seem phased by the woman with her trousers down in the middle of his living room. But then, if he was another paramedic. He wouldn't be.

For a moment she couldn't shake the feeling that Adrian was somehow cheating on her with this burly eastern European. She'd never so much as learned the names of the few relief staff she'd worked with, let alone learned their addresses.

'Don't worry about it,' Lucy said. 'Thanks for the tea.'

Pavel smiled as he carted off a pile of DVDs to another room. He looked every bit as dishevelled as his surroundings, with a week's worth of stubble on his chubby face, his hair messy and unkempt and a month's growth longer than the cut deserved.

Adrian looked up at Lucy, sheepishly. 'This is mostly shock,' he added, returning to the knee. 'You've sprained it good. Two to three weeks and you'll be good as new.'

'Thanks,' she said, trying to shift up on the sofa enough to get more comfortable.

'You want to tell me what the hell's going on?' Adrian asked in a low voice.

'Not right now,' she replied.

He frowned, but she didn't feel overly burdened by a need to tell him everything that was going on. 'Calling in a fake hostage alert,' he muttered under his breath. 'You can get in serious trouble, Luce.'

'One thing at a time,' she said, straightening her leg.

Adrian fussed around in his med bag, took out a syringe and plunged it into her knee. 'That should free it up for a bit. A few hours and you'll be able to walk. But I would suggest...'

'Rest, got it.'

'But you're going to ignore me, anyway.'

'Pretty much.'

'Lucy, love, I know what I saw the other night. What the hell have you gotten mixed up in?'

Lucy was halfway through formulating a response when a knock at the front door saved her the trouble. No gentle, friendly knock, either. The three of them sat up, straight-backed like meerkats.

'Police?' Adrian asked in a hushed whisper.

'Police?' Pawel said, appearing back in the doorway with an increasingly worried expression on his face.

Lucy got to her feet and pulled her trousers back up. The knee already felt easier; she'd be able to limp out of there, should it come to it.

She went over to the window and tried to peer through net curtains so grey it was hard to determine their age. Outside, the sun had set.

The hammering returned.

Pawel shrugged and moved to the door. 'Could be Amazon delivery,' he said. 'New Alien Blu-ray. Steel book.'

'Yes?' she heard Pawel answer.

'Where is she?' came a low, growled response.

Lucy hobbled toward the front door. 'Adam?'

Adam barged past Pawel, who looked startled at the ease with which it happened. 'Hey!' he exclaimed, but Adam ignored him, crossing the distance in a flash to grab Lucy by the shoulders.

'Are you okay?'

'I'm fine,' she said, feeling slightly embarrassed by this sudden show of concern for her. She noted how high Adrian's eyebrows arched.

'What happened?'

Lucy looked around at three sets of eyes on her, each wanting to know what was going on.

She shook her head. 'Fine. You might as well sit down.'

It was Adrian who broke the awkward silence first. 'You don't need to be invited in?'

Adam glared at him. 'No. That's a superstition. A stupid one, at that. You think a magical barrier keeps us out of your homes? Why?'

'Sorry,' Adrian said, realising who and what he was talking to.

'Wait,' Pawel said, looking extremely confused.

'I'm a friend of the patient you took in the other day,' Adam started.

'Who got stolen from the hospital in a coma, putting a nurse in IC?' Adrian interjected.

'I was there,' Lucy said. 'I saw the whole thing. Four of... *them*... came and took Cain.'

'Who's Cain?' Pawel asked. He didn't look any less confused, and Lucy wished he'd just leave them alone to talk. But she could hardly order a man out of his own living room. The simplest thing would be for the ground to swallow them all whole.

'The patient,' Adrian replied. 'And an old flame of Lucy's, apparently.'

'That's... beside the point,' Lucy said. This wasn't going exactly to plan, not that she had one. 'We weren't able to stop them. I've been working with Adam to find out where he is. Well, I was supposed to be. Haven't got very far.'

Adrian and Pawel looked at her with more questions forming on their lips, but Adam spoke first.

'What happened with Elle?' he asked, his voice softer. He looked at her with kindness and sorrow and it made her realise how pleased she was to see him again.

'Who is Elle?' asked Pawel, increasingly exasperated.

Lucy ignored him. She didn't have time for every question, not when she had so many of her own. 'Did you put me with her to get more information?' she asked Adam.

The way he looked at his shoes confirmed the point.

'You knew she wasn't to be trusted?' she asked, a good deal of good feeling evaporating.

'I suspected. Can you tell me what happened?'

'I don't know. I think she drugged me or entranced me, or something. Either way, I spilled my guts about everything that's happened since I met you. She wouldn't let me leave the next morning, so I had to call the police. Adrian helped me escape. I don't know what happened to Elle.'

'That's okay,' he said, but he sounded disappointed.

'I need to go home,' she said, shaking her head. She wanted nothing more than to go home, cuddle up to her cat, watch something mindless.

Her cat.

'Oh, Christ,' she said, the bottom lurching out of her world.

'What?' Adam replied, and she felt his hackles go up. The others seemed to sense it too. They shrank back into the sofa.

'Jones,' she said. 'I left him there. At Elle's.'

'Your cat?'

'Yes, my cat. I need to go back and get him.'

'No,' Adam said, with a finality that shocked her.

'Fuck you,' she replied. 'You do not get to tell me what to do, Adam. I don't give a shit who or what you are. I need to get my cat. That woman might do anything to him.'

'You don't need to worry,' Adam said, chuckling. 'Elle may be many things, but you don't have to worry about her hurting your cat.'

'Easy enough for you to say. It's not your cat.'

'She's a Maenad. She probably thinks more of your cat than she does you or me. And no matter what happened last night, I do not believe her intentions are to do you — or anyone — harm. She's trying to understand what is going on.'

'What's a... meenad?' Pawel asked.

'She's not alone,' Adrian chimed in, ignoring his housemate's question. 'Lucy, this is madness. What are you doing, getting mixed up in this? Your job is to help people, not hang around with people who get their jollies drinking blood.'

'I do not get jollies,' Adam replied, his voice cold and even, 'and I haven't hurt a human being for a long time, though I would make an exception for someone getting in my way.'

'Oh, Christ,' Lucy shouted, bringing the squabble to an end. 'This is ridiculous. Adam, don't be mean to Adrian, he's a good person. Adrian, I'm trying to help someone, remember? Our patient. My friend. He's still out there somewhere.'

The four of them stood in silence for a moment, each too embarrassed to catch the eye of the others. Pawel was the exception, staring at Adam like he was about to turn into a purple dinosaur and start singing.

'What about you?' Lucy asked, turning back to Adam. 'Have you gotten anywhere?'

'Nothing,' he growled. 'I have tried to track Autumn, but to no avail. Come, we will go to Elle and get your cat back and think about our next move.'

'What about work?' Adrian said.

'You said it yourself. I can't work with this knee. I'll call in and explain.'

'And the police?'

'I don't know,' she said, more aggressively than she intended. She sighed. 'I'm sorry, Adrian. And thank you for today.' She crossed over to him and gave him a big hug, which he returned gladly. She felt a pang of regret — she wanted to know how they'd ended up here, rather than at the house he was supposed to share with his husband, but she just didn't have the bandwidth for it.

She pulled away. 'Nice to meet you, Pawel,' she said, as Adam moved toward the front door. 'Sorry for bringing trouble here.'

'No trouble,' the big man said, but he leaned in to Lucy as she passed him. 'Be careful, Lucy. This one may play the mouse, but he is the wolf.'

She smiled and gave him a nod as she pulled away, even as she knew she wouldn't be taking his advice to heart. No matter the truth of it. She said her goodbyes and hobbled to the front door behind Adam. Adam said nothing to the two men, which probably wouldn't endear him to either of them, but she supposed it didn't matter. She was more concerned about keeping up with the tall vampire with her bust leg, an injury she was a little put out he hadn't noticed.

Once outside, however, she realised she wouldn't have to worry about the walk, at least. Parked outside was an old black Morris Minor, lovingly kept and gleaming like the night. Adam stood next to it and flashed her a big smile. 'Do you like it?'

She laughed. 'It's not quite what I'd expected.'

He shrugged. 'It's an original. And I figured you were hurt.' He stepped forward to her and took her hand in his own. It was cold, but soft. 'I'm sorry, Lucy. Truly I am. If you want out of this, I will try to find a way. But if you could stay with me a little while longer, I think we can help Cain.'

She looked up into his eyes. 'Okay,' she said. 'What's next?'

'Get the cat, go back to mine, work out our next move.'

His place. The place where this all started. Just the memory of it brought the stink of meat back to her nostrils. No matter how refined he seemed, or how much that imposing frame of his drew her eye, she always knew it was there, a perpetual reminder of who, and what, he was. The home of a monster.

'Great,' she said, climbing into the front seat.

I4

FEAST OF THE DAMNED

'So, is there an actual plan?' Lucy asked, shifting in her seat uncomfortably. She'd never actually sat in a car with this kind of all-in-one seat, and the lack of seatbelt made her uncomfortable, even as they wound slowly through city centre traffic. People outside stopped and stared at the car, which seemed to please Adam. So much for flying under the radar. Still, the windows were so heavily tinted she doubted they could see her. Thinking about it, the glass was probably as much about keeping the sun's rays at bay as they were about stopping people leering at the friendly neighbourhood vampire.

They'd mask any violence inside, too.

'Elle is powerful,' Adam replied. 'We must tread carefully.'

'What's the deal with her?'

'Elle is what we call an old one, except we wouldn't call it to her face. It's what we call those who were here before us. She is eternal, in her own way, although she has to regenerate.'

'What, like Doctor Who?'

'Not exactly, no.'

'What does she want? Whose side is she on?'

'Elle is on her own side, and nobody else's. Her interests might align with others from time to time, but mostly she keeps herself to herself. She usually has a companion, but they stay in the house together. She'll not be happy about you bringing the police to her door, though, so you need to tread carefully. Let me do the talking.'

'I suppose you'd rather I stay in the car?' she grumbled. She was not used to men bossing her around — the fact this one could kill her in an instant didn't make her like it more.

'That would be worse. They would see it as disrespectful. I doubt she'll demand an apology from you, but she'll want you there before her.'

'I hope she doesn't want an apology,' she sulked, 'because she's sure as hell not getting one from me. She kidnapped me, wouldn't let me leave.'

'Lucy, remember you are literally at the bottom of the food chain here. She's an eternal being capable of dark magics. If she wants you to apologise to her, you do it.'

'Oh, and I suppose if she asked you to apologise, you'd do it, would you?'

'Absolutely. There are few things in this world more danger-ous than my kind, but she is one of them.'

'Well then, thank you for leaving me alone with her without warning me,' she sulked.

He said nothing in response.

She stared out of the window. These constant reminders of her low station as a human being grated. There was an arrogance to these so-called supernatural beings, though there was nothing lofty she could see about them beyond their powers and extreme old age.

That even went for Adam. He was terrible at telling her any-thing — every time she thought she was getting a straight answer from him, she'd look back on it a few minutes later and struggle to find information in it. So Elle was old. It didn't exactly tell her anything.

She realised she was staring at him with a furrowed brow when he turned and laughed; the smile lighting up his face.

'What?' he asked, laughing.

'Nothing,' she scowled.

His eyes went back to the road. The smile never completely left his face, though. 'You know,' he said, 'you're very pretty when you're pissed off.'

She turned away and looked back out the window, simultaneously annoyed and glad he couldn't see the blush on her cheek or the smile trying to take over her mouth.

They pulled up outside Elle's house a moment later, and Lucy was pleased to see there was no police presence left. A tiny wooden board covered the smashed glass panel on the front door. She suspected the board was a lot bigger round the back of the house.

The house stood silent, its drawn curtains revealing little to show if the house's inhabitants had returned. Still, Adam pulled up to the curb and let the engine idle for a moment before turning it off, the engine making strange sputtering sounds as it went.

They got out and walked to the front door. She felt silly for bringing herself back here because of Jones, to a house of unimaginably powerful beings, protected only by a vampire who'd told her their power was great than his.

Adam knocked, and the door opened. Missy, holding Jones in her arms. The cat looked a picture of contentment, and Lucy felt a pang of jealousy. Missy broke into a wide smile when she saw Lucy; it fell from her face when she remembered she was supposed to be cross, moving to a scowl instead.

Elle appeared behind Missy, a good two feet taller than her companion and a hundred times more glamourous. She wore the same fake smile she'd worn the last time she'd opened the door to the pair of them. 'Ah, you've returned?' she said breezily.

'Came for my cat,' Lucy said, feeling Adam bristle alongside her.

'Elle,' Adam said. 'The fault is mine. I didn't give Lucy adequate information when she came here. Please, do not hold her responsible for my ill-judgement.'

'It would seem to me,' Elle said, looking down her nose at Lucy, 'that this girl *is* your ill judgement, Adam.'

It was Lucy's turn to bristle, but she held her tongue. She also noted there was no move to hand Jones back to her, and the traitorous little furball didn't exactly seem in a rush to escape, either.

Adam ignored the atmosphere completely, leaning in to speak to the witch in an even softer, deeper tone. 'Have you heard anything about Cain, Elle?'

Elle paused, looked out at the road above both their heads, and sighed. 'Autumn and her people have taken over a building, one of those ugly modern things near the station. She and her followers have set up camp there. Cain will be there, too. They'll be watching the turn, and they'll set him loose.' She handed Adam a scrap of paper, which he looked at briefly before pocketing.

'What do you mean?' Lucy asked, but Elle ignored her.

'Thank you,' Adam said, and started back toward the car, leaving Lucy stranded for a second. She wanted to reach forward and grab Jones from Missy's arms, but that hardly seemed wise. Besides, it didn't look like she was going home. Elle stared at her with haughty disdain, seemingly willing her to make some kind of move. Lucy guessed being allowed to leave at all after calling the cops should be seen as a win, but it didn't feel that way.

Without a word, she got back into the car. She watched from the side window as Jones leapt down from Missy's arms and headed back inside the witch's house without so much as a look behind him. Traitorous little bastard.

'So,' she said, as Adam turned the engine over and threw the car into reverse to make a three-point turn out of the street. 'You going to tell me what she meant by that?'

'About Cain?'

'Yeah.'

'I told you that the turn can be a hard process for us. Don't think of it in the way you've seen in the movies. It's more like an infection. It kills the host and brings them back; a more symbiotic relationship than a disease. When you come back, at first you can barely find your way. It's painful, and confusing, and the other part of you, the new part of you, needs blood. You need it too, because everything that was keeping you alive — food, calories, oxygen, water — none of those things matter anymore. You need blood.'

He shifted in his seat, glancing over to judge her reaction before continuing. 'After you wake, there is little control. The thirst is everything. Almost every tale of vampires you have heard has come from someone becoming. After a while, once you are sated, you come back. And you remember what you have done. We are still the same people, once the change comes. There is no demon. We have to live with the guilt of what we do for centuries. For most of us, it keeps us in the shadows, drinking to survive, and rarely killing. Blood is not hard to find.'

'What about those who don't?' she asked.

He sighed. 'They become like Autumn.'

'So, what do they want with Cain?'

'I don't know. Perhaps they want to bring me into the fight, but I can't think why. Or it's a punishment. But Cain doesn't deserve this. He's a sweet man. Funny. Kind. If it comes to it and we're too late, he would hate to become one of us.'

'Isn't that strange? I mean, I would have thought most people who hang around vampires would do it because they want to be one?'

'Some, sure.' He shifted around in his seat once more — this was clearly a subject he found uncomfortable. 'There are people drawn to the darkness, what they see as the romantic side of us. Eternal night. They don't last long.'

'What about Cain?'

'He knew what I was, and didn't want it for himself. He believed in me, more than he believed in our kind.'

'Believed in you how?'

'I have a different view from some of my brethren about the future of our people.'

She waited for him to elaborate further, but he pulled the car in at a junction; near three huge modern buildings, each sticking out like monstrous brick sore thumbs amongst the houses of this city suburb. 'We're here,' he said.

'Holy shit,' she said, realising where they were. 'I used to work here.'

'Where?'

She pointed out the first building. It looked fully deserted, without a single light on inside. 'That one. I used to do telesales in there.'

'What's telesales?'

'People used to phone us to activate their bank card, and we'd try to flog them insurance. The place shut down a few years back when everyone realised it was a giant scam.'

'And you worked there?'

'I didn't realise until I was already working there. It was a part-time job while I was at University. God, I hated the place. I quit after they gave me an almighty bollocking for refusing to sell identity fraud protection to an old lady so confused she thought I was the post office.'

'Looks deserted,' Adam said. 'Probably where they've taken him.'

'That's where I knew Cain. Where we met. I heard it closed a few years after I left. They had to wind it up pretty quick. My guess is they couldn't shift the building before they went under.'

Adam started the car once more, driving it away from the building in question, into the adjacent building's car park. Lights blazed in that one — a medical company, by the logo outside.

He parked up, and both got out.

As they walked back across the car park past the dozen other cars, a flashlight scanned the ground before them before shining up into Lucy's eyes. She held her hand out in front of her, and saw the rough outline of a security guard, skinny and tall, crossing toward them.

'You can't park there,' he called out, still a distance away.

'Sorry,' Lucy said. 'Look, we're going to be ten minutes. Surely it's no bother?'

'Sorry, miss,' he replied. She squinted to get a better look at him, but all she could make out was the grey of his uniform. 'But I'm afraid it's company policy to allow...'

Shadows moved within shadows, too fast for Lucy to see. An arm grabbed the guard from nowhere, whisking him off his feet. His torch tumbled to the ground. It took a few seconds for Lucy's eyes to adjust after the flashlight, but when they did, she wished they hadn't.

A vampire pounced onto the fallen guard, who did his level best to fight it off. The monster ripped into his neck with a move of such ferocious violence it splattered Lucy in a spray of arterial blood.

'No!' she screamed, but as she moved toward the injured man, Adam stepped in front of her. Half a dozen vampires moved in. They seemed to melt out of the surrounding night. The vampire leading the attack straightened up, her face wet with red, her eyes seeming to burn into the dark.

Autumn.

The man on the floor gurgled for a moment, drowning in his own blood, before laying still. Lucy's stomach turned; her heart pounded in her chest.

'Adam,' Autumn said, her extended teeth gleaming in the night. 'How good of you to join us. And you've brought us food. How generous of you. I had the feeling you wouldn't want to miss the turning.'

Lucy looked up into the face of her protector, but he wasn't looking at her. He stared at Autumn with an animalistic hunger, his teeth out, his eyes seeming almost to glow.

'Of course,' he said, grabbing Lucy by the arm in a move that brought a silent scream of pain bubbling up her throat. 'I wouldn't have missed it for the world.'

The bottom of Lucy's stomach dissolved into numbness as she realised how badly she'd been played.

15
BLOOD SPILLER

The old offices of the Card Protection Scheme had changed a fair bit in the years since she'd last been here. The room was the same one she'd sat in day after day at the same desk, looking across at the same cocaine-addled managers as they tried to gee up their disinterested sales force. Those desks were burned and broken and scattered about. The walls were grimy and splattered with things Lucy didn't even want to contemplate, and an icy darkness permeated everything.

As for Lucy, she'd have settled for her old desk over her current setup — wrists bound and hung from the ceiling by metal chains that dug into her flesh. If she took the weight off her feet for even a second, she felt like her hands might break apart under the pressure, and her swollen knee protested at being called back into action.

Tears ran down her face, snot hung from her nose, and sweat dripped down cold skin at an incessant rate. The whole place smelled like spoiled meat, and there was a haze in the air, like all the old dust had joined up with the death on the air for a little party.

Adam had disappeared to the far end of the room with Autumn and the others, leaving her hanging on a chain with the diminishing hope he was playing for effect.

Laughter drifted up from where the vampires huddled, discussing Christ knew what. Had anything Adam told her been true? Every ounce of effort not spent keeping herself on her feet ran over her collected moments with him. Everything she knew about Autumn came from him. Everything she knew about Cain she took at his word. She replayed events at the hospital again and again in her head, trying to work out if she'd misread the situation. Had he been waiting for Autumn the whole time? He didn't exactly intervene.

How could she have been so stupid? Her first encounter with a supernatural being, and she'd... trusted him? Because he filled out his clothes well and had a brooding intensity? Was she that shallow?

A noise came from behind. She tried to inch round to see the source, but before she could, a man appeared by her side. Pale skin, waves of power coming off him like dry ice at a concert.

'What do we have here?' the man said, leaning into her ear and placing a hand on her hips. 'Dinner?' She shuddered, but that seemed to encourage him more. He pressed himself against her. He might not have breath, but the smell coming from his mouth was rancid enough, more spoiled meat and copper.

Lucy said nothing, gritting her teeth against her desire to answer back.

'I can hear your heart,' the vampire whispered, tracing a long fingernail across her ribcage, hand moving up under her top. Lucy's flesh crawled with goosebumps with every movement. She shut her eyes, bracing for what came next. Could be the last hope left was to die with dignity.

Or not.

Whipping her head backward, the back of her skull connected with the vampire's nose with a crunch of bone and cartilage. He squealed, a horrified high-pitched wail that fell back with him.

In a flash he was back on her, his hand going round her throat, squeezing so hard Lucy thought he might rip her head clean from its moorings. The weight he put on her dragged her hands down, and she'd have screamed if she could get the sounds through her throat.

'Hey,' Adam called from somewhere, and the vamp let go.

Her feet went out from underneath her, putting even more weight on her hands — he'd been keeping her up, and she struggled both to get back her breath, and to get her legs working again, the former coming in ragged shallow breaths, the latter stumbling like a drunk walking across ice.

'She's not for you,' Autumn hissed at the newcomer. 'She's for the ritual.'

Ritual. Not a word you wanted to hear in relation to yourself, especially not while trussed up in an abandoned building.

Adam walked toward her. 'I'm sorry,' he said, without sounding it.

'Go fuck yourself,' she replied, wanting to muster a hearty spit in his face, but not having the moisture in her mouth to do so.

'This isn't personal,' he continued, his hands out as though to defend himself, even though her single possible recourse was harsh language.

'It feels pretty personal to me,' she said, struggling for breath. The pain in her knee and wrists threatened to overwhelm her. 'Please,' she said. 'My hands, my knee.'

Adam turned to Autumn. 'Let me help her,' he pleaded.

'She's food,' Autumn replied, sounding bored. 'All we need from her is a pulse. Knock her out cold and be done with it.'

Adam looked back at Lucy, a look of pain on his face. This enraged Lucy more.

'You piece of shit!' she spat. 'Try to come and knock me out, you coward.'

'Bring him in,' Autumn said.

The other vamps in the room disappeared, leaving the three of them alone in awkward silence. Autumn looked across at Adam warily. It looked like she trusted Adam about as much as Lucy did.

Lucy continued her struggle against the pain threatening to drag her under — the only way out of this alive was to stay awake.

The other vamps returned, carrying between them a makeshift stretcher, upon which lay the corpse of Cain. Lucy's heart sank. So here it was. She had failed. The body had been gone for a little while, clearly. The skin had taken on a vaguely grey hue, and there was a peaceful riposte to him that marked him entirely at odds with the room they carried him into. He'd not been dead long enough yet to bloat, and she suspected he never would. Soon he'd be something else, something hungry. And there she was, trussed up and ready to eat.

They moved the body onto a table, one of the few that hadn't been overturned or smashed for firewood. Once he was laid out, other vamps appeared, arranging candles around the head, and a variety of small urns. Another brought out a shawl and covered the body — it was gossamer thin.

'The ritual requires the body be buried,' Autumn said in a grave voice. 'Even the most cursory of burials provides us with the covering required.'

'Like I give a fuck,' Lucy replied. She got control back in her legs, standing up on her tiptoes to release some of the pressure on her wrists. The chains had dug into her skin, and the wrist itself was wet with blood. Panicking, she looked up to check the damage, but all she could see was a slight cut amongst the red lines on her wrist. Thankfully, it was on the top of her wrist rather than the carpal tunnel.

Working her hand, she tried to see if the lubrication might allow her to free her hand, careful not to pull on the cut and make it worse. The last thing she wanted was to de-glove herself. That might be the only thing worse than the alternative before her. At first, it seemed futile, but as more blood oozed from the cut, she worked it more until her hand was almost free.

The preparation of Cain's body had Autumn distracted, but Adam watched her with a cool eye. She didn't care. If he had to come over and silence her, stop her, she would make the bastard regret it.

He watched her slide her hand out and shook his head ever so slightly. 'Not yet,' he mouthed, stopping Lucy in her tracks.

She stared at him, not daring to hope. Another trick? Another way to keep her in line? Or was he playing this all along? It wouldn't be the first time he sent her into a situation without letting on his intentions. Maybe he didn't trust her not to reveal the truth. Was that so unreasonable? She knew nothing about these beings, where their powers lay. The vampires of myth and legend could control minds, so why not read them, too? Just because they didn't fear crosses didn't mean it was all lies.

If that were true, she'd endangered the whole thing by working it out. Autumn might read her, take Adam out of the picture, and she'd be screwed, even if one hand was out of her restraints.

Or he could be messing with her, not wanting her to mess up his chance to get back in with Autumn and the others. This could be his atonement for killing the blonde vampire. Or his revenge. She had no way of knowing, and there was too much at stake to improvise.

She stared at him, wanting his intentions to become clear. He shook his head once more, almost imperceptibly, and she realised the bloody hand was still out of its binding. Cautiously, she wiped some of the blood onto the wrist of her other hand and slipped the free hand halfway into the shackle.

The extra few inches this afforded took some of the stress off her knee, so it was worth it for that, if nothing else. Using the blood from her free hand, she worked the other one, squeezing her hand as small as she could to squeeze it through. The restraints were steel, but designed for bigger hands than hers. She worked it slowly free, easing it back in halfway, holding onto her position. The wrists still burned, and the knee still hurt like a bastard, but it was better than before.

Adam gave a wry smile and turned back to watching the proceedings. All the vampires were — evidently the main course wasn't as exciting as the table setting. Lucy might have found it fascinating, too, but under the circumstances, it was difficult to muster anything other than blind panic. Even if Adam was on her side — and that was a mighty big if — it didn't change the fact there were nearly a dozen vampires here, and only her and Adam to fight them. That was before you counted in the freshly risen vampire with a bloodlust due to arrive any moment.

Adam backed away from Autumn, slowly moving toward Lucy. She wished she knew what the hell he was planning — she might stuff it up if she didn't know her role.

The vampires at the other end of the hall began their ritual, each taking one of the pottery urns and holding it aloft. At this end of the room, it didn't sound like anything more than some vague mumbling, but they seemed pleased with themselves.

Autumn turned, her face lit up with excitement until she saw Adam. Saw how far he'd moved toward Lucy.

Her face fell.

She crossed the distance between her and Adam in a flash, but her vampire friend was not her destination — Lucy was.

Adam's arm shot out, grabbing Autumn round the throat. The female vampire gave a startled scream, and brought round her hand in response, slashing at Adam's face, leaving dark red traces across his skin. He let out his own wail of pain, and Autumn broke free, turning her attention back to Lucy. The distance between them shrank to nothing in a flash, and Autumn reached out her hand to grab Lucy.

Slipping her hands out of the manacles, Lucy dropped to the floor, going into a crouch. Autumn, unprepared for the move and travelling with great speed and rage, crashed into Lucy, the force knocking the air from Lucy's lungs. Autumn regained her poise somewhere before she hit the ground, like a cat landing on all paws. The two of them faced each other, one armed with teeth and claws and superhuman strength, the other armed with a sprained knee.

'I'm going to enjoy this,' Autumn said.

16

ALL HAIL THE NEW FLESH

Even as Lucy tried to work out how to survive the next thirty seconds, another blur of movement shot past. Adam, his already imposing body spread out to its full, ferocious capacity. He wound back his fist as he went, bringing it forward to meet Autumn's chest.

The crack of bones rang out like a rifle shot. Autumn flew backward, blood misting in a trail from her mouth behind her as she went. She crashed onto the floor with considerably less grace this time, her head smacking against cold industrial carpet. If she was going to get back up, it wouldn't be soon.

Adam turned back, face feral with rage. His teeth were extended, his eyes burned with rage. He snarled with ferocious intent. Spreading his arms wide, for a second Lucy thought he might turn his attention to her, driven so mad with rage she looked like a meal once more.

'Get behind me,' he growled, the words barely human, like gravel scraped along a driveway.

Lucy turned. She'd forgotten about the ritual behind her. As had the vampires conducting it. They turned from Cain's corpse, their attention on her, advancing slowly across the call centre floor toward her and Adam. Their teeth were out, their eyes alight, snarling cautiously as they approached.

Stumbling back, Lucy moved behind Adam, relieved to have him between her and the advancing vamps.

'Finish her,' Adam snarled, and for a moment Lucy didn't know what he meant.

She looked down at the broken body of Autumn. She was still. Lucy looked around for something to finish the job. A shard of broken desk lay a few feet away. She scooped it up and advanced on the female vamp. She wasn't sure if this would be real wood, but Adam had said it didn't matter, anyway. Her kitchen knife had been good enough for the blonde, after all.

Lucy straddled Autumn, pinning the vampire's legs under her own, the ribcage left exposed. Autumn's hand came round like lightning, grabbing at Lucy's throat, squeezing with such intensity Lucy dropped the shard, both her hands going to the woman's wrist, pulling to free her windpipe.

Air rapidly depleting, Lucy could feel her head swelling, her eyes bulging. She desperately clawed at the wrist, but she might as well be scratching at solid rock.

Rolling her over, a rictus grin spread over Autumn's face as she brought her other arm round and effortlessly pulled away one of Lucy's flailing limbs, shoving it against the hard floor hard enough to make the bones crunch. Lucy let go a moan of pain.

Abandoning the attempt to tear the arms from her throat, Lucy groped wildly at the floor with her one free arm, desperate to locate the shard she'd dropped.

'I know you're supposed to be Cain's first meal,' Autumn said, 'but I think I might need to take a taste. I'm sure he won't mind, before he mauls you to a death of unimaginable misery and pain.'

Moving her head down, she used the hand around Lucy's throat to turn her head away, exposing her neck.

Lucy's fingers closed around what she hoped was the shard of wood. She couldn't see where it was going, certainly couldn't aim it at the vampire's ribcage, so she had to hit out and hope.

The wood swung up, finding fleshy resistance at the top of its arc as it plunged into Autumn's neck. The vampire let go of Lucy, her hands going to the gaping wound pouring blood over Lucy. It splashed her face, covered her eyes, ran into her mouth, filling it with the taste of coppery death.

Lucy pulled the shard back out, liberating yet more dark blood. She plunged it back in again, harder this time, the anger and rage at her own impotence against this woman welling up inside her.

Autumn fell back, sliding off Lucy as she fell to the ground, hands going to her wrecked throat to try desperately to undo what had been done, her eyes full of panic.

Getting to her feet, Lucy leaned over Autumn as she scrabbled at her throat, and plunged the shard into her, working it under the ribcage. Autumn thrashed, but Lucy knew what she was doing this time, working the makeshift wooden blade until it pierced the vampire's heart.

Autumn's wild movements stopped abruptly. Lucy pulled her hand back out, covered in gore. She looked up from the corpse to tell Adam about her victory, to find him with a few problems of his own.

Besieged by half a dozen vampires, Adam cartwheeled around the room, shaking them off him like a man trying to shoo the wasps spoiling his picnic. Much larger than his assailants, when he landed a punch the punchee stayed down, but there were too many for him to get a foothold in the fight.

Even as he landed another punch, one so hard the vampire receiving it dropped as though his strings had been cut from the ceiling, something stirred on the table at the far end of the room.

Cain.

The shroud moved, sliding off the body. There was already evidence of the transformation, even as he groggily returned to life. The skin had lost its grey hue, taking on the same porcelain hue of the other vamps. His muscle definition was different, too, like thick cables taking on too much tension.

He wasn't, as Lucy thought, sitting up. No, he was cramping in pain. As his face came up, she could see the pain etched across it. His arms and legs curled in on themselves as though recoiling from fire. It was almost enough to have Lucy run to the man across the long room, were it not from the newly minted fangs protruding from his mouth, and the violent red of his eyes.

The other vampires seemed to sense the rising behind them — they broke off their attack long enough for Adam to get back to his feet. He stumbled toward Lucy, covered in cuts and bruises, his face looking more like pounded meat than recognisable human features. He fell to the ground a few feet away from her, and she rushed to help him up.

Cain let out a scream. A terrible sound, like the dying call of a hundred animals.

She looked around. The best exit was behind her — she knew it well as the way she'd come in and out each afternoon when she'd worked here. If there was anything this place had taught her, it was how to leave in a hurry — most days it was to run to a shower to wash the grubby feeling from her soul.

She headed for the door, but in her haste she forgot her knackered knee, spilling over onto the floor. As she scrambled back to her feet, she chanced a look back across the room, and immediately wished she hadn't. Cain was on his feet, the full effects of his blood lust clear as he bore down on the first thing he saw; a vampire who a moment ago had been pounding his fist into Adam's face. The older vampire, wrong-footed by being attacked by own of his own, held his hand out to ward off the new vampire. Cain grabbed the outstretched hand and clamped his jaws around it, ripping away as he did, tearing the flesh. Before his victim could react, Cain moved with ruthless efficiency to the man's throat, tearing it open and letting the blood spill down his face.

Stopping, dropping the dead or dying vamp to a heap on the floor, Cain paused. He convulsed, spraying the blood he'd taken across the floor in a torrent.

Vampire blood. Of course. Cain needed human blood, but he was too feral, too wild to realise it. How long until he realised, and how long until he realised there was one excellent source of it in the same room as him?

Getting back to her feet, ignoring the scream of pain in her knee, Lucy ran for the doors. Adam was a fraction behind her — he could easily overtake her at full strength, so either he was protecting her, or too weak to move at speed. Given Cain's blood lust, she hoped it was the former.

They made it through the door, a fresh burst of screams following through. Cain's attention had turned to the other vampires. She tried to block out the sounds of crunching bones and splashing blood and headed for the stairwell. There was no use going for the lift, it was one floor down.

Limping together they went down, the only sound the squeak of her trainers, wet with blood and gore. It covered her, but that wasn't something to think about, no matter how disgusting it smelled, as her wet hair slapped against her cheeks. As they reached the bottom, the door above them slapped open noisily. Cain was in pursuit.

'Go,' Adam hissed, though Lucy hardly needed the encouragement. Together they limped through into the central atrium, which looked half as trashed as the floor upstairs, but was still a long way from the sleek entrance she'd walked through each day. The barriers were still in place, swipe card access sentinels she'd sleepwalked through every day, their glass barriers preventing them an easy exit. They would have to vault them, which was easier imagined than achieved in their current states. She looked over Adam, who held his arm at a funny position.

'Jesus,' she said, 'let me look.' It was broken. She didn't know if vampires felt pain, but if they did, it would be excruciating.

'It's fine,' he replied, staring at the barriers. 'I heal quick.'

The doors behind them opened, and Cain ran into the lobby. As soon as he saw the pair before him, he stopped, baring his fangs and spreading his arms wide.

'Cain,' Adam said, holding his hand in front of him as he moved himself between her and his old friend.

But there was nothing left of the man they once knew. He looked terrible — his clothes soaked in blood, tattered, dirty. Deep cuts on his arms and face dripped fresh red onto old. His new muscles still bulged out like someone had attached electrodes to them, and there was nothing human in his face. Still, as Adam spoke, he did not advance.

'Listen to me,' Adam continued. 'I know how you feel. We can help you, okay? We need to get you some blood. If you come with us, we can get you some, and nobody needs to get hurt.'

If these words impacted on Cain, he didn't show it. He stood, staring, some measure of recognition in there, something holding him back from attacking. Lucy and Adam stood across from him, the three of them caught in some kind of holding pattern.

'Cain,' Lucy said. 'It's me, Lucy. From work. Remember?'

Cain let out a howl of anguished pain, clutching at his torso. Hunger. He stood up straight, snarling like a wild animal, and launched himself forward.

He aimed for Lucy, but didn't make it that far. With surprising grace, Adam pulled him from the air as one receiving a ball, pulling him down and slamming him against the barrier. Cain let out a scream, a more human sound than anything he'd produced to date. The glass barrier cracked and shattered, spilling Cain to the floor with another moan.

Adam positioned himself between Cain and Lucy once more, as the new vampire got to his feet. He looked at Adam again, a puzzled look on his face.

'Cain,' Adam said. 'It's me. It's Adam. We can get through this.'

Cain looked between them once more. With a snarl he turned, running straight through a plate glass door and into the dark night.

17

THE GATHERING DARK

Adam stumbled through the broken barrier, but before he could get to the door, he collapsed to the ground, falling into the shattered glass. Lucy hobbled toward him and pulled him away from the ground of shards. Her paramedic's instinct kicked in, and she examined him cooly to see how bad his wounds were.

She wedged him with his back to the wall and placed the damaged arm across his lap so it fell into the good one. She expected tears, sweat, panting, exhaustion, but he sat placidly, staring out after Cain's retreat. 'We have to go after him,' he said in a low voice.

'We can't,' Lucy said. 'We're in no shape. Least of all you.'

He looked at her, a look of shock crossing his face, as though he hadn't expected to see her standing over him. 'You're covered in blood,' he said.

'Autumn's.'

'Did you...' he started to ask, but seemed unwilling to follow through on his thought.

'What?' she asked.

'Did her blood get in your mouth? In your wounds?'

She recalled the acrid taste, some of which lingered still at the back of her throat. 'Some.'

Adam reached up tenderly with his good hand, and took her wrist, the one cut by the manacles that had allowed her escape. Thick black blood caked the cut, a deep ridge of it lining the wound. Carefully, Adam pulled away at it, peeling it like a layer of dead skin. It came away, revealing the skin beneath unbroken.

'How?' she asked, although she already knew the reason. Blood. Blood that turned Cain from corpse to monster. When they found Cain, he had blood around his mouth, as she did. 'Wait, am I?'

He shook his head, but his eyes told a different story. 'I don't know. I wish I could say. This is not an exact science. Rituals and ways that have not changed for centuries govern us. I've never turned someone, so I don't know how it works, exactly. I mean, I dimly recall, but...' He was babbling, this man made almost entirely from muscles and composure. Babbling like an idiot. He was scared, and his fear wormed its way into her.

Was she about to lose everything? Was her fate the same as Cain's? She'd faced death so many times over the years she no longer truly feared it. She'd looked into the eyes of those who'd gone quickly, and those who went hard, and none of that scared her. But this did. Turning into that, whatever Cain was. She wasn't sure she could handle the thought of it.

Adam closed his eyes, sighed, and opened them again. 'We have to find him,' he said.

'Your arm is broken, and my knee is pretty fucked.'

He smiled. 'That knee?'

She looked down; she'd had her weight on her bad knee for the past few minutes, with nary a twinge of pain in sight. Her fingers moved over her jeans and found the swelling had disappeared.

As she checked herself over, finding evidence of the traumas of the last few days miraculously absent, Adam stood, still cradling his arm. 'This will take a few hours,' he said. 'But we don't have that long.'

'What will Cain do?'

'That's not Cain anymore. He's in there, sure, but he's not at the wheel. There is no choice for him but to satisfy the thirst. He broke off from attacking you because he sensed he'd find easier pickings elsewhere. Animal instinct. We have to find him and stop him.'

'How?'

'He's strong, but not used to his power yet. He'll kill easily, but make mistakes.'

Sirens sounded in the distance. Not far in the distance. Lucy straightened herself out, brushing herself down despite it doing nothing to improve her look. She wanted to run and find a shower, stay in there for days, wash this off. But it wasn't an option. 'Let's go find him.'

Facing the broken glass, Lucy felt power coursing through her, raw, animalistic. She hated it. Loved it. Wanted more. To die. To live. Racing into the night, she wondered where the hell she could get more.

18

THE MIDNIGHT SUN

Cain's blood lust was far from subtle. Cars had dents where he'd run across them, which at least gave Adam and Lucy some direction. Toward the far end of the car park was a fresh hole in the fence ripped apart seemingly by bare hands, revealing a path down to the abandoned train tracks used by the Railway Museum to shuttle stock back and forth. Overgrown, dark, silent. Distant sirens extinguished any hope the tranquillity of the scene might quell Cain's rampage. He had a few minutes' head start on them, but must be moving fast.

Somewhere ahead of them, across the tracks and beyond the buildings on the other side, a scream tore through the night. Lucy and Adam doubled their efforts, crossing over the tracks and climbing the other side, through a broken fence and out onto a street.

The first body they found breathed its last even as they came across it. Lucy felt naked approaching it without her med kit, her ambulance, her partner, but none of that would have saved this woman. Even without the massive blood loss, half this woman's neck was gone, ripped out with unimaginable fury. The woman, a middle-aged looking white lady with the slightly worn respectable clothes of someone returning home from work, lay face up, glassy eyed and utterly dead.

'Come on,' Adam said. 'There's nothing we can do for her.'

She left the body, feeling the same pull of guilt that came every time she had to prioritise one patient over another. Sometimes, especially at an RTC, you had to choose the life you were more likely to save. Down the street were people she might save.

Usually her green uniform was enough to get people out of her way in a hurry, now the fact she looked like an escapee from a lunatic asylum by way of the end of the movie Carrie cleared people out of her way. They moved onto the main streets, where people were aware of an intangible something happening on their quiet streets, eyes darting around looking for danger or excitement.

The second body already had people crowded around it. She pushed her way to the front of them, shouting 'paramedic' as she went, ignoring the revulsion and confusion on the faces of the people she shoved.

The body was a young man, black, his perfectly crisp white t-shirt stained red from the wound on his neck, which he desperately covered with his own hand. The boy had a panicked look in his eyes, and when he saw Lucy looming over him, he tried to move along the pavement where he lay to get away from her.

'It's okay,' Lucy said, offering him a smile. 'I'm a paramedic.'

'You look...' the boy said.

'I know. Not a pretty sight, huh? What's your name?'

'Nathan.'

'Okay Nathan, can I take a quick look?'

The boy took his hand away. Cain was getting more precise in his attacks — this was no ugly, torn off chuck of flesh — this was more precise. A circle, two punctures on one side, oozing blood.

She smiled at him. 'This isn't too bad, but we need to get you to a hospital.' She turned to the crowd. 'Has anyone rung for an ambulance?'

Lots of shaking heads, until one woman took out her phone and stepped away from the group.

'Okay, does anyone have a scarf or a piece of fabric?'

'We haven't got time for this,' Adam growled, stalking back and forth, looking angrily up the street. 'He'll be fine.'

She shot him a look, but said nothing else.

One of the other bystanders, an elderly woman with a stroller covered in stickers of scotty dogs, reached into her thick coat, and pulled out a beautiful-looking scarf, handing it over. 'Will this do?' she asked.

Lucy gave the woman a smile and folded the scarf over on itself until she had a small, thick square. 'Lift your hand,' she said to Nathan. She placed the scarf over the wound, making Nathan wince and kick out. She turned to a man who stood beside her. 'Hold it there until the ambulance comes, okay? Firm pressure, but don't choke him. And don't lift it for anything.'

The man offered a nod. Lucy turned to the group. 'Stay with him. He should be okay, but if this man can't keep the pressure on, one of you will have to do it.'

A lot of nodding. The woman on the phone rejoined the group. 'Ambulance is on its way.'

'Hey kid,' Adam growled, leaning over Nathan and making his eyes go wide in fright again. 'Did you see which way he went?'

Nathan shook his head, but at that moment an enormous boom shook the street, and a fireball went up above the surrounding houses.

'Go,' Nathan said to Lucy.

They ran, Adam holding his arm less as he came back to full strength. Her head still buzzed from whatever Autumn's blood had done to her.

They headed down one side street and another. The fireball dissipated, but the smoke left in its wake a clear signal where they should go. Lucy ran at full pelt, but Adam drew ahead of her easily, turning the corner a dozen metres ahead of her.

Something moved out of the corner of her eye, off to her right, before she too took the turn. For a second she saw a young girl, a wide smile on her face. Missy. But even as she looked back at the space she'd been, there was nothing there.

What the hell was *she* doing there?

Turning the corner, the full devastation of the explosion sprawled before her. A terraced street, except one end was on fire. A takeaway pizza place, except the inside of that building lay spread across the street. Glass, wood, brick, people. Half a dozen of the latter, at least. Adam stood amongst them, looking around.

Lucy rushed to the first person she found, but they were gone already, the explosion taking half their torso out, leaving the rest as a blackened, charred mess. She checked the pulse to be sure, but there was no helping him. She moved to the next. A large man sat on the kerb, coughing, his head in his hands, burns and scorch marks across his bald head. His left arm was burned, the flesh exposed by flame and charred, still smoking.

'He's not here,' Adam shouted, above the roar of the fire.

In the overwhelming suddenness of the fire, Lucy had forgotten about Cain. 'Are you okay?' she asked the man, reaching out to touch his shoulder. He jumped, and she saw blood in both his ears. He must have been right by the blast. She noted his clothes and the apron around his waist.

He looked up at her, eyes full of tears. 'I don't know what happened,' he said, his voice thick with an eastern European accent.

She stood. He was in shock.

'This is a waste of time,' Adam said.

'Oh, fuck off,' Lucy said, shaking her head. 'Can't you see what's going on around you?'

'It's not him, though. We need to find Cain. We need to stop Cain.'

'I need to stay here and help,' she said. 'I can't leave these people.'

'Fine,' he said. 'I'll go on. Meet me where we first met.'

Before she could respond, he was gone, headed back down the way he'd come. She bit down on her lip, shaking her head. She headed toward the other bodies.

The first one she found was a woman, maybe in her forties. She didn't have visible burns, but there were dozens of tiny cuts on her olive skin, and her clothes were cut to shreds. She must have been walking past the window as it exploded. Lucy checked her pulse — nothing.

Arranging the body, she tilted the head back, and started giving mouth to mouth. It felt right, peaceful, serene, to be back doing what she knew. A scene of calamity and death and trauma — that was where she was most comfortable, where there were no nagging doubts, no loneliness — no vampires, just her and a patient.

Three rounds of compressions were all it took. The woman spluttered smoky breath back into Lucy's mouth as she exhaled, sitting up and drawing a huge breath, her eyes darting about wildly in panic.

'Hey,' Lucy said, placing an arm around the woman's back to stop her from falling back. 'You were in an explosion.'

'Where did she go?' the woman said between ragged breaths.

'Who?'

'The woman. Tall. Pretty. She stood right there. I don't know how she did it, but she threw... fire? Red fire?'

Lucy stood, looking around. She hadn't imagined Missy. She'd been lookout. So where the hell was Elle?

Sirens approached, winding through the back streets toward them, close enough that their lights filled the sky, if not the street.

The woman sat up on her own and began picking out glass shards from her skin.

'Are you okay?' Lucy asked.

The woman nodded, looking around. 'I was gone, wasn't I?' she asked.

'You're back now.'

'Thank you. They're nearly here. Maybe you should run.'

Lucy looked back at the woman.

'You look like someone who doesn't want to be here when the police come,' she said. 'Look like you might have a few questions to answer.'

'You're right,' she said. 'A few to ask, too.'

The blue lights were at the far end of the street. She could still make it. Offering the woman a smile of thanks, she turned and headed back down the street the way she'd come, heading back deep into the night.

19

WIND BELOW

Whether it was no longer having Adam by her side or the effect of Autumn's blood wearing off, as she found herself alone in the York night — covered in dried blood, without direction or leads — Lucy became lost in the warren of back streets.

People moved away from her in disgust; she even passed two of her old university friends out on a date at their local Indian restaurant without them recognising her, giving her the same looks of absolute horror she got from the other strangers. She ignored them, trudging on down the street on ever-more-tired legs.

Not one person stopped to ask if she was alright. Here she was, a woman on her own in a city centre, walking around like she'd escaped a bloodbath, which she supposed was exactly right. Nobody asked her if she was okay. Everyone crossed the street. Would she do the same, she wondered idly, as she turned off a main street into a residential area? She'd like to think not, but who knew? Fear was a bigger motivator than empathy, she knew. She'd seen it so many times with people at the scene of an accident who didn't want to intervene, hadn't wanted to do what they knew would help, for fear of making things worse — for them or the person in front of them. Human nature, she supposed.

There were no signs of Cain anywhere. No sirens blaring, no trail of destruction. Whatever turn she'd taken was away from the action. She was too tired to care. Adam was on his trail. Let him deal with it. Cain was one of them now. Maybe it was best if she stayed out of it.

She should head home, get changed, have a shower. Climb into bed and stay there. She didn't know how she'd get in; she'd lost her phone and her keys somewhere in the night's course — no doubt on the floor of the call centre where she used to work.

Yet home wasn't where she found herself, when she bothered to look around her to see where her mindless meandering had taken her. No, she was back on the street where this had begun, standing outside the shabby old broken down building that was Adam's home.

She knocked on the doorway, knowing full well he wasn't there. In fact, if someone came to the door, she'd likely bolt, but nobody came. She tried the door, but it was resolutely locked. Wedging herself into the doorway, she pulled her knees up and cuddled up to herself. For the first time, she noticed how cold the night was. The blood covering her clothes and hair was dry, but it still clung uncomfortably to her skin. She tried to keep as still as possible, but that made things worse when she did finally move, as the tacky clothing grabbed at her skin and sent shivers down her spine.

As she drifted toward sleep, Adam appeared from nowhere, a quizzical look in his eye. 'Hey,' he said, bending down to her level. 'You okay?'

When she tried to move, she realised what felt like drifting toward sleep had been more like being knocked out cold. Her mouth felt like the inside of a sock, and her clothes had turned completely rigid, along with every single one of her joints, as she tried to move.

'I'm fine,' she lied. 'I could do with a shower.'

'Let's go to mine,' he said. 'I still don't trust your place isn't being watched.'

'I don't have my keys, anyway,' she said.

He pulled her keys and phone from the inside pocket of his jacket, handing them over.

'Thanks,' she said. 'Did you find him?'

'No,' he said. 'He must have fed enough for the first night. But it's not over. He'll be back out tomorrow night.'

'I can't think that far ahead,' she replied, swaying slightly as she tried to stand still. She turned to face the door, waiting for Adam to unlock it.

'Uh, what are you doing?'

'Waiting for you to let me in to your house.'

He laughed. 'What, you thought I lived in there? Give me some credit. No, I'm round the corner.' He walked down the steps, back onto the quiet street.

Confused, she traipsed after him. 'If this isn't your home, why were you and Cain here?'

'Investigation,' he replied, offering nothing further on the matter.

She couldn't help but feel a sense of relief when he led her up a series of stone steps to a perfectly normal and respectable looking town house on the next street over.

He opened the door, letting her in. He took his shoes off in the hallway so she did the same, amused by the notion of a vampire — creature of the night, beast of Satan — taking off their shoes so as not to mess up the carpet. Once he turned the light on, however, she understood.

If the house's exterior was vaguely anonymous, the inside was anything but. The hallway — lined with oak panels and finely detailed wallpaper — was home to art that spanned, to Lucy's limited knowledge, hundreds of years of innovative pieces. It was like walking into the world's homeliest museum.

'Come on in,' he said.

'Wait,' she said, motioning to the gore stuck to every conceivable surface of her. 'I can't traipse all this through your home.'

He laughed. 'As appealing as the prospect of you stripping off in my hallway is, I think I can handle any mess you might make on your way upstairs. Come up, you can use the shower.'

He turned away, sparing Lucy from him seeing her blushes. She followed him up the staircase, trying to touch as little as possible. He turned on lights as he went, revealing more of the exquisite home, and the treasures within. Antiques sat alongside more modern pieces, bookshelves dotted the walls, crammed with books.

Further comment was off the table. She felt far too exposed in this place, and off balance from his comment downstairs. She didn't think she'd ever looked less attractive than she did right now.

This was confirmed when he led her quickly through his bedroom, into a bathroom. Old yet pristine white tile, with a grand mirror at its centre. It reflected the utter carnage inflicted upon her, and that on Adam, who was reflected right back at her. She looked up at him.

'Not expecting a reflection?' he asked. 'That myth has gotten me out of trouble more than once.'

He opened a cupboard door and pulled out two towels, placing them on the rim of the beautiful Victorian bathtub next to her.

'Thanks,' she said.

'I'll try to find some clothes for you,' he said. He gave her another awkward smile, and she wondered if he, too, was embarrassed by the line downstairs. 'You should find anything you need above the tub.' He flashed another weak smile, and left her, pulling the door closed behind her.

She marvelled at the state she was in. Her face was streaked with sweat and blood and grime, and her hair hung in straggled black, with chunks of deep unpleasantness caught within. It looked like she'd crawled through hell, which she supposed wasn't far off. She peeled off the top first. The blood had soaked through to her bra, which looked like a nightmarish tie dye. She ran the shower, peeled off the rest of her clothes and climbed in.

Never in her life had she encountered anything so refreshing as the blast of hot water which followed. She stood there, turning the shower curtain red, turning the bath red, letting the water power over her. Chunks of matted blood fell from her hair, and she stood, eyes closed, letting it wash away.

She stayed in there for what seemed like an age, marvelling that an old Victorian building like this could achieve and sustain such water pressure.

Some dark vampiric magics, no doubt, but she didn't care. At that moment, she didn't care about anything that had happened so far. She could allow herself a few quick moments of not caring, because caring was exhausting. She could even allow herself, for the briefest of moments, to consider that line from Adam, and how she felt about it. Revulsion, possibly? He was dead. A walking corpse, an impossible thing, something against God and nature and science. And yet...

And yet.

She picked up a bar of soap and washed everywhere with a thoroughness as much about luxuriating in the moment as getting rid of the filth clinging to her.

He was handsome, for starters. Tall, muscled without looking ripped. Nice eyes. A Slightly hooked nose and a slightly weak chin were the sole flaws. That and the fact he literally had to eat people to survive and was old enough for the prefix to be great-great-great.

Jesus, what was she thinking? There was a psychotic killer on the loose, an undead psychopath who'd already killed several people. She still couldn't work out where Elle and Missy fit into everything. Their creepy witchy fingers were all over it, but she couldn't work out how, or why. Whatever Autumn had been planning for Cain, that plan backfired. If they could bring Cain in without further death, that should be the end of it. So why did that feel... wrong?

She was letting it creep back in, she realised, wanting to go back to the moment of quiet bliss. But it was gone, replaced by fear and not a little loathing. Finally, feeling something approaching clean, she turned her attention to her hair, hoping the shampoo in the elegant containers at the side of the bath wasn't some terrifying vampire shampoo that would kill her hair. It seemed to lather up okay, so she spent a while rinsing, getting more and more gunk out until her hair practically squeaked.

In place of her clothes there was a fluffy white hotel bathrobe and an equally fluffy towel. She dried herself off and wrapped the robe around herself, luxuriating in it for a second. She found fluffy white slippers; it was as though Adam had transported her to a lush day spa. She checked herself in the mirror. Well, she looked a damn sight better than she had twenty minutes earlier, or however long she'd been in there.

She opened the bathroom door and stepped out. She was in his bedroom, alone. Having barely glanced at it before, without him here, she could take a better look around. It was beautiful. Whatever else Adam was, he was a man of refined taste. Intricate gilded patterns detailed the wallpaper, and the furniture complimented everything else in the room. Carved oak panels covered the lower part of the wall. If even a few of the details here had been wrong, it would have been ugly, but it was a room entirely in balance with itself.

At the heart of the room stood a vast bed, its oak frame sitting under what looked like an enormous mattress, and a duvet thick enough to have brought about the deaths of many geese. The whole thing gave off a masculine air, but not overpoweringly so.

'Were you expecting a coffin?' Adam asked behind her.

She jumped. Turning to face him, she wrapped her robe tighter. 'You like sneaking up on people, huh?'

'Perk of the job,' he said. 'Here.' He held out a bag containing entirely new clothes, straight from the store. What the hell kind of clothes shop opened at this time of night? Certainly none she knew of in York.

'Thanks.' She took the bag.

He wore different clothes, but there was still blood on his neck and face. 'If you get dressed, come down. I could do with a shower myself.'

She nodded, he left. She pulled the clothes out. Nothing particularly exciting, but it impressed her he had both her size and her style down pretty well. Black jeans, and a top both cute and functional. New Converse trainers to round it off. She raised a bit of an eyebrow at the underwear he'd chosen, much frillier than she would have picked. But it was expensive, at least. Not that she could tell the price — there were no labels, let alone price tags.

She dressed, wondering what to do with her discarded robe. Taking it and her towel back into the bathroom, and realised she'd left it in a bit of a state. She tidied it up, giving the bath a quick rinse with the shower.

By the time she came back out, Adam stood in the doorway again, leaning on the wooden frame. 'Thanks,' he said, motioning to her efforts in the bathroom. 'Head downstairs. I rarely have food, but I got you something to eat.'

'I'm not hungry,' she replied.

'There if you want it. I'm going to jump in the shower. Snoop about the place.'

'Thanks.'

She moved past him, into the hallway. He pulled the doorway closed, and she stood there, uselessly, for a moment, staring at the door.

Shaking her head, she headed downstairs.

20

APOCALYPSE MORNING

There were no televisions, she noted. Bookcases in every room, and more than one old stereo setup. Records. Art. No television, no computers, no wi-fi router she could see. She wandered from room to room, running her finger along immaculately clean sideboards, looking at the bookcases to see if there were titles she recognised, which invariably there weren't. Most of the books looked to be decades old, centuries sometimes. The records were mostly jazz and classical, with some nods to vague modernity here and there — Depeche Mode's Violator stuffed amongst the Duke Ellington and Etta James around it.

There were pictures, too. Adam did not hide his age — there were pictures of him alongside men and women probably dead before her grandparents were even born. Lots of nightlife snaps, some in America in what looked like the 1920s. One with his arm around a sweaty black man with a trumpet in his hand, each beaming at each other in delight.

Lots of women, too. In solo poses in fine dresses at first, but increasingly candid ones as they crept closer to the present. The newest seemed to be from around the fifties or sixties, back in England, if she had to guess. A stunning woman, curvaceous, blonde. For a moment, she wondered if it might be Elle, but the face was the wrong shape.

There were other artefacts for a life lived long. A signed poster from a boxing match, two fighters she'd never heard of. An old pipe in a box, the inscription on the brass plaque beneath it lost to the sands of time.

At one end of the hallway, one painting stood out against the others. A woman in what looked like Victorian dress, perhaps even older. A white wide collar sat above a black corset and greed dress, and the face above that was plain, her hair done up in a braid of some kind. An utterly unremarkable portrait, against such perfectly balanced decor it seemed incongruous, somehow. In the top corner was what looked like the letter E. She made a note to ask Adam about it.

In the kitchen, an incongruous white plastic bag sat on the wide wooden table. If there was a room that lacked the attention of the rest of the house, it was this one, but compared to the kitchen in her living room, it was still lush. It even had an Aga, albeit one wearing its years of neglect.

She looked in the bag. A chicken and bacon sandwich and a bag of Fanta. She laughed, the sound ringing hollow in the empty room. It seemed so pathetic in the surroundings, like she should be presented with quail eggs on artisanal bread slices.

'I wasn't sure what you liked,' Adam said, sneaking up on her again. She didn't jump out of her skin this time, at least.

'This is fine,' she said. 'I'm not hungry.'

He motioned for her to take a seat, and he did the same. They sat across the wide wooden table in silence for a moment, Lucy thinking it seemed a shame for this to be the room in the house they ended up in.

'You have a lovely home,' she said, cursing herself for sounding like her mother the moment she said it.

'Thank you,' he said. 'I've been here quite a long time, so I've been able to make it how I like it.'

'How long?'

'Uh, I came back from America, so... Nineteen-fifty-eight?'

'Where are you from, originally?'

'Poland.'

'You don't have an accent.'

'I've had a bit of time to lose it.'

She returned his smirk, and they fell back into silence.

'That painting, in the hallway,' she said, glad of something to break the silence. Who is that? Distant relative?'

He smiled, but a half-sad smile. 'Of a kind,' he said quietly. 'Something of an old obsession of mine,' he said. 'It's how I met Cain, actually. I should have taken it down years ago.'

She smiled. 'Doesn't exactly fit the rest of the place.'

He nodded, but said nothing more. They lapsed back into silence, with less comfort in it than before.

'It's been a strange few days,' she said.

'It has. Even by my standards. You must be exhausted.'

She laughed. 'I think I left exhausted some way behind me.'

'The sun will be up in a few minutes. Cain will not be out again until tonight. You should get some sleep. You are welcome to do so here.'

Did she catch a hint of a smirk in the offer? 'I should head home,' she said.

'I'm not sure it's safe for you to go home. Elle and Missy are still out there, and we don't know their place in this. I don't believe they would harm you, but I... would like to be sure.'

'They were there, you know?' she said, realising she'd not told him that part of the evening's festivities yet. She'd been so tired and shell-shocked.

'Where?' he asked.

'The explosion. Witness said a woman threw a ball of red fire.'

He took this in but said nothing.

'What happens next?' she asked.

'Tonight, I find Cain. I will almost certainly have to kill him.'

'You can't save him?'

He sighed, a long, weary sound that seemed to feel up from deep inside. He looked haunted. 'It's too late for him,' he said. 'The ritual you saw goes back centuries. When we fail to adhere to it, there is a danger...'

They sat for a second, as Lucy tried to find an artful framing for the question she wanted to ask. 'Is there always a... sacrifice?' she asked, failing to find it.

He considered it for a second. 'We are what we are,' he replied with sorrow in his voice. 'It is the reason we rarely make more of us. The cost is too high. In the early hours, the first days, usually one person would be enough. Perhaps two. The point of the ritual is to awaken surrounded by your brethren, but to have them limit the damage you do. It is a lot easier, once you come out of the early days, to rationalise what you have done. Remember, we are the same people we were before, and most of us are as uncomfortable with causing death as we were when we were people.'

'How do you feed?' she asked, unsure whether she wanted an answer.

'I'm not quite an elder, but I've been around for a long time now. The older we get, the less we need to feed. I need to drink perhaps once a week, and I can do so without killing. Modern medicine makes blood freely available.'

'What about other blood?'

'Pigs? It can keep one alive, if needed, but it can cause sickness. The same with other animals. No, it must be human blood.'

'So why do you think you'll need to kill Cain? He's going to come through this, right?'

Adam frowned. 'He might, but it's likely he won't find his way back without support. It may already be too late. In the meantime, he will remain feral, a beast. When you go through the ritual, we keep you separate. One body can last. It is... not pleasant. But you come through it and pick up the parts of yourself remaining. But that's not why I'm worried for him.'

'Why?'

'His reaction when he woke was not like anything I have ever seen. He went straight for other vampires. It was beyond feral. There was something else at work there.'

'Elle?'

'Could be. But it makes no sense to me. Elle and her kind walk the same long path as us, but never the same lane. We co-exist, but do not mix. Elle and I are probably as close as any vampire and maenad have ever been.' He furrowed his brow. 'I did not know she was involved. She has ways of knowing things I do not, and I thought she would be as... interested... by you as I. You must believe me; I never thought she would be a danger to you. If I had, I wouldn't have left you there.'

She stared at the Fanta can, wondering whether to open it, contemplating his words. 'The explosion at the restaurant,' she said. 'I think it was a diversion. Like they wanted Cain to escape. To slow us down.'

'To what end?' Adam asked, rocking back in his chair.

'What can you tell me about Missy?'

He got up from the table. 'Not much. She's a wicca, not a maenad like Elle. But she is not the child she appears to be.' He shifted in his seat. 'When I came to York for the first time, Elle was a junior power. There was a warlock who ruled these parts, and many more vampires than there are today. When I came back a second time, Elle had risen. The warlock disappeared, and she took his place, with Missy by her side. The word was the young girl was a human, a talented wicca from a young age, but Elle cast a magic to grant her the long life of a born mystic like herself. It worked, but by casting her in frozen time. Never to grow old, never to die. An eternal child. It's a dangerous thing. I have seen it myself with vampires.'

He stood, ill at ease with the stillness required to stay in his chair. 'Since then, the two mystics have mostly kept to themselves. Most of the vampires native to the city moved on or died. We move around a lot.'

'What's the difference between a Wicca and a Maenad?'

'Wicca are what you would term as witches. They are human, but they have access to the mystic. They draw power, the kind of power that can allow them to live far beyond normal humans. It is something a Wicca usually comes to later in life. Missy is unusual in that regard, and there's been much discussion in certain circles about how much power is hers, how much is drawn from Elle.'

'Okay, so what is Elle?'

'Maenads are not human. I don't know what they are. They have a dark history. They are the ancient worshippers of Dionysus, although Elle is pretty straight laced for someone in thrall to the god of wine and fertility.'

Lucy cracked, her own thirst reaching the point of no return, and pulled the ring on the Fanta. Adam's nose wrinkled as the smell of chemical orange flavouring hit his nostrils.

'What about Cain?' she asked, before taking a long sip. The bubbles stung her throat where the woman vampire had grabbed it. 'Shouldn't we try to bring him in? Surely he'd have a better idea what's going on than anyone?'

He sighed. 'It's too late for that. He was my friend. And trust me, he would want me to end the misery he's in. He would never forgive himself for the deaths he's caused. He was a man of... extraordinary peace.'

'Shouldn't you try?'

He shook his head. 'No.'

The finality of his response was like a slap across the cheek. 'I can't believe you'd give up on him. I thought you were his friend?'

Her words seemed to hit him right back. He stared at her a second, wounded, and she felt an immediate grip of realisation that this was not a man to piss off. After all, this was not a man.

'Tell me,' he said, gripping the back of the chair before him, staring at her. 'Do you try to resuscitate every patient without a pulse?'

'If I think there's even the remotest chance I can save them, yes.'

'Exactly,' he shouted back. 'The remotest chance. You do not know what you are talking about here. Cain is gone. There is no remote chance of bringing him back. He would want this.'

'What makes you so sure?'

'Because he hated vampires!' He banged the chair on the floor, and for a moment his eyes seemed to burn. He closed his eyes for a second, gripping the back of the chair so hard it looked like it might splinter in his hands. 'Almost as much as I do.'

'What?'

He shook his head. 'I have lived away from my people for a long time. When I was in America, I... fell in with a hard crowd. Did terrible things. I thought of myself above the rest of my kind, but when it came down to it, I was every bit as bad as they were. I came back to England, shamed. Resolved to stay out of everyone's way. Cain convinced me otherwise. He wanted me to join his crusade.'

He sat back down, staring at the table.

She turned this over in her head. 'That's why they took him. Why they turned him. You aren't able to kill each other, correct?'

'Not easily,' he replied, his voice quieter.

'They wanted him in the one place they knew he couldn't hurt them.'

'If that's true,' Adam said, looking up. 'It didn't work. Cain took out several vampires in the first few minutes of his rebirth.'

'Do you think he did it deliberately?' she asked.

Adam shook his head. 'No. There was no thought there. Instinct, perhaps. Hatred. But there's no conscious thought for the first few days. Which is why he's so dangerous.'

'But don't you see?' Lucy said. 'He's the key. They've set you against everyone else, Adam. You're being played. We both are.'

'It changes nothing,' Adam roared. 'I am his friend. I have to do this.'

'Can we not at least try?' Lucy roared back. 'You know, he was my friend, too.'

Adam crossed the table in a flash, his hand around her throat and her feet lifted clear off the floor in a heartbeat. Before she could protest, she was fighting for air.

Anger flashed across his face for a second and left as quick as it came. He put her down.

'Lucy,' he said, but before he could say anything further, she shoved him as hard as she could. He tripped on a chair, tumbling back. The path between her and the doorway was clear, and he didn't need a second invitation. She ran from the room, heart pounding in her chest. God, she'd trusted this man and once more, he'd shown her what he'd already told her — he was a monster.

If he was a monster, Cain was a monster, too, one she owed nothing to. She needed to get out of this sick game. It had no bearing on her, and she had no skin in it.

And yet...

Even as she reached the front door and began fumbling at the various locks across the wide wooden panelling, Adam followed her through.

'Lucy, I'm sorry,' he stammered, his body too close to hers.

'Go to hell,' she said. She managed the last of the locks and pulled the door open. Sunlight spilled through the door. Adam fell back, reeling from the light. She stepped happily into it, relief washing over her as she reached its relative safety.

'Lucy, wait,' Adam implored.

She turned to face him. He squinted against the sun's rays, his hand held up to protect his eyes. He looked utterly pathetic, smaller somehow.

'You might not want to help him,' she said. 'But don't expect me not to try.'

She turned on her heels and headed down the street, ignoring the door slamming shut in frustration behind her.

21

BORN TO RAISE HELL

Lucy would risk returning home, she decided. She wanted to see what state Elle and Missy had left the place in, and if the pair of them were waiting for her, she'd at least get closer to working out what the hell was going on. She'd stake the place out first, make sure there were no police, or anyone else. At least she'd be safe from vampire reprisals for a few hours. She was more worried about the police in the light of day. Two crime scenes had to have her bloody fingerprints over them, and that DI would want to talk to her about his raid on an empty house.

There was a cafe across the street from her apartment, and despite turning down the sandwich at Adam's, a deep hunger was gnawing away at her insides. Why hadn't she eaten? Stupid. The realisation that followed — that she hadn't wanted the handsome vampire to see her munching through a chicken and sweetcorn sandwich — didn't make her feel any better.

Pulling up a chair in the café, she positioned herself with a view of the entrance to her building. She would have breakfast, have a couple of coffees, watch the world as it went about its business, and see if that business was her. When the café's perennial serving staff, Angie, approached, she ordered a full English breakfast and a black coffee.

If anyone was watching, they were subtle. The best vantage point was right here, and unless Angie was a secret police informant, there was nobody else here. She doubted the police could spare round-the-clock surveillance. That kind of thing happened in movies, not real life. The police were so thinly stretched these days they could barely keep up with the constant volume of fresh cases, let alone spend hours watching the empty homes of people they were interested in. She saw it enough first hand every time the police protecting her as she attended some domestic violence case or city centre brawl got pulled away to another crisis.

'Here you go, love,' Angie said, handing over a plate so laden with fried meat it made Lucy's stomach lurch with anticipation.

'Cheers, Angie.'

'You alright, love?' the tiny woman asked. 'You look like you had a rough night.'

'Bit tired,' she replied, honestly. 'Been a long one. Hey, have you noticed anything weird around here the last few days?'

'Oh, you know me. I keep my head down, love. Although, there were a lot of police here the other day, milling about outside your building. Not right sure what was going on, might have been a drugs raid.'

'Really?' Lucy asked, cutting up a sausage and stuffing it in her mouth to find it was hotter than the sun's surface.

'Oh yeah. Loads of them. Big wagon of them. Armed ones and everything. They don't half scare me, though I guess you're more used to them than I am.'

'I dunno,' Lucy replied, watching as a man in a dark jacket approached the building and rang on the buzzer. He was buzzed inside. 'Not sure you ever get used to it.'

'Well, I think it's the Lord's work you do, love.'

She disappeared back into the kitchen, leaving Lucy alone in the café. She ploughed into the breakfast with gusto, her stomach protesting at the sudden influx of meat, eggs, fried bread, and beans.

Nobody was watching, she decided by the time half of her pot of coffee remained. Adam was worried about her, but it didn't seem likely Elle or Missy were actually interested in her. If the gnawing feeling in her stomach was right, they were wrapped up in this, but did their interest in her end the moment Cain didn't eat her?

She left some money on the table — Angie never brought a bill out to her, but Lucy refused not to pay. This was their elegant solution, with neither having to back down from their positions of deference to each other. Lucy respected the hell out of the fact Angie kept this place going, a proper old-school café in a city fast running out of old-school anything.

Having put the money on the table, she knew Angie wouldn't come out and collect her plate, so she took a few more minutes to finish her coffee and headed back across the street. She punched in the entry code and took the stairs up to her flat.

Elle hadn't lied about cleaning up the place, but she'd neglected to mention the fresh door she'd put up to replace the shattered one, replete with a fresh lock Lucy didn't have the key for. Lucy laughed. Of course. No need to watch the place when she'd made it so Lucy had to go back to Elle to get the key.

Even as she stood before it, scratching her head as to what the hell to do next, the door to the flat behind her opened and Mrs Phatak poked her head out.

'I've got the key for you,' she said, looking somewhat harassed. The sound of manic children at play rang out from behind her.

'Oh, great,' Lucy said, and headed over to her neighbour. 'Who gave you it?'

'Tall woman. Pretty. I assumed it was your landlord?'

'Something like that. Are you okay?'

Mrs Phatak rolled her eyes. 'Birthday party. There are twelve children in here and they're making more noise than I thought it possible to make.'

Lucy laughed. 'You have my sympathy. Wish Nadim a happy birthday from me.'

'Will do.' A frown furrowed her brow. 'I'm not sure what happened with your door. I keep trying to remember, but it... slips away, somehow.'

'Burglary attempt,' Lucy said. 'I've been with friends for a few days since.'

'Oh,' she said, looking relieved, before realising it was not an explanation that gave much solace to a single mother living in the same building.

'Someone I knew,' Lucy added hastily. 'Ex-boyfriend. Said I still had something that belonged to him. All sorted. He won't be back.'

She gave a nod of solidarity, and the frown disappeared. Something smashed behind her, followed by a scream. She rolled her eyes. 'I'd better get back in there,' she said, and handed over Lucy's new key.

'Thanks, and good luck,' Lucy said, even as the door closed behind her.

Lucy looked at the key in her hand — perfectly nondescript. It even had the generic plastic tab on it that locksmiths always put on. Even so, it felt strange. Opening the door into her apartment, the sense of otherness deepened. Everything looked exactly as she'd left it, or how it had looked approximately ten minutes before a deranged vampire crashed through the door and tried to kill her. No evidence of blood, no evidence of a struggle, no evidence of anything replaced. It was as though the damage had been simply... undone.

She looked in the previously smashed mirror. It wasn't a new mirror; it was the old one. Restored without the faintest evidence of repair, it still had the foggy corner on the top right that had been there for years. The same went for the sofa — the fight had ripped it asunder, but as she sank into the familiar groove of her own arse, she knew instantly it was *hers*.

Even with everything returned to normal, Lucy couldn't shake the feeling of a place no longer entirely her own. She couldn't put her finger on it, but there was a definite sense something had violated her dominion over this place. The urge rose to run from the place, close her door and turn her back on everything within it, but she didn't have the luxury. What had Elle and Missy left in their wake — were there spells here? Were they watching her? It was enough to send a shiver down her spine that kept cycling through on itself in a feedback loop.

Whatever she felt, though, she was too tired to fight it. Kicking off her shoes, she moved through to her bedroom. In here, at least, it felt like home still — but the fight never came in here. She pulled off her new jeans, took off her top and bra, and climbed straight into bed. The sheets were cool, and she pulled them up over herself, cocooning herself inside their comfort. She closed her eyes and fell instantly to sleep.

Sleep seemed on the edge of reach when something in the room snapped her back to consciousness. All was still and calm, and daylight still streamed through her curtain. Drool at the edge of her mouth suggested she had slept some, and a quick glance at her clock confirmed it was mid-afternoon.

Laying perfectly still, she listened. There was no Jones to have pounced on the bed to wake her — she was completely alone in the flat. She didn't feel it — she felt eyes on her, somewhere. Listening so hard she could hear her heart and the bustle of day life below her window, she lay there.

Nothing.

She got out of bed, pulled back on her new clothes, and set about inspecting her room. It seemed exactly as she'd left it. Nothing disturbed in her drawers, nothing moved in her wardrobe. The thin layer of dust on her mantelpiece looked undisturbed... almost.

Her eye skipped over it at first. It looked such a part of her room; she looked right at it half a dozen times before realising.

There on the mantelpiece, nestled between pictures of her mum and the two best friends from university who she spoke to on Facebook once in an aeon, sat an urn. Small, ceramic. Quite pretty, and in keeping with the rest of the room. But not hers. She was sure she'd seen one before, but struggled to place where.

Staring at it, she wondered what to do. The presence of the damn thing was unsettling enough, and the thought of touching it seemed like entirely the wrong thing to do. If this was a gift from Elle, God knew what was inside.

She crept up to it slowly, as though it might fire spiders at her face. Careful not to touch it, she peered inside. It was empty save for some kind of dark residue. There was no scent when she sniffed the air above it. She was about to reach inside with her fingers, but thought better of it. Moving through to the kitchen, she picked out a long spatula, wrapping it in kitchen towel and taking it back through to the bedroom. She hit the lights and opened the curtains, wanting as much light as possible.

Without touching the pot, she dipped the spatula in, scraping it against the bottom and the sides, almost losing control and sending the pot to the ground to shatter into pieces and bad mojo. She stopped it at the edge of the sill, holding her breath as she manoeuvred it back into place. Carefully withdrawing the spatula, she took a better look at what was inside.

Blood, if she had to guess. Old, practically gone to powder. Maybe mixed with something else for some dark purpose, but blood nonetheless. She unwrapped the paper towel, careful not to touch the powdery paste, and took it through to the kitchen bin, dumping it into an empty bag.

Grabbing some tongs, she went back into the bedroom and carefully lifted the urn up, carrying it through to the kitchen and placing it carefully inside the open bin. She might not know what the hell the thing was for, but she knew she didn't want it in her house. Lifting the bin and tying the handle, she took it outside her door and placed it in the corridor.

Closing the door behind her, she felt an amazing sense of relief, a weight lifting off her shoulder and flying out of her flat, taking the bad vibes with it. She felt at home again.

Or did she?

A few minutes later, the dread returned, along with the sense of loss... loss of what was hers. She didn't feel at home in her own home, like the ownership had transferred away from herself. It didn't help that Jones wasn't here, either. She wondered how he was enjoying what seemed to be his new home, wandering through the legs of ancient beings. It wasn't fair. Sure, she and Jones treated each other like housemates who'd long since stopped spending much time together, but she still loved the little fuck. He was hers. She was his. It was as close as she'd come to a meaningful relationship in as long as she could remember.

'Fuck this,' she said to the empty house. 'I'm going to get my cat back.' She picked up her purse and jacket and headed out the door.

22

THE RECKONING

The afternoon was clear and crisp, and she found herself across town before she could form a coherent strategy in her mind. She didn't think banging on the door and demanding Jones back would work, and if the witches used their power on her, she wasn't sure what she could do to stop it. Stopping at the end of the street with the old house within view, she crouched down behind the hedgerow of a neighbour, hoping the lack of a car in their driveway signalled they weren't in.

After watching long enough for her knees to ache, she decided on the bold strategy of sneaking up to the rear of the house and crossing her fingers. Checking there was no curtain twitching at the windows, she crept out into the road and through the side gate, the latch of which was still broken from the Police's incursion. Maybe she'd get lucky and the house would be the same, although if the witches could fix the grim scene of her flat, she reckoned they could fix a single pane of glass.

The house looked empty. No lights within, no movement in the windows save for Jones. He sat in what little sunshine shone through the replaced rear window, considering Lucy with his usual mix of disdain and boredom.

He was inside; she was outside. Short of smashing the same window the police had put through, she didn't see a way of redressing the imbalance. Certainly, Jones didn't seem to give two fucks about the situation. After flashing her his most disdainful stare, he lifted his tail, showed her his puckered arse, and sauntered off into the house.

After a period of crouching behind a shrub that was unkind to her creaking knees, she decided there was nobody home and wandered to the back door. She tried the lock, but it was firmly closed. She put her hands to the window, cupping them to allow her a better view of the inside.

Of the devastation within.

The walls were splattered with thick red, the furniture up-turned and broken. She watched as Jones lazily walked through a thick pool of congealing blood, sanguinary footprints leading away across the carpet until he stopped and licked his paws.

She tried the door again, but unsurprisingly, it hadn't magically unlocked in the space of moments. Magic. Was that what this was? Or had Elle and Missy's magic not been able to protect them from some wild beast?

Cain. It had to be. Whatever Adam said about the man not having access to the critical faculties of his human self, something here was different. Cain had attacked vampires during his awakening. Was it such a stretch he'd come after witches, too? She may not like Elle, or Missy, but they didn't deserve whatever had happened in there.

She had to get in.

To the side of the main door was a smaller window — from the kitchen, perhaps? Trying to remember the layout of the house from her time before, she fished out her old door key, trying to lever the ancient wood frame, but it wouldn't budge. She might fit through the gap if it were open, but crawling through smashed glass was a one-way ticket to getting her guts sliced open.

No, the best way in was the same way the Police did it. She supposed there was a decent argument for breaking in — she'd come to retrieve her stolen cat and found what looked like a murder scene. As a trained paramedic, she had a duty of care. That had the advantage of being true, but the problem was not so much her justification for being there, more that she'd already stacked up questions from the police that would be tricky to answer, without adding more to the list.

The skies above darkened; night was not far away. She looked through the window once more — whatever was inside had likely not survived the assault. She could call 999 and get them to send as many flashing lights as they had in their station houses, but what if Cain was still in there? Would the police be able to deal with a feral vampire?

Would she?

It didn't matter. Paramedic instinct took over, and she picked up a stone and smashed the pane. The noise reverberated across the garden, splintering the still of the early afternoon. Careful to avoid the shards sticking out from the wooden frame, she stepped inside.

The smell of death hit quick; a putrid, sickly sweet smell she'd encountered so many times before. Once more she felt naked without her med bag, the shield of armour she used to get her through this world of death. Her hands felt empty without it.

She was no forensic examiner, but she could read the signs here easily enough. The hallway showed arterial spray patterns from extreme violence, with additional pooling from the points of impact. The hallway beyond showed further signs of struggle. Pooled blood suggested bodies bleeding out. Bodies, it had to be said, who were no longer there. Had Cain moved them, maybe, to continue feeding?

Two pools of blood; two victims, at least. Each was disturbed at one end where someone had dragged them deeper into the house. Following the direction of travel, she listened for any sign of imminent danger, but struggled to hear anything above the pounding of her heart in her chest, a sound that seemed to thrum in her ears and her throat. She swallowed. God, she could do with a glass of water. The blood continued through to the grand staircase and up. She followed, wincing with every creaking floorboard.

Jones appeared at her feet, brushing against her leg like it was a Sunday morning and he wanted some nibbles. She ignored him, and the urge to pick him up and run clean out of the house.

She carried on up. A faint sound danced at the edge of her heightened senses. The closer she got to the top of the stairs, the sound of scraping became clearer. Dull, repetitive, like someone scraping a butter knife across wood. She wished she had thought to pick up a weapon — all she could see were more of Elle's urns. In fact, there were dozens of them tucked away into every nook and cranny of the house. If either Elle or Missy were alive, Lucy would have to ask what the hell they were.

As if either of them could be.

The prospect seemed dimmer the higher she climbed. By the time she reached the top of the stairs, she'd all but given up on it. The door to the guest room that had been her own brief prison was wide open, the scraping sound issuing from inside. Carefully, she approached the door and peered inside.

It was dark, but she could make out one pair of legs sticking out from the other side of the bed. A child's legs, clad in white tights, mottled with dark spots. Missy. She couldn't see the second body, but she wasn't about to go looking for it. Especially not given the sight directly before her.

Slumped against the wall, legs sticking out into the light but the rest in shadow, was Cain. Breathing heavily, his rasping breaths the source of the scraping sound she'd heard. He was still in the same clothes he'd worn at the ceremony the night before, caked in gore.

His hands looked broken and raw, and he stared ahead with a dead-eyed intensity.

'Hurts,' he said, as Lucy whipped back her head to avoid being seen. She cursed herself under her breath and stepped into the doorway.

'What hurts?' she asked, not moving beyond the wooden doorframe.

'Everything.' His voice was full of pain, on the edge of breaking.

Carefully, she approached. 'What do you remember, Cain? Do you remember me?'

He nodded, wincing as he did so. He looked less a feral creature than a broken child, albeit one covered in the blood of their victims. 'I....'

'Do you remember the ambulance? You remember getting bitten?'

He frowned. 'No. I went to meet Adam... I don't remember.'

'What do you remember?'

'Pain. And anger. Rage. I... there are things. Memories. They can't be mine.'

Her first instinct was to get Adam, somehow, but she remembered what he'd said. He would kill Cain, thought that was what his friend would want. But what Lucy saw before her was a broken, traumatised person, deep in shock. If she could reach him, maybe she could save him.

'I can help you,' she said, moving slowly forward.

He growled, and she stopped.

'I'm not going to hurt you,' she said.

'It's not you I'm afraid of.'

They had that in common. 'Can you tell me what you were doing before you went to meet Adam?' she asked. If she could ground his memories and thoughts in the time before he turned, maybe she could keep his mind there.

'I... there was a tunnel.' He frowned, trying to remember. At least he'd stopped growling. Still, she didn't risk advancing further.

'A tunnel?' She had to keep him talking.

'They were there. They were whispering. Chanting.'

'Who was there?'

'They wanted me to turn on him, said the consequences....'
His voice descended into a growl. His hands pumped into fists
in his lap.

Backing away, she held her arms out. 'Cain,' she said, fighting
to keep the terror out of her voice, trying to be commanding and
failing. 'Remember who you are.'

'Who I was,' he growled.

He got to his feet in a flash, prowling around the space beside
the bed. His fists kept pumping, and he moved his shoulders like
a fighter getting ready to step into the ring.

'They took that from me,' he growled.

'And they've paid the price,' she replied. 'If you go over to
what they wanted you to be, you're giving them what they would
have wanted.'

He gave a confused look, looking for a second almost the man
who sat across from her in a pub and talked too much about his
ex-wife. It lasted for half a second until the rage returned.

He crossed the gap before she could react, grabbing her by the
arms and shaking her so violently she thought her neck might
snap.

'You're just like them,' he hissed, spraying her face with flecks
of foul-smelling spittle. 'Controlling little bitch.'

'No,' she tried to say, but nothing came out but a gargled noise
of panic.

Cain's eyes burned furiously, his pupils dilated, his nostrils
flared. His teeth were out, and she realised in a flash that her
body would soon be on the other side of the bed, alongside the
two dead witches. Cain screamed, holding onto Lucy so hard
she thought he might snap the bones in her arms. She wept, a
moan of her own bubbling up from within her as white-hot pain
flooded her. She waited for those jaws to close around her neck,
for it to be over.

Cain threw her, tossed her at the bed with such force she rebounded up and slammed into the wall, face first. She crashed down on the bed in a heap.

Raising her head with all the strength she could muster, she looked up.

Cain was gone. She was alone on the blood-soaked bed.

23

VENOM HELL

Peeling herself off the bed, she moved her arms gingerly, sure they would flare in pain, but nothing more than a dull ache spread from them. She checked her clothing. Some of the blood had gotten on her, mostly too dry to stick. Whatever happened here must have been hours ago now. Still, her DNA had to be everywhere. Another thing for her to explain.

Getting off the bed, she peered over at the two bodies stuffed in the space between the wall and the other side. Both smeared in blood. It was hard to make out their faces, but they certainly dressed like Elle and Missy.

Dead.

She wanted nothing more than to run and hide, make this some distant memory. Move to the countryside, live in ignorance and peace. But how many more people would end up like Missy and Elle here, if she couldn't get through to Cain?

Lucy'd had him for a moment — a glimpse of the man she knew. She could reach him, she was sure of it. She was used to losing patients; here was her chance to lose one yet bring them back. Not from cardiac, but from death itself. Cain was a good man, and he still could be. What had Adam said? He hated vampires, wanted to bring them down. If she could reach that part of him, team up with Adam, they could be a force for good between them.

Under the immediate threat and danger to life, something else tugged at her — scientific curiosity. She'd long ago given up on her dream of becoming a doctor; she liked the thrill of the streets too much and knew she'd likely saved as many lives as any doctor in any hospital. But she was still the same girl who, at nine years old, sat in her room surrounded by anatomy books, wanting to know the secrets of how people were put together. These last few days upended everything she thought she knew about the human body, and everything she'd seen in Cain overturned what she thought she knew once more. It was like standing on the other side of a doorway to a world of knowledge with a whisper of cloud stopping you from getting anything more than a glimpse. She had to follow Cain, talk him down. She'd seen enough of his humanity to know there was a way back for him. Adam made it back, with help.

She wasn't ready to give up on Cain yet.

Making her way slowly back through the house, she listened for signs of Cain, though she knew there was no way he was still in the house. Her heart hammered at every movement in the shadows, and when Jones appeared at her feet, she nearly leapt high enough in the air to send him running for the hills. He soon came back, weaving through her legs in a bid for attention. She stopped, picking him up. There was blood on his paws and whiskers, which made her gag. She didn't want to leave him here, but she couldn't take him where she was going. She couldn't put him out, either. He was an indoor cat, if ever there was one.

'I will come back for you, okay?' she told the disinterested ball of fur. 'You stay here, and when this is over, I will come back for you.'

She put him down and he sauntered off, clearly satisfied by her brief attention. He headed into the kitchen, where she saw an uneaten bowl of cat food. She didn't want to leave him with those bodies, but what choice did she have?

She ran back upstairs and closed the door to the bedroom with the bodies inside. That would have to do. Heading back downstairs, she found the front door bolted, so Cain must have fled the way she came in. That raised the question of exactly how he'd come into the house in the first place, but she figured there was no way to answer that question now.

Heading through the shattered glass door into the garden, she tried to figure which way Cain headed. Heavy rain clouds blotted out the sky, pouring endless torrents of cold wet into the garden. Shit. Pulling her jacket closed, she headed out into it.

The streets were empty of all but the hardiest traveller, and there were no screams or sirens to point her in a particular direction. It was not yet night, but with the heavy clouds above her, did it even matter? There was no sunlight coming from above. Cain left no clue, so she trudged back into the city. If he was looking to drink, that'd be his best bet. Although he hadn't exactly screamed bloodthirsty rage back there. Anger, yes. But no bloodlust. Maybe he'd been sated by the two witches.

Could it be she was going about this all wrong? Assuming he had a greater cognitive reasoning than Adam assumed possible from him, why had Cain gone to the home of two witches, above anyone else? He must have wanted answers — answers he didn't get, judging by the corpses left in his wake.

Where else might he go for answers? Autumn? Dead. Adam? He could seek his old friend, although Lucy thought he knew even less about what the hell was going on than he let on.

No, she was better off retracing Cain's steps. If she was looking for answers, he was likely doing the same. The best two options were the house where she found him, and the call centre. Unless he went further into his own past. In which case she'd be screwed, and she'd never find him. It's not like he'd be sitting at his old table at The Fox, nursing a watery pint of John Smiths and staring forlornly out at the sky.

Chances were he wanted the same answers she did. Why turn him? Who benefited? If there were answers, maybe they were at the place he turned. Pulling her collar close, she set off on foot toward her old employer.

By the time she got there, every inch of her was soaked. The unrelenting rain seeped into every crevice and drenched every fibre of clothing on her. She was glad to receive the blessed relief of shelter for at least three seconds — until she remembered where she was, and how she barely got out alive last time.

The destruction wreaked last time was still evident. It felt like months since she'd been here, but it was one night. She thought about how badly injured she'd been, and how none of those injuries had left even a dent on her. Autumn's blood. She'd lost the sense of euphoric power that came straight after it, but she wondered how much long-term effect it might have on her. On the plus side, her teeth seemed the normal length, for now.

She walked through the broken barrier, careful not to tread on broken glass and give herself away. She moved through into the long corridor and decided on the stairwell over the lifts, no matter how cramped and dark they might be.

'He's here,' Adam said, stepping out of a shadow she'd not even noticed.

'Jesus fucking Christ, Adam,' she hissed. 'One of these times, you're going to give me a heart attack.'

'Sorry,' he replied. He wasn't just apologising for surprising her, if his lowered head was anything to go by.

'I'm not killing him,' she said, hoping to add a note of finality to her voice that might convince her as much as it might him. 'He was at Elle's house. I spoke to him. I can reach him.'

'You saw Elle?'

'What's left of her.'

'Oh.' His lips tightened. 'Come on,' he said, and held the door open to the stairs.

The smell of rotting meat stung the back of her nostrils. This was not the standard stench of death, but something worse.

'Vampire death,' Adam said in a low voice, by way of explanation.

The smell intensified as she stepped closer, and she wondered if her flat would have smelled like this if the witches hadn't magicked away the problem for her. What would happen to that magic now they were dead?

The double doors onto the first-floor corridor hung from their hinges in an un-door-like fashion. Slowly, they moved in. Once again, Lucy realised she was walking into a fight with a far superior force, armed with nothing more than the lint gathering at the bottom of her pockets. She wished Adrian was there with her, the two of them walking in with their green armour and righteous purpose. She thought about the resignation letter somewhere in the pockets of another pair of jeans and wondered if she couldn't just resign from this old mess instead.

Looking about for a weapon, she found a long shard of table leg that seemed right for the job. Not that she wanted to use it.

The doors to the call centre floor were every bit as smashed as the last set, revealing the world of utter horror beyond. The rotting corpses of the vampires killed at Cain's hands lay about the place, with Autumn the closest to them. A stark reminder of the last time Lucy held a weapon in her hands. Her stomach turned at the sight of her — skin tightened, body falling quickly into decay, her already thin face looked ancient, its skin spotted and pulled into a rictus grin, the eyes already turned to jelly spilling from the sockets.

Adam stepped over the corpse with no apparent note of its existence. Lucy opted for as wide a berth as possible, not taking her eyes off the body for a second until she was past it. Once she did so, she saw the rest of the room.

The altar on which Cain had been raised lay overturned, and the pots that had surrounded him lay in shattered pieces on the floor. Each shattered pot lay in a pool of thick red spilled from its inside. The same pots as the one she'd found in her bedroom. Whatever the truth of this was, there were two dead witches at its centre.

Beyond, sitting on an office swivel chair with head in hand, was Cain. The same rasping breath came from him as it had in the house, and Lucy thought what a contrast it was to Adam, who never seemed to need to breathe.

Adam moved in front of Lucy instinctively, holding up a hand to signal her to stop.

'Cain,' he said.

The other vampire's head came up slowly. Caked in blood, with so little bare skin left on display, she could barely make out his eyes. 'Adam?' he replied, the name sounding like it crossed a vast ocean of memory to get to his lips.

'Yeah, it's me.' Adam kept moving forward toward his old friend, slowly, cautiously, his hands raised in front of him like an offering.

'I thought they'd done for you already,' Cain spluttered, the words followed by a rattling cough that sounded like a ball bearing wreaking an engine block.

'It'll take more than Autumn to bring me down,' Adam said. The warmth in his voice took Lucy by surprise.

'I don't know what's happening with me,' Cain replied, a note of obvious pain in his voice. 'It's not like I thought. I feel... stuck.'

'They did not observe the ritual,' Adam said. 'And there were other...' he shot a look at Lucy, 'complications.'

'I never wanted this, Adam.'

'I know.'

Cain's head bowed.

'Cain,' Lucy said, appearing from behind Adam.

Cain raised his head again, slowly. 'Lucy,' he said, and he gave a wry smile. 'Hello love. Strange to see you back here. I seem to remember joking with you that neither of us would get out of this place alive.' A darkness crossed his face. 'You should go,' he added.

'These pots,' she said, moving toward him as carefully as she could. 'You spilled them when you came back, correct?'

'I don't remember,' he replied sulkily.

'Try,' she said.

'Lucy,' Adam said, getting back between them.

Cain looked up once more, the sadness replaced by something colder. 'What the hell does it matter?'

'Did you drink from them?' she asked.

'Drink? I....' He shook his head, as though trying to shake some memory loose.

'Where are you going with this?' Adam asked.

'Elle,' Lucy replied. 'These urns, they came from her. She sent Missy to my apartment to clean it after what happened, and when I went back, I found one of these in there. It had some kind of residue in it. I think it might have been blood. And there were lots of them in her house. And they're here, too? Are they always a part of the ritual? What do they do?'

'Slow down,' Adam said.

Cain changed in a flash, rage filling him in an instant. He jumped out of his chair, fists balled at his side. 'Jugs? Pots? What the hell are you talking about?'

'Calm down, Cain,' Adam said, pulling Lucy behind him. 'Think about...'

Before Adam could tell him what to think about, Cain sprung forward, bowling into Adam, grabbing his skull in his blood-soaked hands and smashing it into the ground. Adam's body twitched, then stopped. Cain crouched on his old friend's chest and looked up into the horrified face of Lucy, stumbling back.

'Your turn,' he said through grinning teeth.

24

RUN

*R**un.*

*R*un.
Even as she turned and bolted for the door, Cain's rasping breaths closed in enough to feel his breath on her neck, the fetid stench of spoiled meat fogging her skin. Before she could get away, his fingers closed around her hair, pulling her backward.

She screamed as she fell back. He pulled with such force her hair pulled right out of her scalp. Before she had even a second to get her breath, however, he was on her, his hands tightening around her throat.

'You think I'm the man you knew?' he hissed. 'He's dead. We're all dead. There's nothing left but echoes, dust, and blood.'

Gasping for air, she tried to find her weapon. She didn't remember dropping it, but it was no longer in her hand. She groped around on the dusty, filthy floor, fingers searching for something, anything. Cain pressed down harder on her throat.

Adam charged Cain with a bellow, knocking him from astride Lucy, sending him flying backward across the filthy ground. Adam roared, and ran at Cain even as the newer vamp was getting up, knocking him over.

Lucy tried to drag air through the ruined place her throat once was, panicking as she struggled to fill her lungs. She turned onto her front, crawling on hands and knees, coughing, crying, desperate to breathe.

Air came back, too slowly, hurting so much she almost choked on it, breaths taken so close to the floor they sucked up the dust from the filthy carpet, which added to her coughing.

Water. She had to have a drink, or she wouldn't make it long enough to see who won the battle behind her.

A distant memory unwound of a daily walk to the water fountain on the other side of the room — usually while trying to get the attention of Dave, the cute guy with tattoos who sat right by it, who always ruined it by looking at her tits. Where was that? It was hard to reconcile her memories of this place with the reality, especially with everything swimming in and out of focus.

Over there. It had been knocked over, and the clear plastic had gone brown, but there was liquid in there, still. Crawling on her hands and knees, she desperately clawed her way across the room even as she struggled to breathe.

Somewhere behind her, the roar of two vampires in full battle roared. Crashing, thudding, their attacks on each other sounded like wood hitting wet meat.

Knees scraping against the detritus of the wrecked office, she inched closer. Every ounce of her fixated on one thing alone. With every gained inch, she could make out the bottle that much clearer. Retching, coughing, she had to keep going.

Her fingers closed around the neck of what was once blue plastic. She barely had strength to lift it, but she tried anyway. Pulling herself to her knees, with trembling hands she lifted it, reassured by the sounds of sloshing liquid inside. There wasn't much water left in there, and she could see through the plastic it wasn't remotely clean, but when in a desert....

The water tasted acrid, spoiled, like liquified mouldy vegetables. She gagged on it, spitting the mouthful onto the dusty floor as a reflex. She forced herself to go on. Christ knew what bacteria she was ingesting, but water was life, and she needed it.

It tasted beyond grim, but it did the trick. She sat there on her knees a few moments more, breath rasping but not feeling like swallowed knives, and regained her composure. If she made it through this, she would put herself on a course of antibiotics, but that seemed far away from this place. Wiping her eyes, she turned her attention toward the two old friends, tearing seven shades of shit out of each other on the other side of the room. As she did so, Cain threw Adam like a rag doll against a desk, his face badly broken and swollen. He was losing the battle against his old friend, who barely looked to have suffered damage beyond a bloody nose.

Adam got to his feet and lashed out with fists half blurred by speed, but it wasn't quick enough. Cain deflected easily, turning Adam's strength against him on the turn, snapping the other vampire's arm. Adam screamed, countering with a punch to where Cain's kidneys may have been before. Cain stumbled back, hissing at Adam.

'Cain,' she said, her voice coming out more croak than shout. It was enough to draw Cain's attention, though.

'Lucy,' he said. 'Brave Lucy. Run into a burning building, you would. But that's how you burn.' He began walking toward her, as Adam stumbled behind him, desperately trying to get back to his feet, cradling his broken arm, wild fear in his eyes as he watched what was about to unfold.

'Stop this, Cain,' she said. 'I know you're still in there.'

Cain laughed, and it hit Lucy; he wasn't in there, not anymore. Not the Cain she knew. She'd never heard a laugh like it. 'Stupid Lucy,' he said, laughing a mirthless laugh. 'You don't get it, do you? I'm not me. Not the man you knew. Not the man he knew.' He motioned toward Adam. 'Cain died, and those witches brought something different back.'

She stopped, but Cain kept advancing. A smirk spread across his face.

'And the best thing is,' he continued, 'there's enough of him left in here that killing you will be even more enjoyable.'

He jumped at her, driving his shoulder into her chest, knocking her backward. She tried to raise her stick to fight him off, but he batted it away easily, sending it spinning off across the floor.

She writhed under him, trying to buck him off her. 'Careful, love,' he said. 'You don't want to go giving me ideas.'

'Get off me!' she shouted.

Instead, he gripped tighter, his knees crushing her ribcage. His fangs glistened, and he smiled at her. 'Prichádza tma,' he said, and leaned in for the kill.

Lucy fought the urge to shut her eyes. She wanted to squeeze them shut and wait for death, wait for her throat to be torn out, wait to drown in her own blood as it filled her windpipe.

Behind Cain, Adam's good arm wrapped around Cain's neck, pulling him backward.

Lucy's hand shot out, grasping for her discarded weapon. She grabbed it and whipped it up, knowing exactly where to place it. Stabbing up through Cain's diaphragm, she punctured through it, driving her hand upward until she found her mark.

Cain howled and thrashed, held in place by Adam as Lucy drove the shard home until it punctured his heart. His eyes went from wild to empty; his knees stopped squeezing. He went limp in Adam's upward pull; both dead and undead vampire fell back, sprawling on the floor. Adam gave a howl of pain as Cain's corpse landed on his broken arm.

Panting, Lucy lay there for a second, trying to get her breath back.

It was over.

Cain was dead. The witches were dead. The other vampires were dead or fled.

She allowed herself a moment of congratulation before the crushing realisation she'd stabbed Cain in the heart washed over her.

Wiping away the tears from her face, she told herself there'd be plenty of time to mull it over. She had to get the hell out of this place. Sitting up, she found Adam sat cross-legged on the floor. It was an odd sight, seeing a powerful vampire who easily cleared six feet sitting cross-legged on the floor. He looked like he'd been through hell. His face looked pulverised, and his arm hung at a funny angle.

He looked at her. 'We should get out of here,' he said.

'Your arm,' she said.

'It'll be fine,' he said, but it looked anything but. He couldn't move it easily, and it hung limp.

'Let me look,' she said. She got to her feet and crossed to him. He winced as she lifted it gently, assessing it. 'Clean break,' she said. 'Normally I'd say to straighten it and head to the A&E, but I'm guessing if I can set it, you'll heal, right?'

He shrugged. 'I guess. I knew one once who broke his fingers and did nothing about it. They healed in the broken positions.'

'Okay, let's get this set. It might hurt a bit.'

'I'll be...'

She snapped the bone back into place before he could finish. He howled, gritting his teeth so hard his fangs punctured his bottom lip. Two separate streams of thick red flowed from the wound, leaving deep red marks down his chin. He closed his eyes for a few seconds, face scrunched up in pain, but as soon as his eyes pinged back open, he was over it. His face returned to the usual stoic mask.

'Thank you,' he said.

'You saved my life back there,' she replied. 'Least I can do.'

'I'd say we both saved each other. He had me.' He looked Lucy over. 'Are you okay?'

She laughed. 'I don't know. Okay is a while off. I'm glad it's over.'

'Come on,' he said. 'What say I walk you home?'

25

TRAUMA BONDS

As much as she wanted to invite Adam inside, not wanting to be alone, she was glad when he said goodbye at the door.

'Do you want me to take your rubbish out?' he asked, picking up the white bag outside her door.

'Full service hero,' she replied, leaning against the doorway. His face was already healing, though the two holes in his bottom lip were still there, like badly placed dimples.

He frowned and sniffed at the air as though sensing something disgusting. 'You going to be alright here? I could have the spare bedroom made up at mine for as long as you want.'

'I'll be fine,' she said. 'Everyone who wanted to kill me is dead, and the police can wait another day. Careful with that,' she said, pointing to the bag. He looked confused, but said nothing.

Closing the door behind her, she headed back into the flat, aware she'd not left Adam with any impression he'd see her again. That was fine, as far as she was concerned.

Heading into the bedroom, she closed the door behind her and peeled off her dirty clothes. She fished out fresh pyjamas from a drawer — old comfortable ones with the elastic all but gone, rather than the newer ones that came out on the rare occasion she thought someone might see her in them — and pulled them on. In the mirror, she looked herself in the eye. She could do with a shower, but even that seemed like too much effort.

Was there still a bottle of wine in the fridge? If there was, she was going to climb onto the sofa and sleep there with some dreadful tat on the television to keep her company. She fished her slippers out from under the bed, put them on her feet, and opened her bedroom door. She couldn't help but let out a yelp of panic as she took in the scene of complete destruction.

What remained of her door hung loose from its broken frame. The rest lay in splintered pieces across the inside of her flat, cast into the general chaos of her once-again-wrecked apartment. Her sofa lay broken, and plaster lay scattered from the wound in her wall where she'd slammed the blonde vampire into it. She stared at the chaos for a moment, trying to take it in — she'd gone into her room two minutes earlier, and there'd been no sound coming from the lounge.

It was as though time had rewound, back days to after... the witches had magically cleansed her apartment. Or, in fact, not cleansed. It was an illusion, nothing more, and the illusion was gone. Her stomach sank as she thought back to the vampire corpse in her hallway.

She peered out. No decomposing corpse, at least, but that was where the good news ended. Pools of dried and decaying vampire blood lay over the floor, huge bluebottle flies arcing lazily around them. The stench she'd run into in the call centre was here, too, a rancid decay that hit the back of her throat and made her gag.

There were trail marks through the blood, two sets of footprints — one normal, one like a child's. There was, however, no sign of the times she'd been back to her apartment. It was as though this reality had been shunted off to one side, and another replaced it, one in which the events of a few nights earlier never occurred.

The trail of the bloody footprints led right to Mrs Phatak's door. Stomach turning again, she walked toward it. The door latch was broken, as though the lock had been blasted right out of the door. Lucy pushed it open slowly, revealing darkness inside.

Bloody footprints — Missy's, by the looks of it — led inside. She followed them into the lounge. On a beautiful rug in the centre of the living room, two small blood pools. They were the sole sign of violence in the house, but they were enough.

She'd seen Mrs Phatak yesterday morning, or had she? Her head swam with too much to take in. Did the magic bring her back?

The magic. The urn.

She left her neighbour's flat, careful to pull the door to behind her, heart pounding. Adam took the urn in the bin liner outside her flat, said he'd throw her rubbish out for her. Where would he have taken it?

Still in her pyjamas, she stepped carefully across the floor so as not to get grimness on her slippers. She eased through the fire door and ran down the stairs. The main bins were situated outside the side entrance to her modest block of flats. Adam might well not have known, might have taken the bag with him to throw into a public bin. The bag wasn't full, barely had anything inside. Could be he was still walking down the street with it by his side.

Propping open the door with a brick, she ducked round the side of the building to the three green wheelie bins that serviced the building. She lifted each lid in turn, putting her head inside each to see what was at the bottom. The light here was crap, though, so she had to get her head inside to see to the bottom. The smell of rotten food stung her nostrils at every attempt.

At the bottom of the final bin, she found a single bag. It was hard to tell in this wretched gloom, but it might be hers. Leaning the bin over, she reached inside, but her arm wasn't long enough to reach. Carefully, she tipped the bin over and lifted the bottom. Accumulated bin juice ran out — she had to move her slippers in quick fashion to avoid it. She almost dropped the bin, catching it at the last second, as the sound of the bag sliding down the wet plastic rang out above the noise from the road.

It thunked onto the concrete. What if it had broken? She set the bin the right way up and picked up the bag. It was wet with bin secretions, but she could already tell it was hers. Touching the wet bag as little as possible, she untied the plastic knot, revealing the urn inside, fully intact.

Picking it up gingerly, she half expected lightning flashes or deadly magic attacks, but there was nothing but cold pottery. The bag had even kept it dry. Sighing a vast sigh of relief, she wrapped her hand around it and headed back into the building.

She took the stairs slowly, wanting desperately for this to work, for this little pot to make it so that nothing terrible had happened to her neighbour, wanting even more to convince herself this would be the case.

Opening the door from the stairwell, her heart soared.

Everything was as it should be. She could even hear Nadim playing in the next flat over. The sound gave her a moment of peace until she remembered the time. It was gone midnight — far too late for the eminently sensible Mrs Phatak to be letting Nadim play. She was the kind of neighbour who you never learned their first name, let alone heard noise from past midnight. And were those other kids in there?

Heart sinking, Lucy knocked on the door.

Mrs Phatak opened the door, dressed, harassed. 'Oh, Lucy, hi. I've got a key for you,' she said, flustered.

'You already gave me it,' Lucy said. 'Do you not remember?'

She furrowed her brow. 'Did I?'

'Is everything okay?'

'I... Nadim's having a party,' she said, but her face showed nothing but confusion. 'There are twelve children in here, making more noise than I thought it possible to make.'

Lucy reached forward, compelled to touch her neighbour, unsure if her hand would pass right through her.

'I...' Mrs Phatak started, pulling away.

'Mrs Phatak,' Lucy said. 'You know, I never learned your first name.'

Mrs Phatak stared at her, dumbfounded. 'I don't...'

They stared at each other for a second, Mrs Phatak looking caught in total panic.

'Well, good night,' Lucy said.

Mrs Phatak's ghost remnant gave a curt smile and closed the door.

As the door closed, Lucy couldn't help the tears welling in her eyes, nor the squirming in her stomach. Mrs Phatak was dead, and she'd had a conversation with her... her what? Her ghost? Her avatar? Was she still on the other side of the door? Or did she disappear into nothing? Looking down at the small vase in her hand, Lucy almost dropped it in disgust.

Wiping her eyes on her sleeves, she went back to her door, finding it locked. She had left through a broken door and returned to a whole one. She tried the handle and found it firmly locked.

Even through her tears, she had to laugh, a startled sound that rang out in the empty, sterile, completely fake corridor around her. She looked at the vase. Maybe if she smashed it to the ground, the magic would evaporate, and she'd be left with a shattered door she could walk through. Did she want that?

How the hell did she get back in? The door was back, and locked, the key inside the flat — probably still shoved into the back pocket of her jeans.

Shaking her head, she took the vase to the bottom of the stairs and left it on the window ledge. Running back up the stairs, she found her corridor decimated once more. She walked gingerly around the blood, through the shattered door, and headed for her bedroom. She grabbed her jeans and fished around the pockets for the key.

No key.

She laughed again. Great. Her magic door had a magic key, which only existed when she was close enough to need it. It was impressive, if slightly maddening. She picked up the jeans and placed them outside the wrecked door before heading back downstairs. Once the vase was in her hand once more, she ran back upstairs. The jeans were outside the repaired door. She checked the pocket and found the key, replete with a little blue tag.

You had to hand it to the witches; they had an eye for detail. She opened the ghost door with her ghost key and went back inside. All was as it should be, except she could put her finger on the feeling from before. She had lost ownership of this place, of her things. How could she sit on a sofa she knew to be a magical construct? How could she walk past Mrs Phatak's door?

This wasn't home. In either state, this wasn't home. And she couldn't stay here with the weird animatronic neighbour, or the heartbreak of knowing her actions had gotten the real Mrs Phatak and her son killed.

If Cain hadn't done the job already, she could kill Missy and Elle.

She sank onto the sofa; the thought troubling her. Had she become so accustomed to killing she wanted to up her body count? Not that it mattered anymore. She couldn't live here, in this... artifice. But neither could she whisk it away and put it in the bin. She got up from the sofa and placed the vase on her mantelpiece. It could stay here for a while, at least. Lucy did not know if the thing living next to her had a semblance of Mrs Phatak's reality, but on the off chance it did, she couldn't wipe it from existence, either.

She went into the bedroom and packed a bag. Enough things for a few days. She had to gather her thoughts. She got dressed once more, pocketed the ghost key, and left her flat. Halfway down the stairs, the lump of plastic pressing against her leg disappeared. She paused, went back up a few steps, and it reappeared. So that was the threshold.

Out in the chilly night, she realised she'd not decided a destination other than it had to be away from here. She thought briefly about her parents, of travelling down to Gloucester to stay with them. But that would lead to too many questions, not about anything that had happened over the last few days, but about why she hadn't settled down yet, replete with endless hints about getting too old to be grandparents. She could go to Adam, but he was too close to all this. Hell, he *was* all this. No, she needed a friend.

26

THE GENTLE ART OF MAKING ENEMIES

Checking her watch, she cursed herself. Stupid time to be knocking on people's doors. This was a bad idea. She raised her hand and knocked, softly at first. Barking erupted from within the house; the frenzied fury that came from small, yapper-type dogs. Lights came on slowly throughout the house, the dog quietening as the hallway light came on, its job as protector completed at the appearance of the fuzzy shape through the frosted glass.

The door opened, revealing a burly man with a long grey beard and a frilly pink dressing gown. He held the dog in his arms, trying his best to ignore its frantic attempts to wriggle its way out and get back to the floor so it could sniff or terrorise the new arrival.

'Lucy?' the man asked, bleary-eyed.

'Hi Dan,' she said. 'I'm so sorry to disturb you at this hour. Is Adrian in?'

'He's on shift,' Dan said, finally, looking around the street, whether checking for lurking evil or the snide looks of his neighbours, Lucy couldn't be sure. 'Are you okay?'

'Yeah, I'm fine. Sorry, I've been off for a few days, so I forgot the rota,' she said, though in her head she tried to orientate if she was supposed to be at work right now. She got the sinking feeling that she'd just stumbled across some dark truth about her friend's relationship. Was Adrian on the outs with his husband? He had taken her to some random colleague's house when she was injured, rather than his own.

'Come on inside,' Dan said.

'No, it's fine,' Lucy replied, cursing herself. The guilt of her failing to give so much as a passing thought as to the troubles of the man who was probably her closest friend hit her despite the knowledge that she didn't have the emotional bandwidth for it. She also knew that she needed her friend right now, not the boyfriend she'd never really gotten along with.

'Don't be silly,' Dan said. 'You need somewhere to crash?'

She was so tired...

'If that's okay?' she said. 'I'm having some... issues with my apartment.'

'Of course,' Dan said, ushering her inside.

'Thanks, Dan.'

'Don't be silly.' He placed the dog on the floor, and it instantly transformed itself into a ball of manic fur.

Lucy reached down to pet it, ruffling its hair until it calmed down a bit.

'Please, come inside. Sit on the sofa, and I'll make up the spare bed.'

'No, it's okay, I'll take the sofa.'

'Nonsense. You don't want Adrian coming back from his shift and sitting on you while he eats a peanut butter sandwich at six in the morning.'

She smiled. 'Thanks. I'm sorry for putting you out.' She sat on the sofa. The tiny dog jumped into her lap and demanded more attention, licking at her face when it wasn't instantly forthcoming. As tired as she was, it felt quite nice to be the centre of something's unfettered adoration. He was still at it a few minutes later when Dan came back through. Lucy noted there were pyjamas on under the pink dressing gown where before there were none.

'All set,' he said, hovering near the sofa. 'Do you need anything else? Food, drink?'

'I'm fine, thank you. I won't keep you. You have work tomorrow.' She got up from the sofa, and Dan guided her toward the guest room. Once she got past the lounge, Lucy realised she'd never made it this far into Adrian's house, and felt another tiny shard of guilt that maybe she wasn't as good a friend as she thought she was.

He smiled. 'Well, good night.' He showed her into the spare room, which doubled as their office. Like the rest of their house, it was well maintained, with framed posters of musical theatre, opera, and RSC works on the walls. Next to the desk was a small bookshelf, full of books on running a small business and ways to improve one's self.

She put the bag she'd brought with her on the bed, pulled out the folded pyjamas, and changed. Not wanting to disturb Dan more than she needed to, she left her washrag on the side and climbed straight into bed. For a moment, sleep felt like the furthest thing from a possibility, separated from her by an ocean of tumultuous thoughts and waves of anxiety. But the weariness nestled in her core soon took control, pulling her down into a deep sleep.

She woke in darkness with the vague sensation of someone perching at the end of her bed. Floating back to consciousness as though surfacing from deep waters, she opened her eyes with a start once she'd crested the water's surface.

Adrian sat at the edge of the bed, a cup of tea in his hand. 'Good morning,' he said.

It wasn't dark, after all. Daylight streamed through the thin curtains, changing the demeanour of the room entirely. No longer cosy and warm, it was thin, cramped.

'Morning,' she said, scooting up in the bed. 'Adrian, I'm so sorry. I forgot that...'

He held his hand up, his gaze flitting to the door as he did. 'Don't be silly. Most exciting thing that's happened here in ages. Neighbours are abuzz with the news of a woman calling at the gays in the dead of night.'

'Is Dan pissed?'

'He's fine. Stop worrying.'

'Are you guys....'

He smiled. 'You did me a favour. Gave me a reason to come back and have a good talk.'

'So you weren't on shift last night? What's going on with you two?'

He smiled. 'No, I was on shift, he wasn't lying. But I hadn't been back here for a few days. I've been staying at Pawel's.'

She frowned. 'I've been a shit friend.'

He smiled. 'Nonsense.'

'What's going on?'

'Another time. It's really not that exciting. Couple stuff, but nothing like what you've had going on.'

She sighed. 'I've been a shit friend,' she repeated.

He laughed, and the sound of his warmth moved through her. 'Don't be silly. I'll tell you all about it, but I've got to get to work.'

'What?'

'That thing I said about it being morning? Not exactly true.'

'What time is it?'

'Four. In the afternoon. You seemed like you needed to sleep.'

She took a sip from her tea. She'd need a lot more sleep before she'd feel whole again. Or a lot more tea.

'So,' he said, looking down at his knees and brushing some imaginary lint from the beige corduroy cladding them. 'Are you going to tell me what's going on?'

She sighed. 'I don't know,' she replied, truthfully. She'd not thought as far as this, just knew Adrian was as close to a genuine friend as she had in the world. Her other friends seemed like adult children once she had to consider who to go to in a crisis. Adrian was a grownup. 'I don't know if you'd even want to know. Truth be told.'

'Are you in trouble?'

She laughed. 'That probably covers it, yeah.'

He reached across and took her hand. 'Lucy, whatever it is, you need to get yourself clear of it. You look like... well, to be charitable you look like shit.'

'Gee, thanks,' she said, smiling at him.

He smiled back, but it faded quickly. 'You know I love you, Lucy. But I have to ask. Is you being here putting Dan and I in danger?'

'No,' she replied in a small voice. 'It's done. No more danger. Well, apart from the police will probably want to talk to me.'

'Tell me,' he said. 'Let me help.'

She sighed and gave him a look. Those kind eyes. He'd barely acknowledged what he'd seen on that first night, had walked away from that house and barely given a backward glance. Now he wanted to know all of it; the bare, grizzly truth. She closed her eyes, and poured forth every remarkable, terrible thing that had happened in the last few days since they'd shared an ambulance.

With the tale fully told, he looked at her in silent astonishment, as though looking at her with fresh eyes. It was disconcerting, on top of which her tea had gone cold in the retelling.

'Well, that's it,' she said, smoothing the duvet covering her legs. She hadn't left out anything, except perhaps the conflicted thoughts she'd been having about the man... vampire... at the heart of the tale. Probably best if she didn't go down that route, either with Adrian, or in her own head.

'You know,' Adrian said, 'if that story had come from someone in the back of the van, I'd be diverting course to Bootham.'

'You don't believe me?' she said, recoiling at the thought of being taken anywhere near York's infamous mental institution.

'No,' he said with a grim smile. 'I believe every word.'

'What do you think I should do?'

He considered this a second. 'I think you need to smash the vase. Clean the place up. Repair the damage and find somewhere new to live. You can stay here for a few days while we sort it out.'

'Thanks,' she said.

'You need to straighten things out with the police. I don't know how, but Mrs Phatak's family deserves to know what's happened. What's going to happen when someone turns up to visit her and she's a... a hologram, or something? They might never get justice, but at least they can investigate. That investigation will probably focus on you, mainly. And your friend.'

All sensible. All things the thought of doing filled her with unspeakable dread.

'And,' he continued, as though the shopping list wasn't long enough, 'you need to cut your ties with Adam.'

That one, the easiest to accomplish, hit her like a stone dropped into her core.

'And another thing,' he said, getting up from the bed. 'I think you should come back to work tonight.'

'I can't,' she said. There was too much to do. Too much to think about.

'You can. This can wait one night. You need to get back out there and help people. That's what you do, Luce, you help people. You save lives. You're not... a vampire hunter.' The word dripped from his tongue with disdain. He still couldn't quite wrap his head around the concept. No wonder he wanted her back. He wanted normal back, too.

'Let me think about it,' she said.

'We're out in two hours,' he replied. 'Go take a shower. I'll fix us some bacon sandwiches.' He headed back to the door.

'Adrian,' she said, stopping him in the doorway. 'This is because you don't want to go out on another shift with Pawel, right?'

He laughed. 'So transparent.'

She smiled, and he smiled right back at her. 'Thank you,' she said.

The shower felt good, and the bacon felt better. By the time she wiped up the last of the ketchup with the crust of her bread, she knew Adrian was right.

By the time they got to the ambulance depot, enough people asked about her bad knee that she felt obliged to put on a bit of a limp. She'd never covered with Adrian the bit about Autumn's blood and her miraculous recovery, and he didn't ask, either. In fact, besides the information she'd given him, he didn't ask for any further details, just as she didn't ask him about why he'd been kicked out of his house.

The police weren't waiting for her when she started, nor were there any calls to them when she showed up to work, just a sigh of relief from the overstretched duty manager. Pawel turned up to ride with Adrian, but was more pleased to see she was alright than he was disappointed to be sent out with someone else. She climbed into her greens, and felt a surge of relief at the normality of it all.

Their first call was to a fall — an elderly man who'd taken a tumble from his bed and was stuck. He'd been there since the night before, discovered by his grandson coming to visit. The grandson fussed and doted on the old man, who hid his fear behind a wall of witty banter and mild misogyny. It took them a full hour to get him onto a stretcher, worried he'd shattered his hip. They took him to the hospital, where once again she was met by a chorus of people pleased to see her. It was warming; reminding her of what she'd missed during the isolation of the last few days.

Next was a nasty RTC, a bad smash on the ring road that took every ounce of Lucy's concentration for nearly three hours, during which she saved two people from death, at least long enough to get them to A&E. One of the police on the scene gave her a sideways glance and wandered off to talk into her radio, but beyond that, the scene was too busy to talk to anyone except Adrian, the two of them slipping back into their efficient cooperative manner. As horrific as the scene was — for the two they saved, they lost two more — it felt right to be working again. There was purpose in what she did, and she realised the foolishness of chasing Cain's redemption around when he'd dismissed it himself.

'That was intense,' she said, climbing back into the cab once they'd delivered their incredibly fragile cargo back to the hospital.

'I need a new top,' Adrian replied, looking at his blood splattered uniform with dismay. He jumped into the back and quickly changed. Lucy climbed over into the driver's seat and stared at the workman's entrance to the hospital. A nurse came out and lit up a cheeky cigarette, obviously not arsed to make the long walk to the smoking shelter in the cold. Lucy couldn't blame her. The nurse saw Lucy watching and offered a tired grimace, an oh-god-don't-tell-on-me look that made Lucy smile. The nurse turned away, fishing her phone out and scrolling aimlessly through some distraction or another.

Adrian returned, climbing into the passenger seat. 'Calls?'

'Nothing.' Together, they watched the nurse smoking. She evidently didn't like the attention, throwing the cigarette away in frustration and flashing them a dirty look on her way back into the hospital. They both chuckled.

'Thanks,' she said, putting her hand on his.

'It's okay,' he said. 'I told you; this is where you belong. This other stuff, you run around, thinking you're making things right, but it's an illusion. Ask yourself, is there anyone you actually helped?'

She stared out the window, tears welling in her eyes. He was right, and she knew it. She'd known it all along. She'd gone through this whole thing trying to save one man, a man who died before she even set foot in the room.

An illusion, like he said. One she'd played on herself.

An illusion.

Fuck.

Of course.

She started the engine and put her seatbelt on. Confused, Adrian did the same.

How could she have been so stupid not to see it?

She put the big van into gear and reversed out of the ambulance bay. She drove out with enough speed for the speed bump to send the both of them out of their chair.

'What are you doing?' Adrian asked, as she turned right out of the hospital, causing the traffic in either direction to slam on their brakes.

She hit the blues, the sound of the sirens disrupting the surrounding calm.

'Lucy!' Adrian shouted. 'What the hell are you doing?'

'I still need to get my cat back.'

27

EVERYONE DIES

She killed the lights long before she reached the witches' house. If she was right — and she was certain she was — she'd need to approach this carefully. If she was wrong, well, then she'd made a terrible mistake and was probably about to ruin her only the friendship in the world. Hell, who was she kidding, she seemed on a collision course to do that anyway. She parked, as Adrian had, a few doors down, facing toward the house this time. No lights inside; no signs anything had changed since she was last there.

'What are we doing here?' Adrian asked, seemingly unable or unwilling to keep the exasperation out of his voice. Some fear mixed in there, too. Good. He'd need that, probably.

'I told you,' she replied. 'I need to get Jones back.'

'Bullshit, Lucy. Besides, if you think you're going to keep him at my house, you'd better think on. Dan's got allergies.'

She tutted. 'Dan doesn't like cats,' she said. 'When you came round mine for dinner, he didn't even know there was a cat in the house until Jones got out. I'm pretty sure Jones used Dan's coat as a pillow, too.'

'I'm not letting you bring a cat home,' he said. 'It's not worth the row. I'm in enough trouble with you as it is.'

Lucy looked at him and felt a pang of guilt. She shouldn't be dragging him into this — she should get back to work, come back tomorrow alone. But she had to know. It was like having an itch inside your ear. It didn't matter how much you knew not to put a cotton bud in there, sometimes it was the only way.

'Okay,' she said. 'It's not about Jones. Though I want my cat back while I'm here.'

'What's it about?'

'Let me show you.' She opened her door and got out of the cab.

Adrian shook his head, muttering something under his breath as he undid his seatbelt and climbed down from the passenger seat.

The back entrance was as she'd left it — rear patio door smashed, glass littering inside and out. Silently, they picked their way through it, going straight into the kitchen. The smell of death still filled the room.

'Jesus,' Adrian said. 'Who died in here?'

'If I'm right? Nothing.' She pushed open a door, doubling the smell of death and decay instantly. She tried to remember if she'd left the lights on but saw burnt-out stub of candles dotting the wall, pools of molten wax laying beneath them. It was a miracle none of them started a fire.

Or was it?

Ahead of them, movement. She steeled herself.

'Hello shithead,' she said, as Jones nuzzled into her. He shivered as he pressed his body against hers. 'Sorry I left you here. Let's find you some food.' She carried Jones back through to the kitchen, looked through the cupboards and found a stack of cat food tins. She opened one onto a plate and left it on the floor. Jones eyed up the back door but thought better of it.

'Come on,' Lucy said to Adrian, who still loitered near the back door uncertainly. As she headed inside, he followed.

Slowly, they worked their way upstairs, Lucy straining to hear any noise in the darkness, but there was nothing but eerie still-ness. If she was right, this showed the level of detail the witches could weave.

Into the bedroom, heart pounding with each step, she switched on the lights, flooding the macabre scene with bright yellow, revealing the true devastation.

The two bodies lay where she'd left them, bloated with decay. A burst of flies reacted to the change in light, buzzing furiously to protect their meal.

Still, she was right. She had to be.

'Oh, my God,' Adrian said. 'I... I can't. I'm calling the police.'

'Wait,' Lucy said, her eyes darting around the room to find... there, on the bookcase. Three vases. Each identical to the one in her room.

Picking up the first one, looking inside and seeing the same residue as in her own, she brought it down to the ground in a crash of splintered porcelain. She looked at the legs sticking out from the other side of the bed. No change.

'What the hell are you doing?' Adrian hissed. 'You're contaminating a crime scene,' he added, in answer to his own question.

'There's no crime,' she answered, and picked up the second vase. Smashing it on the ground, it spilled something else from within as it broke — it looked like thick, gloopy glitter paint.

There was no change in the horror beyond the bed.

Breathing deeply, she picked up the final vase. She closed her eyes for a second, offering some silent prayer to a deity of non-specific origin, and brought it down.

It shattered, as the rest had, but there was no subsequent reordering of reality. Dead legs still jutted from beyond the bed. Blood still lay in pools and spatter around them. Jones wandered into the room with a look of disdain and headed to Adrian to weave between his legs.

'I think you need to admit,' Adrian said, picking up the cat, 'you've gotten mixed up in some bad stuff here, Luce.'

'I know,' she said in a low voice, eyes darting around to look for more vases. She shook her head. It couldn't be. She was so sure. If Elle and Missy could bend reality at her apartment, they were as capable of faking their own deaths. She might not know why, but she knew the two witches were at the heart of this whole thing; whatever their plan, she doubted it involved them being mauled by their own creation before they could see their plan through to fruition.

And yet...

She moved around the bed. The decomposition on the two bodies looked real, and the smell clawing at the back of her throat felt real, too.

It was real.

The curtains to the room were drawn, but as the blue lights pulled up outside, there were no sirens, only sweeping arcs of blue shining through the gaps and dancing on the ceiling.

'Oh God,' Adrian moaned.

Lucy sat on the edge of the bed. Her head dropped into her hands. She felt tired. So tired. She'd been so certain. But why? Could it be that somehow she didn't want this to end? That she was trapped in a hell that she was choosing to return to. And as a consequence, the police were here.

What the hell was she going to say to them? It would be bad enough having to explain her connection to everything that'd happened without them finding her here, surrounded by death.

'Lucy,' Adrian said, 'I'm sorry, honey, I am, but I don't think I can lie to the police.'

Could she? She played it out in her head. Either she held back the truth of what happened, in which case she was at the scene of a crime in a location she'd called the police to, standing over the bodies of the two women (one woman, one child) who she'd accused of kidnapping. Throw in what happened at the hospital, the probability of her prints, her blood inside the call centre, not to mention what they'd find at her apartment if they smashed the urn on her bookcase, and she looked guilty of something. But if she came clean about everything — vampires, witches, potions

— they'd likely cart her away in the back of her own ambulance, off to be greeted by some nice people in white coats.

Careful not to leave footprints in the blood, she peered through a curtain. They'd gone for the full works. Three squad cars and a meat wagon. Oh, and, yep, there was the flying squad, turning up en masse with their thick black rifles and heavy armour.

There was no option but to run. Well, no that wasn't quite true, but it seemed the only viable one.

She turned back to Adrian. 'I'm so sorry about this,' she said. 'Tell them everything you know. Don't mention vampires. Don't worry about me. Can you look after Jones for me?'

He stood, aghast, trying to find some response to her request. She never gave him the chance. Without thinking, she lunged forward, swinging her right arm round in a wide arc, ending at his chin.

He flew back, Jones flying from his hands in a startled bid for freedom.

Before he had hit the ground — at least he'd land on dry carpet — she was on the move, taking the stairs two at a time. Flashlights already pried through the closed curtains downstairs, one beam of light searching the wide hallway through the frosted glass on the front door. She ducked under it and made for the kitchen and the garden beyond.

Shoes crunching on the broken glass, she jumped through the shattered edges still hanging in the frame of the sliding door. Without thinking, she ran to the rear of the garden, not chancing even a look back toward the back gate — it would be a matter of seconds before police poured through it.

Tall bushes framed the garden, higher than she was, impossible to look over to see what lay on the other side. Unthinkable to climb, but she had to try. Reaching the back of the garden, she paused for a second, listening for a helicopter in the night sky. If they came in this much force for her, they may have set an eye in the sky after her, and there'd be no point running. But she couldn't hear anything.

Reaching forward, she grappled with the wall of green at the furthest point from the house, hoping her own green clothes and the distance would shield her from obvious view. The hedge was less than friendly; hundreds of tiny needles jabbed into her hands and forearms at once as she drove her hand in, trying to find a branch sturdy enough to pull herself up with. Scratched fingers closing around a gnarled branch, she started upward.

She reached the top, every exposed inch of flesh torn by cuts small and wounds deep. Behind her, the bellowed warning of impending entry carried through from the front of the house, followed a few seconds later by the crash of the back gate being unnecessarily kicked in. Laid on top of the hedge, she lay as flat as possible, hands down by her side, wishing the wind would stop swaying her hiding place.

The police ran into the house, and she started her climb down the other side of the hedge. Halfway down, she allowed herself a brief look around. No dogs waited with slavering jaws at the bottom. She was at the end of another affluent-looking garden; the house at the other end of it lit by several windows.

Her concentration elsewhere for a second, her foot slipped. The sudden drop sent deep tangles into her arm, and in a panic she grabbed out, misjudging it and sliding down the harsh face of the bush. She landed with perfect awkwardness on the knee she'd previously turned, doing so again in a sickening grind of muscles and sinew.

She let out a yelp, a frightened howl she tried to bite back the minute it burbled up her throat, to no avail. Forcing herself to stand, she leaned against the hedge, fresh scrapes digging in where blood already flowed. She tried to remain as still as possible, waiting for someone to burst through the hedge to throw handcuffs on her.

When nobody did so, she moved across the garden, careful to put as little weight on her knee as possible; it hurt but seemed stable enough to walk on. Skirting the edge of the garden, she tried to find a gate out onto the road, but the only door led into the house.

She peered through a gap in the curtain, careful not to press her face forward enough to be visible. A family sat in the living room, lit by the light of a television, the sound of laughter coming through the glass. Three people — an older couple and their child, a teenager. The teen had headphones in; the husband was asleep, and the wife was transfixed on the screen. Laughter came from her, lighting up her face as much as the glow from the television.

Crawling on her hands and knees, the ground biting into deep cuts on her palm, she manoeuvred herself under the window so she was next to the rear door. Through that door was an enormous kitchen. All she had to do was get in, walk through the house undetected, and go out the front door. Easy. She'd broken into dozens of houses over the years, but always in an emergency that justified the entrance. She wasn't sure her greens would explain her entrance here.

Deep cuts ran along the length of her palms, blood still flowing freely from them. She needed to stem the tide, or she'd be in danger of passing out. There were more on her forearms, too, and she could feel the sting of more cuts on her face, blood running down her cheeks.

A burst of canned laughter erupted from the television. She tried the handle, which twisted uneasily in her bloody hand, but opened.

She stepped inside.

It took a few seconds for her eyes to adjust to the bright interior, but when they did, she was confronted by a vision of herself reflected in the mirror placed above a shabby-chic dining table. She looked a complete wreck, like something tumbled out of the screen of a movie, maybe some slasher film. If she stepped out in the street looking like this, she'd not get far without drawing notice. Experience told her little of that notice would lead to help, but it might lead to police.

Blood dripped from her hands onto the tiled floor. Shit. She headed for the sink, and quietly turned the tap, placing her wrecked hands under the flow of cold water to stem the noise and wash off some of the blood. The water stung like acid, and she winced. Taking one of the tea towels stacked up in a small white cubby hole, she wrapped it around the worst affected hand. She'd have to add stealing to her list of offences, too, she guessed.

Wetting some kitchen towel under the tap, she dabbed at the wounds on her face. They weren't too deep, but they bled profusely — as soon as she cleared the blood from her cheek, it was wet once more.

So preoccupied was she with cleaning herself up, she forgot her surroundings. She turned the tap off and turned to head to the front door, finding herself confronted by a teenage boy, his face white, headphones still in his ears as he gripped the phone in his hand.

'Muuuum!' he shouted.

28

RIGHT TURN

Before Lucy could open her mouth to beg for silence from the boy, his mother rushed into the kitchen, letting out a little squeal of fright at the bedraggled sight of Lucy bleeding over her lovely kitchen.

'I'm sorry,' Lucy said. 'I...'

'Who are you?' the woman asked, pulling the boy close in toward her like a shield. He shrugged off the physical contact. Lucy recognised the woman, vaguely, but couldn't place her.

'Sorry,' Lucy reiterated, still unsure what magical combination of words might come next would unlock the situation and allow her to leave through the front door without cuffs on her wrists. 'I've... escaped. Ended up in your garden. Sorry.'

'Are you okay?' the boy asked, his eyes on the tea towel wrapped around her hand.

'You're hurt,' the mother said, her voice wary.

'I...' was all Lucy could manage. The first tendrils of dizziness took hold. She needed to stop bleeding, and judging by the darkening red of the towel, her hand was no closer to doing that.

'The house behind, was that where you came from?' the mother asked.

Lucy nodded.

'Strange people at that house. Parties all night. Other...' She ran out of words, as though realising something she'd always known to be true. 'Are you?'

'One of them? No. I was…'

The boy crossed to her and caught her in time. He was older than she'd realised at first, probably heading for his GCSE's. He guided her toward a chair around the table.

'Thanks,' Lucy said, her mouth dry. 'Could I have some water?'

'We don't want trouble,' the mother said.

'Me either,' Lucy said.

'She's hurt, Mum,' the boy said, running over to the sink.

'No trouble,' Lucy said, wondering even as it left her mouth how much of a lie it might prove to be. She took the glass offered by the boy and drank deep, noting blood left like a lipstick mark on the glass's rim. 'Thank you. Do you have a first aid kit?'

Without waiting for permission, the boy rushed off to a different cupboard while his mother stood awkwardly in the doorway, frozen solid by the fear battling with her sense of British politeness.

'I'm not sure how well stocked it is,' the boy said, returning with a small green bag stuffed to the gills. He placed it on the table, opening up the bag and spreading its contents out. Like most people, they kept it full of plasters, bandages, and little else. It would do. 'You need help?' the boy asked, as Lucy unwound the sodden tea towel.

'I'm good, thanks,' Lucy replied. 'I'm a paramedic.' She felt stupid saying it, seeing as she was in her green uniform.

'Paramedic?' the woman said, her brow wrinkling, before her face lit up in revelation. 'I thought I recognised you,' she said excitedly, moving from her rooted spot for the first time. 'You were here a year ago.'

Lucy looked around the kitchen, but didn't remember it. 'I was?'

'You saw the lounge. My husband had a heart attack.'

'You saved his life,' the son said. 'I recognise you.'

'I'm glad to hear it,' Lucy said. 'How's he doing?'

'Better,' the mother said, the spell apparently broken. She moved toward Lucy, looking half as though she might reach over and hug her.

Cleaning the wounds out with an almost dry antiseptic wipe, Lucy winced at the pain and tried to recall the man. Last year, a heart attack. Nice part of town. She dimly recalled a big man, younger looking than the man she'd glimpsed asleep in his chair. She remembered the mother, too, fussing around, barking a thousand different things that could be wrong with him, desperately wanting for it not to be a heart attack. He'd left them at one point, and she'd done ressus.

'I'm glad to hear it. I remember him.'

'I always wanted to say thank you,' the son said.

The mother leaned in. 'those cuts on your face need cleaning. I'll get a bowl of water.'

The three of them sat there in silence for a few moments, the son staring at her as she bandaged up her hands and forearms, while the mother cleaned the cuts on her face, giving her awkward smiles every time they made eye contact.

A hard knock on the door broke the silence.

All three looked up at once, so preoccupied with the task at hand, none of them had noticed the blue lights flashing through the pull-down blind at the front of the kitchen. Both mother and son froze, staring at Lucy. All Lucy could do was give the tiniest shake of her head.

'Come with me,' the boy said, pulling Lucy up by both hands and moving her toward the back of the house. 'Mum, get the door. Say nothing.'

The mother looked flustered but made no reply, but even as she moved toward the door, the hammering returned, greeted by another voice, coming from inside the house. 'Alright, alright, keep 'yer bloody hat on.' Lucy barely glimpsed an old man walking through to answer the door with his walking stick before the boy opened a small door next to the fridge and pushed Lucy through. She stood in darkness, a tiny slither of light from under the door the sole hint as to her surroundings. A food pantry; as she adjusted to the cool air, she smelled something vaguely bready and the musk of soil from the sack of potatoes by her side.

'Yes, officers?' she heard the old man say breezily, his voice thankfully loud enough to hear. The same could not be said of whomever answered, their response lost through the distance and the door.

'There's nobody here, I'm afraid, and you've woke me up. Whoever you're looking for, they're not here.'

A pause.

'Back garden? Ain't nobody poking in my back garden, officer, I can assure you. We've got high hedges, and there's no back gate.'

Another pause, during which she heard the shuffling of the mother and son tidying up the kitchen hurriedly.

'I suppose you can come in and check the garden, if you must.'

Lucy's heart leapt into her mouth. Even with the clean-up, there was blood on the kitchen floor, and on the handle to the back door. An even half-alert officer could spot it easily enough.

'Sorry, Dad,' the boy said, moving through to the hallway, his voice more distant. 'What's going on?'

Another silence, as the officer on the doorstep no doubt explained what was going on a second time, possibly with an air of added frustration.

'Listen, Officer, I'm sorry, but you've woken my Dad. He's been quite ill recently, and we can't have this kind of excitement, or a load of police officers trudging through the house in the middle of the night. The back door is locked, and there's nobody in our garden.'

Another pause, in which she thought she could make out the mother leading the father away from the conversation, presumably back to his sofa or up to his bed.

Lucy tried hard not to so much as breathe, her heart pounding. This constant turmoil couldn't be good for her. Or maybe it could; it was like having a constant cardio workout.

'Yes, officer,' the boy said. 'I'm sure. I'm sorry, but I have to think of my dad's health first.'

Another pause.

The boy's tone changed. 'Excuse me, officer, but we've got rights here, right? You can't barge in.'

Pause. Lucy felt sure this family would end up in a jail cell on her behalf. She felt like jumping out of the cupboard and shouting that the family knew nothing, but swallowed the impulse back down into the pit of her stomach.

'I will, officer. And thank you for being understanding.'

The sound of the door closing, footsteps crossing the kitchen toward her.

'I don't think they've gone yet,' the boy said in a low voice. 'Maybe stay put for a few minutes.'

Another pause, and a tap came on. The boy busied himself, presumably wiping her blood off the floor. Her heart continued to pound like a nightclub bass bin, but she stayed there, silent. At least the dizziness had passed; the bandages she'd put on herself were not half bad for someone having to use broken hands to mend their own broken hands. She reached up to her face and found the cut there no longer spilling blood.

'They're still outside,' the mother said, re-joining her son. 'Doesn't look like they're paying particular attention to us, but you can't be sure.'

'They've been flashing lights over the back hedge,' the boy said, the words almost lost over the clattering of dishes. He was washing up, using it as an excuse to stare out the back window. Smart. 'How's Dad?'

'He's fine. I got him to bed.'

A long pause fell between them, and Lucy could imagine the looks passing between mother and son. Of fear. Of wondering what the hell they'd gotten themselves in for. Of the realisation they'd lied to the police for a stranger who broke into their house. She stood, her head as close to the door as possible without nudging it open, straining to hear. What if she opened the door and found a room full of armed police? She didn't know these people, didn't know what they were capable of.

'Okay,' the mother said, finally, 'I think they've left.'

The boy opened the door, revealing a kitchen empty save for the three of them. 'I think they're gone,' he said with a smile.

'Thanks,' she said, stepping out gingerly into the bright light. 'I'm so sorry,' she said. 'I didn't mean for this.'

The mother nodded, but her expression suggested any good-will Lucy might have been entitled to for saving her husband's life ran out the minute the police left.

'Maybe you should stay here tonight,' the boy suggested.

'Oh, no, thank you,' Lucy replied, not giving the mother the opportunity to protest her son's suggestion. 'Honestly, thank you both so much. But I need to get on my way.'

Without giving the boy a chance to lodge his own counter-protest, she walked toward the door. She hoped the police were gone, or this was a stupid idea. 'Thank you,' she said once more at the front door. 'You have a lovely home,' she added, not sure where it came from. It seemed to work on the mother, though — she positively beamed.

Stepping out into the dark night, Lucy pulled her coat around herself, zipping up the front to protect against the night's cold, and headed off down the street.

29

THORN IN MY SIDE

The bandages were helpful for keeping her hands warm as much as for covering her wounds — the night had developed a definite chill. She kept her head down and walked with purpose out of the residential street, turning back toward town as she tried to work out what the hell to do next. Her theory about the death of the two witches may have been wrong, but it didn't help shake the feeling there was something deeply fucking rotten in Denmark.

If the last few days had taught her anything, it was that facts and reality were a malleable mix. And yet, the facts were clear. Autumn was dead, as were most of her vampire gang, including the odd blonde one who seemed to be on his own mission. Both witches were dead, no doubt taking the secret of their involvement in matters to the grave with them, or wherever it was witches went. Cain was dead, too, and if he was the centrepiece of their grand plan, she'd foiled it with a shard of flat pack office furniture.

She'd won. So why didn't it feel that way?

Maybe it was the gnawing guilt at punching Adrian and leaving him at a murder scene for the police to find. It grew the longer she walked along the dark streets, watching out for police activity round every corner. Or maybe it was knowing that before this could truly be over, she'd need to see the inside of a police cell and find a plausible explanation for the events of the last few days.

What exactly was her plan? Go on the lam? Move to Mexico? She had a life, such as it was, and even if the events of the last few days had her reconsidering the resignation letter that she'd carried around in her pocket, she didn't want to have to drop everything and go into hiding because she was the only remaining tie to several crime scenes.

Adam. He was the one to speak to. Given his offer to her, and the fact her own apartment was a haunted hell hole papered over by weird magic, he might offer a place to lay her head for a few hours. Hell, she might actually prise some new truths out of him. And, as the nagging heat at the back of her neck reminded her, he might give her more than that.

Before that last idea had more than a second to take root, something out on the street caught enough of her subconsciousness's attention to make the hairs on the back of her neck stand on end. As her senses heightened their alert, she realised she was not alone on the street.

She'd drifted away from the safe residential part of the city's outskirts, onto the industrial seam of buildings running alongside the railway line. It was twenty feet away, but the road she walked down was cut off from it but a series of small industrial businesses. Garages, used-tyre shops, a furniture shop that looked like someone had thrown three shop's worth of junk into a building and hurriedly locked the door before it could spill back out again.

The road was narrow, and she was not walking it alone. Her pursuer was far enough back to be another late night traveller, but something about their footsteps said otherwise. They matched Lucy for pace, staying far back but close enough to put fear into her, driving her forward.

Forward toward what?

Up ahead, another person loitered at the corner, nonchalantly lighting a cigarette and leaning against the wall. Lucy had two options; keep going toward the second person, or take the next left. She figured that was exactly what her pursuers wanted — she did not know where the left-hand path led, and didn't much feel like finding out. The problem was she didn't seem to have much in the way of alternative options.

Directly across the street, one of the warehouse shops had a side path leading to a car park — labelled for customers of RiteSafe. It seemed as good a sign as any. She bolted for the gap, moving as fast as she could muster. That was, her knackered knee reminded her, not fast at all.

Car park was perhaps an overly grandiose term for what she found — roughly ten feet squared of pitted, uneven concrete with a decent corner taken up by a pile of scrap metal. Wire fencing ringed the car park on all sides, and there was no way out but the way she came.

She was trapped.

On the other side of the chain-link fence — over razor wire — were train tracks. So close.

She whirled around, desperately looking for some fire escape or anything else that might offer the vaguest flicker of hope. Any trace of that upped and left the moment the two figures sauntered into the car park after her, wearing their nonchalance in every stride. She wanted to think they might be muggers — that this might end with an empty wallet — but she knew better. She got a look at the pair of them for the first time, realising one was a woman — a realisation that would normally take the top layer off her fear. It would have done if they hadn't both been vampires.

Lucy was getting pretty good at spotting them. It wasn't so much anything they looked like, more something in their way, their demeanour. Something beyond arrogance, beyond humanity.

'What do you want?' she called out across the uneven grey between her and them, a space growing smaller with every ambled footstep closer. She made no effort to quiet her voice, hoping it might draw some kind Samaritan.

The woman smirked. She wasn't worried about heroes. She wasn't worried about anything.

The sound of metal clanking on metal heralded more trouble. Two more vamps, vaulting the fence and razor wire as though it were a low fence, crouching as they landed silently on the uneven concrete.

Four vampires advanced.

'Who are you?' Lucy asked, trying unsuccessfully to keep all four in her view, twisting and turning and utterly failing.

'Darkness,' one of the original two said; the man. Skin as black as oil, it shimmered in the moonlight. His eyes matched a leather jacket that looked a hundred years old, worn beyond the point of distress. Well built, his imposing frame was offset by the woman by his side. Smaller than Lucy, squat, her skin not as dark as the man's but a rich umber.

The other two looked close enough to each other to make Lucy think they were brothers. Shaved heads, skin so white it reflected the light of lamp and moon, their heft more than muscle. Both men you'd leave a pub rather than chance them talking to you. The kind of men who radiated violence, and had probably done so long before their deaths.

'Darkness, right,' Lucy said. 'Listen, I don't know what's going on here, but I'd be perfectly happy to go home and pretend none of this has happened, if that works for everyone?'

'You've had your chance,' the black man replied. 'More than one. You keep sticking your nose where it doesn't belong.'

'Sorry about that,' Lucy said, still whirling. The four vampires stopped advancing — they didn't have to. Each could easily reach forward and grab her by the throat, and there were no escapes left for her unless she could talk her way out of there. 'Seriously. Consider me warned.'

'No warnings,' the woman said. 'This ends.'

'You're right about that,' came a voice from behind the female vampire. Lucy's heart soared.

Adam.

The circle broke apart to face him, but even as it did so, one brother grabbed her roughly, his thick arm wrapping round her throat before she could so much as take a breath. She struggled, but might as well have been fighting a tree.

'Put her down, Boris,' Adam growled, his eyes fixed on Lucy and her captor.

'Come and make me,' Boris replied. His accent surprised her: posh English, Oxbridge educated, if she had to guess. Adam's command must have had some impact, however; he loosened his grip enough to allow her to draw breath, even if she could still feel the raw power of his strength coursing through his thick arm as it weighed on her chest.

'We have to end this,' the black vampire said. 'Centuries of fight, and where has it got us?'

'It's kept us in check,' Adam replied. 'And you used to believe in that fight too, Marcus.'

'And you didn't believe,' the woman said.

'Things change,' Adam growled back. 'But we've always kept the peace between us. Détente. What's changed?'

'Darkness is coming,' Boris growled, unable to keep the glee out of his voice. 'Finally.' He squeezed Lucy's throat again — for a second she thought she might pass out right there, dangling from Boris's arm like a rag doll.

'The age of man is ending,' Marcus said, a wide grin stretching across his face, his fangs sparkling against his dark skin. 'This petty squabble between us will pale into nothing against the coming war. The streets will run red with blood.'

'Seems like a waste of blood,' Adam said. 'You don't get the notion of harmony, do you?'

'Harmony is no longer relevant,' the woman snapped. 'We have left these humans to grow and spread and get fat. What have they done with harmony? They've broken the planet.'

'Oh, spare me the eco-warrior crap,' Adam said. 'Eighty years ago, you were all for using Nazis to justify wiping out humanity. Before that, the French Revolution. And the Russian Revolution. Admit you want to wipe out humanity and be done with it.'

'Not wipe it out,' Marcus said. 'Make it serve. Return this world to harmony with nature and establish ourselves as the true apex of life on this planet.'

'An apex which can't organise anything more complex than a tea party amongst itself without descending into tribal feuds, and which can't go outside when the sun is out. Brilliant plan.' Adam sounded weary of these arguments. Lucy just wanted the arm gone from around her throat.

'You always lacked vision,' Boris said. 'Cretinous puddle of piss with teeth, that's all you are.'

'You're confusing half-baked ideas with vision again, Boris,' Adam replied, laughing.

He wasn't taking this seriously enough for Lucy's liking, but maybe his nonchalance was the best way out of this. She sure as hell didn't like the chances of the two of them taking on four vamps who looked more than ready to put up a fight. There was something about these four that stood out against the others she'd seen. Adam had seemed somehow a step above them — but these four seemed more like equals.

'Sorry,' Lucy squeaked. 'It sounds like you have a lot to catch up on, and I'm busy so...'

The arm tightened, which at least saved her from having to think of an end to that sentence that didn't involve begging for her life. Five sets of eyes fell on her, as though they'd each forgotten there was a human in the mix.

'She is yours?' Marcus asked in a sombre tone.

'I claim her and ask for her return and safe passage,' Adam replied, his voice formal.

'None of it matters,' Boris hissed. 'The old rules are gone. We make our own rules.'

'For an old traditionalist, you don't seem bothered about traditions,' Adam shot back. There was clearly history between them, which made Lucy less than comfortable having Boris's arm round her neck and primed to break her neck with the slightest of movements.

'Enough,' Marcus barked, and Boris's grip loosened slightly. 'Boris, return the human to Adam. Adam, control her. This needs to stop. And you need to pick a side.'

The arm tightened once more. 'I will not hand *this* over to him,' Boris said, disdain for her dripping from his words.

'Marcus,' Adam growled. It was clear there was history between him and Adam, though he struck Lucy as the type who had bad blood with most who had the misfortune to cross his path. He was spoiling for a fight, and no amount of logic would get through that thick brow of his.

'Come,' the other brother said. He shared the same voice as Boris, albeit softer in tone, the tone dipped in honey rather than wasps. As soon as he said that single word, the tension went out of Boris's arm, and Lucy could breathe properly again. Boris didn't let go, exactly, so Lucy couldn't do what she wanted, which was to run into the arms of her own vampire. The realisation that was what she wanted most of all to do grated on her some.

The six of them stood in a puddle of awkward tension for a moment, each waiting for someone else to make a move, allowing themselves to extricate their portion of the group with their lives — and perhaps some dignity — intact.

'Hey, fuckhole,' Boris growled, his grip tightening, cutting off her air supply once more. 'You want her? Come get her.'

30

MUTUAL RUIN

Everything around her became a blur. Adam moved first, diving at Boris. He never made it; the soft-spoken brother beside Boris blocked off the path with a barrelling charge, the two of them crashing into each other as the female vampire sprang forward, sweeping her leg round in a wide arc that took Adam's legs out from underneath him. Between her and Boris's brother, they had him on the ground so quick it was as though someone had edited a slice out of reality before Lucy's eyes.

Before Boris could snap her neck, Lucy kicked backward wildly, connecting with Boris's knee with a crack. As a howl of surprise came from him, she reached behind and grabbed at his face with her nails, scraping down, one finger catching his eye. It was pure, undiluted panic kicking in, but it did the trick.

Howling, he threw her to the ground. She hit with such force it drove the air from her lungs and she coughed, trying to catch her breath. Before she had the chance, Marcus was on her. Her hand scrabbled in the dirt for anything she could use as a weapon; it found nothing but cold concrete.

Marcus hauled her up like she weighed no more than a tin of beans, and punched. The fist landed square in her chest, audibly breaking several ribs as she began her flight backward through the air.

Even before she hit the ground, she could tell something was wrong. Breath came liquid, shallow. She hit the ground awkwardly, doubling up over herself but rolling away from the fight, desperate for breath. Her mouth filled with blood.

She lay still, fighting for air, drowning in the blood filling her lungs. She stared back at the fight, knowing Marcus's attention could spell the final moments of her life. But he'd turned away already, back to the full-on assault against Adam.

The other three vamps had him on the ground at their feet, lashing out with kicks strong enough to move a six-foot, well-built man between them like he was nothing more than a football. Adam let out moans of anguish, more animal than man; his face bloodied and beaten. Each time he tried to stagger up, another boot connected with him, sending him back to the concrete.

Lucy didn't have time to worry about it. Her breathing shallowed, her lung capacity down to almost nothing. She was going to drown here on this concrete, and there was nothing she could do about it.

Her gaze went to the night sky. The stars were out, even with the light pollution from the city. Stars. Always calming. Through a haze of memory, she thought back to nights out under the stars as a teenager, her first boyfriend beside her, both staring up with the same thought in their minds, neither yet willing to act on it. It was a strange memory to come back to, a moment long forgotten, but it brought her a level of serenity, even as her heart pounded in her chest and her lungs deflated with every shallow attempt at breath.

Across the concrete, a roar. The sounds of ongoing violence. Thuds, slap, grunts. That Adam struggled on was admirable, she thought, but he should give it up. Lay down next to her and hold her hand as they slipped away into the night. Maybe the vampires would allow them that.

A downward pull washed over her like a tide tugging her down into the earth. Calm washed over her with each pull. She knew what it was. She'd seen it so many times. Held so many hands and locked eyes with so many people as they went through it, always wondering if it was a comfort for her to be there with them, or if she was intruding on the last private moment they would ever have. She wished someone was there to hold her hand, which answered her question. She'd done good in this life, she knew. A life not entirely wasted. She just took a wrong turn.

Something scooped her up, something she was tangentially aware of. She looked away from the stars. Adam's face was above her, looking around wildly. He was quite handsome, even with blood dripping in cuts from several parts of his face.

Was he rescuing her? That was nice of him. Pointless, perhaps. But nice.

Motion. Was he running? Was that why everything was moving? She was so tired. She closed her eyes. The motion felt like gentle rocking, like being held by her father. Something dripped onto her face. It ran into her mouth, which felt abstractly grim.

'Hold on,' Adam said, his voice pained, stretched, distorted into something weird. He sounded like he needed to chill out. The thought made her laugh inside, but the laugh was no longer connected to her mouth, drifting out of her body to a different plain.

Wow, that was interesting. Maybe there was something to religion, after all. She knew she should have paid more attention in matins in school.

The icky something dribbled down her throat, which convulsed. Her body shook, and she could feel it. Pain blossomed where it had gone numb, and breath rattled through her lung once more.

The pain. By God, it hurt so bad it pulled her off whatever cloud she'd floated off on and crashing back into the body being carried down the road by an injured vampire. She coughed, blood misting up the surrounding breath. His, her own. Who could tell? What she knew was her collapsed lung was healing alongside the ribs holding it, and it felt roughly akin to having her chest cracked open and the insides being scooped out.

She coughed again, blood gargling up in her mouth. It splashed on Adam's face.

Abruptly, he turned down an alleyway, guiding her down from his arms to set her feet down on the floor in one fluid movement, like a dancer putting an inept partner's feet where they need to be for the next move. Before Lucy could react, Adam had her pinned firmly against the wall, his mouth on hers. The taste of copper filled her mouth as his tongue searched out her own.

Hands running through her hair, he pressed himself against her, his kiss urgent, almost violent. His tongue pressed against hers, hungrily. The weight of his body pushed against hers, grinding her against the wall. She tapped on his arm, weakly, unable to stop him. She was too weak to fight him off, but she didn't want to, either. The pain in her chest turned to something else, a tingling sensation that spread out throughout her.

She kissed him back, her tongue exploring his mouth with frantic urgency. His hands reached up to her face, taking it gently but firmly, and the grinding urgency of his pressing into her changed from urgency to sensuality. As the delirium of the moment threatened to overwhelm her, he pulled away, a guilty look on his face. The cut above his eye had mostly healed. Something beyond the exhilaration of the moment coursed through her; his blood as hers ran through him.

'Sorry,' he said, sheepishly. She pulled him back, their second kiss more tender, but growing more urgent by the second.

Pulling away more gently, he smiled. 'We need to get out of here,' he said. 'The others...'

'Where are we going?'

'My place,' he replied, and the ends of her fingers tingled at the prospect.

'Oh, okay.'

They walked on in brisk silence, Lucy stealing glances up at his face whenever she could. She hadn't been this excited since, well, she honestly couldn't remember when, but there would have been posters of pop stars up on her wall. Her heart fluttered in her chest, and the tingling sensation at the end of her fingertips didn't seem to be going anywhere in a hurry. She bit her lower lip as she walked.

'Won't they be looking for you there?' she asked, not wanting to ruin the moment, particularly, but concerned nonetheless.

'They don't know where I live,' he replied. 'And besides, there are protections.'

'Oh,' she said. The last word brought her back to what was about to happen. Could vampires even... would she need...

The whole thing was as exhilarating and terrifying as anything she'd faced over the last few days, and yet there wasn't the remotest hesitation in her mind about it. As they reached Adam's front door, it was all she could to resist throwing him against the door, her toe tapping impatiently against the front step as he unlocked the door.

Across the threshold, they barely had room to close the door behind them before he had her pressed against the wall, his lips finding hers with breathless anticipation. Her fingers fumbled uselessly at his shirt, but before she could pull the fabric apart, he'd lifted her up once more, pressing himself against her in a way that let her know exactly his intentions. He walked her effortlessly up the stairs as they kissed again, softer, her eyes fixing his. No hint of violence, the brooding intensity replaced with wide-eyed excitement. That he looked and felt as excited as she set the flutter in her chest going once more. He opened the bedroom door and carried her through the threshold to his enormous bed, setting her down with gentle grace. She reached up and pulled him down to join her.

31
In My Time of Need

She awoke with a sense of quiet satisfaction, a gentle calm somewhat ruined by the realisation he was staring at her. Instinctively, her hands went to her hair to confirm that, yes, it did indeed look like a ruined bird's nest.

'Good morning,' he said, ignoring her discomfort. 'Well, afternoon, actually.'

She smoothed her hair down as best she could and tried not to think about her morning breath or the state of her makeup. 'Morning,' she said. 'And here's me thinking you'd be in a coffin.'

He smiled. 'Why anyone would sleep in one of those is beyond me, but there are those who do. Tradition, I guess. I spent my first night breaking out of one, and I'll never be in one again.'

He reached forward, tracing the line of her face with his finger. She became aware of both his and her nakedness, and her own discomfort. She pulled away from his touch.

'What's wrong?'

'I dunno. Maybe coffins weren't the best conversation starter.'

'I am who I am, Lucy,' he said, still staring at her with a hint of hunger in his eyes. 'No point in pretending otherwise.'

She turned onto her side to face him and stared into his eyes. 'It's a lot to take in,' she said. 'It's been a hell of a few days. Especially when I've nearly died at least once a day.'

He nodded. 'I know. Well, I don't. But I can imagine. What do you want to know?'

She loved this about him, this openness, willingness to share himself with her, but every time he asked, it left her at a loss. All that came to mind was trivia. Mirrors. Garlic. Lore. Nothing that cut to the truth of the matter, which was that she was laid next to an immortal.

'Will you die?' she asked.

'Everything dies,' he replied. 'We do not suffer the effects of age much, but they are there. Think of it as a disease. A parasite. Symbiotic. It keeps the host alive, in a manner of speaking, so it may live.'

'A parasite?'

He laughed. 'I'm cracking out all the sexy words this morning, aren't I? A virus, then. It lives in the bloodstream, best as we can tell. It suffuses the body with regenerative powers, but it must feed on fresh blood. So we cannot drink from each other — all we are doing is introducing two rival viruses.'

She considered this. It made more sense than demonic possession, at least, but threw up as many questions as it did answers. What about entropy? Cell degeneration? And yet, she had the proof of it, and there was another question tearing through her brain. 'Am I... infected?'

'I don't know,' he said, and the grin left his face for a moment. She could see it was the last thing he wanted for her. 'You were pretty far gone, but your revival was... an accident. A tiny amount. I was going to take you to the emergency room. But if you couple that with what you took from Autumn, there's no way to tell. How do you feel?'

She considered the question. She didn't feel too bad, and the warm glow of last night still radiated through her. Wasn't that strange enough? Hours ago she lay dying in the street with a ribcage like a bag of smashed crabs and lungs reduced to flat pancakes, moments away from a death more tranquil than it had a right to be. Now there was not much beyond a dull ache across her ribs to show for it. 'I feel... fine?'

He leaned over and kissed her shoulder tenderly, and this time, she didn't pull away. At least, not at first.

'How did you find me, last night?' she asked, pulling away again.

'I was following them, not you,' he replied. 'Like you, I am not convinced that we're at the end of... whatever this is.'

'Who were they?' she asked.

'Peers,' he said, somewhat cryptically. 'I told you before, there are hierarchies within our world. We do not grant territory, do not bind the ability of each other to move as we wish, but there are considerations. If a vampire comes to an area where there is another of higher status than you, it is poor form to not inform them of your intentions.'

'How do you know what status you are? Do you get special badges?'

He smiled. 'No. It is not a formal thing. Part of it is based on age, on ability to survive. Some of it is reputation. Some is attitude. Those four last night, individually, they would each be my peer. They have formed a clutch, raising their standing together while diminishing it individually, if you get my meaning?'

'I think so. You call a group of vampires a clutch?'

'It is one term.'

'I notice you didn't answer my other question.'

'Which was?'

'Who are they?'

'Marcus is the strongest amongst him. We have known each other for many years. We were in America together for a time. He was turned there, having been stolen from his homeland.'

'He was a slave?'

'He was.'

Wow, Lucy thought. She'd met a real life slave. It made her wonder how much history the man laid next to her had seen with his own eyes. 'He doesn't sound American.'

'It doesn't take long to shed an accent. Lidia has been Marcus's companion since he came over here. They are partners. They are also fervent believers in their cause, which is where the brothers Bloom come in.'

'Boris?'

'And Benjamin.'

'Boris and Benjamin Bloom?'

'They are much more dangerous than their name suggests.'

'I recall.'

He shifted up in the bed so his eye line was more aligned with her own. His brow furrowed slightly to convey the seriousness of his message. 'It is not entirely their violence that makes them dangerous,' he said. 'They are cruel and devious. Killers even before they turned. They turned in the last few decades, but their reputation proceeds them. I despise them both, but Benjamin especially. They are peers by weight of reputation, not age.'

'The quiet one?'

'Never allow yourself to be alone with him. He has... tastes... that would make your blood run cold. That sadistic streak brought them to Marcus's cause. They are not zealots like the other two; they enjoy the chaos and violence of their work.'

'God,' Lucy said, pulling the covers up to her neck. 'How many vampires are there in York?'

'Usually only a handful,' he said. 'We get... tourists would be the best term. Marcus and the others are not local, and they're not tourists. I need to discover what they want here. They're definitely planning something.'

She sighed. She knew this wasn't over, but the thought of being a part of whatever happened next was exhausting.

Adam leaned over and kissed her again, mouth caressing her neck and up toward her ear. His body pressed against hers. 'You don't have to be involved in this,' he said in a low, husky voice. 'I can fix this. You stay here until it's over and be completely safe.'

Pulling away, she turned to face him, incredulous. 'What? You think I'm going to sit on a chaise lounge and sip tea while you go out and deal with a cult who wants to wipe humanity — *my species*, by the way, not yours — off the map?'

He sat up. 'I meant...'

'I know exactly what you meant, Adam,' she said, swinging her legs out of bed and looking around for the clothes she'd cast off on the way into it. She found knickers and a top within reach, and grabbed at them, pulling them on and jumping out of the bed to face him. 'Let's be frank here. So far, your role in uncovering what's been happening this week has been to follow me about. I'm the one who found the link to Elle. What the hell have you uncovered?'

'Well,' he replied, sitting up and revealing his rather magnificent torso once more, and far less worried than her about displaying his flagrant nakedness. 'Maybe if I didn't have to keep showing up and saving your life, I might have gotten more done.'

'I thought you weren't following me?'

'I have known where you are this whole time.'

She tried to respond, but all she managed to do was stare and gawp at him. Things she wanted to say jostled in her head for prime position. She threw up her hands. 'Look, this is stupid,' she said, pulling on her trousers. 'You do what you've got to do. I'm going to work out why a murderous band of genocidal vampires is here in my city.'

'That's exactly what I want to work out, too,' Adam shouted, standing there en flagrante. 'Lucy, please. I didn't mean to offend you. I want you safe.'

'I'm a paramedic,' she said. 'I've run into burning buildings and active gunman situations without thinking about it, and in the last three days I've killed exactly two more vampires than you have, unless you actually took out last night's assailants?'

'No, but I saved both of us from certain death.'

Her anger ebbed away, and she gave a little laugh. He stood in front of her, completely naked, hands clasped together in apology, contrition written over his face. And yet, that wasn't what drew her eye.

Slowly, she undid her trousers, and as she dragged them down, she saw the contrition on his face turn to a smile, and another reaction, too.

32

I Simply Am Not There

As they lay in the afterglow, any thoughts of anger had well and truly dissipated. 'I'm starving,' she said, her head nuzzling against his chest.

'I don't have food,' he said. 'I guess I'll have to stock up if you're sticking around.'

She smiled. 'I can't imagine you pushing a trolley around Tesco.'

'The lighting does nothing for me.' He absently ran a hand through her hair. 'You can stay, you know. I mean, we'll sort your flat out, too, but you can stay as long as you like.'

'You don't have other lady callers?' she asked, idly playing with the tuft of hair leading up from his belly button, then moving up, tracing the blue vein lines across his chest.

He laughed. 'No. Not for a long time.'

'How long is a long time?'

'Ah...' he said, hesitating. 'If I say since before you were born, does it make me some kind of deviant?'

'I think you're alright with someone once they're in their thirties.'

They lay in silence; her listening to the slow rhythmic beating of his old heart. It was lovely and peaceful, right until her stomach let out a strange rumbling sound. Adam was so shocked by the sound he practically bolted from the bed. She laughed, pulling the covers over herself.

'What was that?' he asked.

'I told you I was hungry.'

He relaxed. 'I thought maybe you were possessed.'

'I should eat,' she said. 'Be a darling and pass me my clothes, will you?'

He did as instructed, offering her a chance to ogle the rear view as he did so. He handed her the clothes in a neat pile before grabbing himself a robe from behind the door. 'I'll leave you to it for a moment,' he said, before heading into the bathroom.

She dressed, listening to the sound of him brushing his teeth. Once he came out, she followed him in, finding a toothbrush, new in its packet, laid on the sink for her.

'What's the plan?' she asked, coming back through to the bedroom where Adam had dressed in his usual array of muted colours. They left the bedroom behind and headed downstairs.

'There are a few places I'd like to investigate,' he said. 'But I can't go out for a few hours yet.'

'I need to get some food,' she said. 'And I want to find out what happened to Adrian.'

'Be careful, will you?'

'I will. Back here at sundown?'

He moved across the room to kiss her. They shared a long, lingering kiss.

'I feel like a teenager,' he said. 'This doesn't happen often for me.'

'So you say,' she said, biting her bottom lip to keep from beaming. She shrugged. 'Me either, truth be told.'

She kissed him once more and opened the front door. Adam was careful to manoeuvre his way out of the sun's glare, and he flashed her another wry smile as she looked back one last time before stepping out into the sunshine. The day was nearing its end, but the low-hanging sun still shone bright enough to bring some much-needed warmth to Lucy's face, and after so many days without its company, she smiled to see it again. She should take advantage of the vitamin D while she could, and the thought crossed her mind that she should head to a beer garden and get some kind of ostentatious gin drink inside her, until the memory of Adrian tumbling backward from her punch came back to her.

God. What kind of friend was she, falling into the bed of a handsome vampire instead of checking on a friend who she'd assaulted and left at a murder scene as the police arrived en masse?

Her stomach rumbled. Food first, then she could think about how to find out if Adrian was alright. Town wasn't too far away, and she figured even if the police were looking for her, as long as she kept her head down, she should be fine. She stopped on the outskirts of town at Montey's, a noisy rock bar that seemed the least likely place to run into police. She nodded to the doorman, who couldn't look less bothered, and headed inside. Even late afternoon and with nary a customer in sight, the music was oppressively loud, some old grunge band warbling away while the video to an entirely unconnected AC/DC song played on the big screen in the corner. She headed to the bar, ordered a beer and a burger, and headed to the back booths, where she had a good view of the front door, access to the beer garden, and could vaguely hear herself think. The table was filthy, but she wasn't planning on eating directly off it.

With guitars pounding all around her, providing a grumbling white noise that she could feel lost in, she watched the bubbles from her cheap lager climbing the glass. The glow of sex ebbed away as she slowly came back to the reality of her situation, and it occurred to her how thoroughly she'd broken every aspect of her life in the last clutch of days. Hiding from the police. Isolated from everyone she loved. Career in tatters. Oh, and the small matter of killing two supernatural beings and being witness to more murder than she'd seen in her years in an ambulance. The joy of a few hours earlier, the fresh flush of romance and excitement, the danger of who Adam was — it all seemed pretty stupid as she stared at her glass.

She could undo this. She had to. But she needed to put things right with Adrian, though that was complicated in and of itself. What if the police were watching him? Or what if he was still in a police cell? She could call his husband Dan, but she suspected that wasn't a conversation she'd particularly enjoy. She could call work to see if he turned up today, but they'd ask her why she wasn't in, or why the cops kept showing up, or why....

Too many whys.

She fished out her phone to find the battery dead. Not surprising — she hadn't charged it in days. Given how essential it seemed most of the time, the fact she'd not even thought about it for days said a lot. She supposed that was good, given the police were after her. Tracking a mobile was child's play these days. Resisting the urge to go into the beer garden and fling it into the bushes to be free from it forever, she put back in her pocket. A bored emo teen brought over her burger — an insanely meaty stack of the kind you couldn't find anywhere other than a sleazy rock bar. It was exactly what she needed. She ate in silence, save for the deafening roar around her. The music cycled through four or five songs and went back to the one playing as she came in.

The burger turned to regret pretty quickly, turning her stomach as it dealt with the sudden influx of meat, bread, and cheese. She felt a sudden need to smoke a cigarette, and as the bored emo who'd brought her lunch out earlier sidled out the back door with a packet in hand, she grabbed her beer and followed.

The benches were more full than the tables inside the club, each filled with laughing and smiling people enjoying the rare winter sun, the heat lamps blaring at full blast despite the relative warmth of the afternoon. Should be able to bum a cigarette off someone, she reckoned. She was about to ask the emo barkeep, but he joined a table of similarly bedecked teenagers, each of whom looked far too cheerful for their wardrobes and too intimidatingly cool to approach. Scanning the other tables, she found a familiar face.

'Pawel?' she said, approaching his table, where several burly men with short hair and far glummer expressions nursed the ends of their pints. She noted Patel was drinking coke and had a flash of guilt — he must have been put onto the rota with Adrian for tonight, in her place.

The big Pole looked up. 'Lucy?' he said, too loud, standing up so quickly he nearly sent the ends of everyone's pints to the floor. He got up from the bench and came round to hug her, which was slightly awkward, something he seemed to realise just as he got to her. He gave her a friendly pat on the shoulder instead. 'Oh,' he said. 'I have your cat!'

'You do? Jones?'

'Yes. Adrian come round last night with him in cat box. Said his husband very angry with him. Couldn't stop sneezing, so he had to take it away. His husband sound like pain in arse. But I said we can look after until he sees you.'

Lucy frowned. If Adrian had taken Jones, he must not be arrested. And if he thought to rescue Jones he couldn't be *that* pissed off at her, could he? 'Could you keep Jones for a bit? A few days?'

He shrugged. 'Sure, if nobody else mind?'

Everyone around the table shrugged their indifference. She took out a tenner to give to him for food, but he waved it away. 'Don't be silly. This is the most excitement I've had since I came here, and I love animals.'

'Can you tell Adrian how sorry I am? That I'll make it up to him, somehow? If you see him?'

'Of course.'

'Thanks, Pawel, I appreciate it.'

He shrugged. 'No problem.'

She got up from the table, no longer needing the cigarette after smelling it on Pawel's housemates.

'You're going?' Pawel asked, disappointed.

'Things to do, Police to avoid,' she said.

Pawel followed her to the door, watched by his table and the table of emos.

'You know,' Pawel said in a low voice, walking close enough behind her she could hear every word. 'Adrian told me what happen. In my home town, we have experience with the things you are dealing with. Witches. Dark Magics. Creatures. In my experience, the people who get wound up in these things never end up well. You be careful.'

'I will,' she said. 'Thanks, Pawel.'

'Another thing. Adrian said a vampire killed the witches, yes?'

'That's what it looked like.'

He stopped her by the door and faced her, leaning in to talk in a low voice over the loud music. 'In the town where I was born, there were two women who lived together. Everyone said they were witches. We younger people supposed they were a couple, that this was the intolerance of our parent's generation. We watched as they tried to drive the pair of them out, but the strangest thing happened. Our parents became convinced they had won. That the women had gone. But it was the opposite. The women bought up the land in town and forced everyone else out. But none of our parents could see it. When we saw these women in town, they smiled at us, like we were in on a joke about our parents. My parents lost their money, my father lost his job. Everything that happened, I... that story keeps coming back to me.'

She took this in and gave him a curt smile. 'Thank you.'

With that, he was gone, bounding back to his table and talking loudly about getting a new cat for a few days before lapsing back into Polish.

His words weighing on her mind, she headed back into the bar.

33

DEAD DREAMS

Lucy finished her beer on her walk back through the bar, setting the empty down at the end of the bar. She headed back out onto the main street, checking first for police, finding only people heading into town to make a early start on the evening's drinking. The Wetherspoons on the other side of the bar walls showed more than a few had a head start on that aim, with girls in sprayed-on dresses and men in salmon shirts gathering outside with glasses in hand, talking with the air of people for whom violence is never far away. She moved past them and headed down along the city wall toward the station. She would head back to Adam's.

The sun was already down and the engine of York's nightlife was already sputtering into life all around her. Thes would mean Adam would be up, she thought, and the thought sparked not a little joy in her heart.

There was a huge police presence outside York Station, doubtless because of some race day nonsense up at the racecourse. Except there weren't races on at this time of year, so God knew. Maybe football, or some other event designed to spill pissed-up bully boys into the town centre to cause havoc and mayhem.

Ignoring them, she blended into a crowd of people being herded past the police back toward the city centre, finding herself squashed against a group of Chinese tourists, who chattered away in their own language, giggling.

'Ten bodies, apparently,' a voice said behind her, one of three young men in Ben Sherman shirts and too much aftershave, a bottle of Corona in each of their hands. 'Can't believe they kicked us out, though. It's not like the bodies were in the pub.'

'Mad that, though. Train pulls into the station almost empty, 'cept for a few bodies and that. Proper fuck with your mind that, wouldn't it?' This second one had much the stronger accent. West Yorkshire by the sounds of it. Three lads from the valley off on a night out in the big town.

'Be glad it weren't the Guiseley train,' the third one chipped in. 'What do we do if they don't open t'lines up again?'

'Find some lasses to put us up for the night,' the first one said excitedly, as though it were the remotest possibility for the three of them. Their conversation drifted off into banter territory, so she blocked it out, turning her attention toward the line of police outside York's grand railway station, trying to see without being seen. There were ambulances in there, too, under the front canopy to the station, well inside the area cordoned off by what had to be most of the police in the area.

This was them, she knew. Either the vampires who'd arrived in town, or the two witches who she couldn't believe were actually dead. There was only one place to find out, either way. She had to go back to that house.

She pressed on, ignoring the tug at the back of her brain telling her to head back to Adam's and batting down the guilt at not running into the station and offering her services. But there wasn't much she could do if the people were already dead. No, whatever was happening was bound to be tied to everything else going on. If she was going to help, she was already on the best course of action.

She hoped.

The way out of town was abuzz with rumour and gossip. News of ten dead on a train had spread through both the real and the digital world, town was filling up with people going to go gawp at a police cordon, with as many deciding an evening in front of Netflix probably wasn't the worst idea in the world streaming home in the other direction. The roads grew increasingly clogged in every direction by the removal of one of the city's few arterial roads, with much honking and parping from impatient drivers who somehow thought hitting their horns might magically disperse the surrounding cars. Police cars wound their way through, sirens blazing, and soon everyone realised something serious was going down in the city. People stopped ignoring each other, chatting animatedly to strangers about what was happening, and others stood staring down toward the station as though on some kind of silent sentry.

Lucy kept going, past the crowds, into the suburban streets where it was as though nothing had happened. She stopped a street away from the house that seemed to keep drawing her back. Noise drifted across the street from some kind of party.

A couple walked past her in the opposite direction, both drunk to the point of collapse, giggling and staggering in wide arcs in and out of the street. Both wore oddly outlandish clothing — Elizabethan finery with oddly modern embellishments; such as the day-glo leggings on the woman, or the glow stick weaved into the headband of the man's trilby hat.

Lucy shrank into a bush, confident they wouldn't see her even if they were to barrel into her, and listened.

Her. 'No, listen, we should go back.'

Him. 'Oh, don't be silly. We turned up. Showed our face. Besides, if we try to get more of the free bar, they're liable to do far worse to us. I mean...'

'What?'

'What?'

'You were saying something...'

'Was I?'

'Free bar.'

'It was, wasn't it? God, I'm pissed. Who knows what was in that punch? Didn't taste strong, but my golly.'

'Stephen.'

'What?'

'I don't feel good.'

'We'll get you home, sleep it off.'

'We shouldn't have left; we don't want to have to explain...'

She burped. He giggled. They were past her, not by far. She slipped out of the bushes and moved down the street. Turning the corner at the end, she rounded onto the cul-de-sac.

Music carried on the air from somewhere. The house looked as still as it had when she'd fled it a second time, not twenty-four hours earlier. Dead, silent, imposing. But with every step it became clearer this was artifice, and not well concealed. The air shimmered as she got closer, until the witch's house was lit up like a beacon, lights shining from every window. The sounds intensified, and it was clear whatever horrors the house held the night before, it held different ones now.

Hiding in the shadows, she watched. The sun was down, but it was still early, too early to see a house lit up like a funhouse on a quiet suburban street. The music wafting on the air was classical, and yet not. There was something hysterical about it, something on the edge of barnstorming bluegrass; an orchestra playing a hoedown. A scream pierced the air, followed by laughter. The skin on the back of her neck went up, and Lucy wanted to run, to flee. Instead, she watched the windows, unable to see into them from her angle, but able to see movement in each one. The house was packed. Either the house had moved on to new inhabitants who were throwing a hell of a welcome party, or she'd been conned. They had conned everyone.

She should call Adam, get him here to see what she was seeing. Or she should run to his house, send him out to deal with it while she hid within its confines. But she couldn't tear herself away. There was a pull to this place, one she couldn't ignore. It was like a siren's call, and for the first time she wondered if it was really her decision to come here.

A curdling scream pierced the air, making every hair on the back of Lucy's neck stand out. She fought both the training and the instinct within her telling her to run toward the sound, especially when followed by a round of raucous cheering and cruel laughter. Whatever was going on in that house, she suspected the couple who'd staggered away from it were lucky to get away when they did.

She had to get inside. Elle and Missy were behind this whole thing. She did not know what their endgame was, but she felt pretty confident it would mean more death, more pain, more misery for the people of this city. If there was anything she could do to stop that, it was her duty to do so. Plus, it pissed her off. She had the feeling of being a pawn in a wider play and found, to her surprise, that she absolutely hated it.

The sun dipped below the horizon, casting the house in the low remnants of the day's light, and it occurred to Lucy the house before her was almost certainly full of the same vampires that stomped her the night before; that the last thing stopping them from coming to kill her had dipped well out of sight. She was exposed, and the vague shelter offered by shrubbery wouldn't cut it.

Adam. She should go back to him, get him, possibly stop by an armoury, and head back here. A solid plan. She could detach herself from the pull she felt in the pit of her stomach that was drawing her toward the front door of that house, and do the sensible thing. Sinking back into the dark, she moved away from the house.

With every step she took away the party grew more distant, less clear, whatever dark magics in place to hide the event gaining strength. It was a disconcerting experience, like walking through a wall of invisible jam.

Across the street, a group of four people headed toward the house, oblivious to her. Her hair stood up once more. Marcus and the other three. Resisting the urge to break into a sprint, she angled her face and kept walking.

It seemed like she'd gotten away with it until she allowed herself a backwards glance. All four stood facing her like coiled springs. Silent.

Resisting the urge to run, she turned the corner at a walking pace, but once she was out of sight, she broke into a run. The main road was close; if she could make it that far they wouldn't take her in open traffic, right?

She glanced behind her and saw shadows moving, not far behind but not gaining, either. Not four, but two. The brothers.

Panting ragged breaths, she made it onto the main street. The road was empty — no pedestrians, no traffic. Nothing to stop them.

Footsteps echoed on the paving stones behind her. Crossing the road, she was glad to see lights cresting the hill beyond, the joy doubling as she realised it was the double-decker Number One bus. Across the street, two shadows waited, watching for her next move.

Down the street was a bus shelter. She could make it.

She ran, right arm waving maniacally to attract the driver's attention as the bus passed her. The indicator flashed on — he was pulling over. It pulled up ten metres ahead, waiting for her.

Shadows closed in. Even as she moved forward; sweat pouring down her face, down the small of her back; she expected fingers to wrap round her arm, her neck. To be pulled back into that shadow.

As her foot lifted onto the doorway to the bus and the cold neon light washed over her, relief washed over her. She wasn't sure why; she was every bit in as much danger as a second earlier. It was like stepping back into real life, out of the realm of monsters.

'You alright, love?' the bus driver asked. A woman, face like the surface of a rusted car, mouth full of broken teeth, lank hair hanging down over sunken cheeks.

'Yeah, fine,' Lucy replied, breathlessly. 'Single to town, please.'

She fished around for change and handed it over, aware how badly she was sweating, and how with every second the risk to her increased, along with everyone else on the bus.

The driver closed the door with a frown. 'No need to run, love, I would have waited,' she grumbled, pulling the bus away from the curb and back out on to the road.

'Thanks,' Lucy said, meaning it more thoroughly than the woman could imagine. She moved through onto the bus. The downstairs was half full, including a set of track-suited boys playing some godawful tinny noise through their phone. She headed to the top deck, finding, to her relief, a few couples and a group of middle-aged women who already seemed halfway toward their drunk for the night.

Ignoring the looks she got from each of them, she took her seat midway down the bus; on the right, away from the pavement where she'd last glimpsed the two shadows. She didn't dare look. She was in the light, around people.

The women resumed their loud discussion of something utterly incomprehensible to her, their Yorkshire accents so thick as to beyond her ken. She closed her eyes and let the sound wash over her. She had to get to Adam.

For the moment, however, she allowed herself to indulge in some of the exhaustion washing over her. This was adrenalin, she knew, washing its way out of the bloodstream. That and the lack of decent sleep last night, obviously. As the indulgence threatened to spill into reminiscence about the night's activities, reality jerked her back with a woman getting to her feet and shouting, 'What the fuck is that?'

The bus was stopped, Lucy realised. She looked around at the darkness beyond the Perspex windows and realised they were only a few hundred metres down from where she'd been picked up.

A scream came from outside.

'It's got the driver,' the woman squealed. Everyone else on the bus was over on the other side, staring out the window at the pavement below. Lucy jumped to her feet and ran downstairs. The door to the bus was open, and everyone on the lower deck looked utterly terrified, each of them cowering in their seats, or in the case of the noisy teenagers crying openly and hiding behind their seats — looking the children they were rather than the adults they were trying to be.

Running to the door, there was nothing around them but silence, and a vague smell of blood and smoke. Looking to the ground, she saw the source of both — a cigarette, barely smoked and still smoking, its filter laid in a spray of blood running across the pavement and up the side of the bus.

'Hello again,' came a voice from behind her, on the bus.

Lucy whirled round, but Boris was quicker. He kicked out, catching Lucy on the hip and sending her flying out into the street.

34

DEAD BETWEEN THE WALLS

How had he got behind her? Her gaze went past his thick neck to the front of the bus, its lights illuminating the dead body of the driver — oozing its last remaining life as its owner stared glassily out to nowhere.

Dragging herself back up as quickly as she could, Lucy turned back to Boris. 'Wait,' she said feebly, her hands cut up once more, the taste of blood on her lip.

'Nobody around to save you,' Boris growled, his eyes red, a sadistic smile on his face. 'If I'm going to miss the most important night of my eternal life, you'd better make it worth my while.' He grabbed her collar, helping her to her feet and a good few inches off the ground.

Swinging the boot wildly, she connected with the big vampire's knee, hoping to bring him down, but it made no impact. There was a noise from above. Boris's brother Benjamin was up on the roof of the bus, prowling around as the passengers on the top deck cowered in their seats below him.

She was running out of air. Moving her hand as forcefully as she could, she chopped at Boris's throat, a move taught in her basic self-defence classes at work.

Boris staggered back, dropping Lucy, but there was no time for celebration. Boris was a half-step on his heels before he lunged forward again, and Benjamin was down off the bus in a flash.

'Hey,' came a voice from the bus. The teenage boys poured out of the door, huddling together for safety in numbers, but there, nonetheless. 'Leave her alone.'

Benjamin turned to face the boys, bedecked in grubby tracksuits, their heads sporting the same regimented close cuts with what looked like wet fringe tips. Normally her heart sank at the sight of their type, but it soared briefly.

'Oh, Jesus, fuck. What's wrong wi 'yer fucking teeth, mate?' another asked.

'Get out of here,' Lucy called.

'Kill them,' Boris hissed, but his brother hesitated, flashing his brother a look of weary disdain for a second. More people poured out of the bus, following the lead of the boys. No. This wasn't what she wanted. They wanted her, not these other people, and she doubted they'd offer more mercy to the new arrivals than Benjamin's arched eyebrow.

'Leave her alone,' the group of half-cut women shouted in unison, moving around the two vampires to join her, doing the thing women instinctively did in a nightclub when they wanted to protect one of their own.

Boris turned to look at his brother, unsure how to proceed.

'Oh shit,' one kid said, pointing behind Lucy. 'There's another one. Toothy motherfucker.'

Adam ambled into view with a disconcerting nonchalance, strolling through the night as though he'd run into them by chance.

'Gentlemen,' he said, addressing the Brothers Bloom. 'I think it's probably wise if everyone walks away from this.'

Benjamin smiled. 'You think we're going to get scared of a bunch of civilians, old man?'

'No,' Adam replied, flashing his own grin in return. 'And the chances are you'd take me, maybe her, too. Hell, you might end up with a veritable buffet. But you can be damn sure we'd kill at least one of you in the effort. And you would spend the rest of eternity alone, half of a missing whole.'

'I don't know,' Lucy said, chancing an arm. 'Strikes me Boris would be no substantial loss to the world. Benjamin? What say you?'

Boris whipped back round to her, snarling, but Benjamin crossed the gap to hold him back. 'Let's go,' he said in a low voice, and the snarl dropped off Boris's face. The brother was the dominant one, no matter how crazed Boris was.

A flash of anger crossed Boris's face, turning to a sneer. 'Prichádza tma,' he said. 'You do not know what's coming. After tonight, nothing will be the same.'

Within a breath, they were gone. Lucy couldn't even work out where they'd gone, let alone how they'd gotten there.

A collective sigh of relief went around the crowd. They stared at each other, trying to work out what the hell had happened, and how they'd summoned the collective bravery.

'Thank you,' Lucy said. 'You saved my life.'

One woman regarded her cautiously, her eye going between Lucy and Adam, a look of disgust on her face. 'Might not have done if I knew you were wi' one'r them.'

'I'm not... He's not... I...' was about as much as Lucy could manage in response.

'No,' Adam whispered, seeing the driver splashed across the road in the path of the bus's headlights.

He rushed to what remained of her, followed by Lucy. Everyone else hung back.

Lucy felt for a pulse, but it was obvious there was no point. The woman's face was ash grey, eyes staring out at nothing; her moth-eaten uniform was covered in her blood.

'Why did that man say that?' one of the other passengers said, an elderly man whose last remaining hairs came from his nose and ears.

'Say what?' Lucy asked.

'Prichádza tma,' he replied. His voice was thick with an Eastern European accent. 'Why would he say that?'

'That's not the first time I've heard it,' Lucy said. She turned to Adam. 'Do you know what that means?'

Adam said nothing.

The old man frowned. 'It means, literally, darkness comes. But that is not so... precise. It is more... the coming dark. But it is not the darkness of light and dark. Of night and day. It means the darkness brought about by...' he struggled with the words, glancing around at the eyes on him. 'I am sorry. I am being foolish. Ignore me.'

'No,' Adam said. 'Where are you from, sir?'

'Piešťany,' he replied. 'Slovakia.'

Adam chuckled. 'I know it.'

The man's face lit up briefly. 'You do?'

'It's been a long time. I never learned the language. I was there for a few years. It was Hungary, back then.'

The man looked confused. 'But...'

'Never mind,' Adam said. 'Tell me about the saying.'

'Piešťany is a wonderful city, full of heritage and culture and history. But darkness, also. Myths. Legends. I think maybe you know of some of these.'

Adam nodded. Everyone from the bus listened with wrapt attention, even the gang of boys, making this probably the longest they'd ever concentrated on anything.

The old man looked around at them, slightly embarrassed, as though about to admit to some terrible secret. 'There is a legend,' he said.

'The Countess Bathory,' Adam said.

The man crossed himself.

'Where do I know that name from?' one of the pissed women asked.

'You might know her as Countess Dracula,' Adam said.

'Oh,' the woman replied, shaking her head. This was a bit much to take in when you were half cut, Lucy imagined.

Adam frowned. 'Countess Bathory was no demon. She was no vampire. She was a madwoman, rich enough to indulge her cruelty. Some think her crime was being a powerful woman when men would allow no such thing.'

'My town is steeped in her legend,' the old man said. 'The castle; it looms. We played as children in its walls, got chased off by elders. But there was a legend, that when they walled Bathory in at Cachtice Castle, she put a blood curse, saying she would return when the world would be ready to bow to her.'

'Witchcraft?' Lucy said, looking at Adam. 'Elle wouldn't?'

'She's dead,' Adam said, coldly.

'I'm not so sure about that,' Lucy said.

'The fuck yous talking about?' one of the young lads said. Sensing an opportunity to get away from there, he turned to his friends. 'Come on, let's fuck off.'

'We can't leave until the police come,' a woman said. None of them seemed drunk anymore. Her words had precisely zero effect on the kids, who pulled their hoods up, hunched their shoulders, and headed off toward town.

'Shit,' Lucy said. 'Has anyone called 999?'

'I'll do it,' one of the other women said, fishing out her mobile. It occurred to Lucy it was a miracle none of this had been filmed. Christ, this many people, there'd usually be multiple angles. She knew well enough driving an ambulance for a living that the best way to find the scene of an accident was to look for the cluster of people looking at the damn thing through their screens.

'We should get out of here,' Lucy said in what she hoped was a low voice to Adam.

'You can't leave,' said the same indignant woman as before. 'This is because of you.'

'You want to try to stop us?' Adam growled.

The woman shrank back.

'Look,' Lucy said, 'you might not believe us, but there are lot more lives at stake here. We have to go.'

The indignant woman demurred.

'We'll stay here, talk to the police,' another woman said, the subtext being *we'll tell them all about you and your weird toothy boyfriend.*

They crossed the road, leaving a group of disgruntled people behind to tend to the murder scene until the police arrived. By the grumbles Lucy could hear across the street, it was dawning on those heading into town for a night on the tiles that they were no longer likely to get it.

Adam walked one step behind her. 'You said things with Elle might not be as they seem,' he said, his voice slipping briefly into a vaguely southern American twang.

'You'll see,' Lucy replied. 'Keep an eye out. I saw Marcus and his date, too. They looked like they were heading for the house.'

'And you didn't think to come to my house, as agreed?'

She shook her head. 'I don't know. I fully intended to, but...'

'There was a pull?'

She frowned, but gave no other answer. 'How did you find me?'

'We are connected now,' he said. 'It will always be easy to find you.'

She wasn't sure she liked the sound of that, but also didn't mind it, either. They walked in silence toward the witches' house, Lucy sure the Blooms would jump out at her.

'What can you tell me about Bathory?' she said, if for no other reason than to break the silence.

'Myth. Legend. She bathed nightly in baths of virgin blood, luring peasants up from the village and brutally murdering them, or so the story goes.'

'Sounds delightful.'

'People have tried to tie her to our legend for centuries. She became a kind of symbol for some among us.'

'You went looking for her?'

He said nothing.

'Wait,' she said, the thread of memory connecting dots she hadn't seen before. 'Your house, there's a portrait hanging on the wall, extremely old.'

'That's her,' he said.

'And you just happened to have gone to her hometown in Slovenia? Or Hungary. What was it? Night time vineyard tours, or were you searching for a legend?'

He frowned. 'I was young once,' he said. 'As I learned more about who I was, I sought the roots of our kind. Her legend springs from the same part of the world as our legend. The timing fit. But when I got there I found mostly rumours, conflagrations of superstitions. A backward people scared of every shadow, thinking every part of their world some occult conspiracy. I left doubting all of it.'

She turned back toward Elle's house. 'Did you ever find them?' she asked.

'Find what?'

'The roots of your kind.'

'No.'

She frowned. 'That's the connection to Cain, right? He was a scholar of her and her history?'

'He had a lot of the same questions as I did, but it was more than that.'

'So you were part of the Darkness cult, once?'

He frowned, his brow furrowing in the dark. 'For a while there, I *was* the cult.'

'But no more?'

'No more.'

They walked the rest of the way in silence, the sounds of the party escaping whatever spell held them away from the real world, until they reached the barrier. As they walked through it Adam shuddered, his teeth coming out. Once they were on the other side, stood in the street looking up at the full-on party raging in Elle's house, he had regained his composure.

'Well,' he said. 'I guess they're not dead after all.'

They watched it for a second. 'How do we get inside?' Lucy asked, not sure she wanted an answer to that question, knowing there was no other option than to go inside and end this.

Adam shrugged. 'I never received an invitation, but I guess we could go knock on the door.'

35

BEAUTY IN FALLING LEAVES

'Not exactly dressed for a party,' Lucy said, checking out her reflection in the side window, pulling her top straight, fussing with her hair to try to vaguely tame it. The people she'd seen staggering away from the party had been in finery, and here she was in blood-stained jeans and a scruffy top.

'Don't worry about it,' Adam said. 'You look fine. You ready?'

'Not even a little.'

He knocked on the heavy door.

They waited in awkward silence, Lucy wondering what hell might await them on the other side of the door. She was halfway to talking herself out of the whole thing when the door finally swung open, revealing the young girl who Lucy had seen dead by the upstairs bed only a few hours earlier.

'Yay,' Missy said, clapping her hands together in a joy that was not exactly what Lucy had expected. 'You made it. Do come inside.'

Missy's childlike frame was clothed in a Lycra bodysuit, with robes far too big for her draped over them. She didn't look remotely displeased or surprised at their appearance.

'Good evening, Missy,' Adam said. 'I guess my invitation got lost in the post?'

Missy's smile wavered for a second, long enough for Lucy to wonder whether vampires and witches used the post office like everyone else.

'Nonsense,' Missy said. 'You've always been on the path to come here, both of you. Come on, the party's barely started.'

As they stepped inside, the volume doubled instantly. The vibe inside was like a carnival, albeit one permanently set on the edge of hysteria. There must have been hundreds of people in there, pressed against each other in groups, most engaged in wildly animated conversation, the gists of which were lost in the music's wake.

'Stay with me,' Adam said in a voice low enough not to carry further than her ears.

'I have no intention of wandering off,' Lucy replied.

'Please,' Missy said, pushing between them, her head barely up to Lucy's chest. 'Do make yourselves at home. There are drinks in the kitchen, and Adam, there's some fine O Neg — responsibly sourced, of course — in the cloakroom. The night's entertainment isn't for an hour, so please mingle and mix.'

Missy moved off effortlessly through the throng, chatting with others as she went. The shy, odd little girl Lucy had met was gone — this new version was deeply unsettling, an adult hostess in a child's body, a body Lucy had seen decomposing.

Adam manoeuvred them through the crowd. Most of the people there seemed like ordinary people, mostly moneyed, all with the same manic intoxication she'd seen on the couple in the street an hour earlier.

'I wouldn't try the punch,' Adam said, eyeing up the people as they moved out of his way, wide-eyed.

'Less punch than potion,' Lucy agreed.

Taking up a position at the far end of the drawing room, they leaned against the wall. There was no sign of Elle, yet, nor of Marcus or the brothers Bloom.

They watched in silence as guests ground seemingly without joy against each other in a rough approximation of the music's rhythm, pained expressions on their faces. After a few minutes of watching, Lucy thought she could split the room into three groups; witches, their power clear, their enjoyment controlled but evident; vampires, all glowering looks and reserve, staring around at each other with much the same look as Adam currently wore; and humans, seemingly here for the entertainment of the other two groups.

The house seemed different from the previous occasions when she'd been here. It certainly seemed bigger. This wide kitchen area hadn't seemed big enough to hold the hundred or more inside it now, and there were double doors at the end when there had been an ordinary one. Magic, no doubt, but it span her head.

The vampires were spread out across the room, not interacting with each other. They had the look of security dispersed through a large crowd, watching everyone without partaking. She suspected the blood on offer had yet to be touched. And yet, their presence seemed not to upset anyone.

'Vampires and witches,' Adam said. 'Never easy bedfellows. Although... well.'

'You guys don't get together and swap stories about eternal life?'

He considered his response. 'There have been times throughout history when there has been a certain political expediency in being allied. But it never lasts and rarely ends well. Witches look down at us. They have power, undeniable power. They see us as what we are, diseased. We look at them as tricksters. Liars. There is no honesty in anything they do, as we have seen. Normally, we stay as clear of each other as we can.'

'What about you and Elle?' Lucy asked.

'York is an old city, and a centre of power for the witches, as well as a natural place for ourselves. We are often drawn to these older cities. They have a familiarity to them. Many of us own property in old cities.'

'How long have you owned your house?'

He laughed. 'I built it. Not with my own hands, perhaps, but my funds paid for the entire street. And the street next to it.'

'Wow,' she said. 'You must be loaded?'

'Maybe if I'd kept hold of some more, yes.'

'You sold them?'

He shrugged. 'Over the years.'

They watched a bit more in silence.

Several vampires were watching, Lucy realised. They were subtle about it, and if Adam had noticed, he wasn't letting on, but there were looks and glances that spoke a thousand angry words. They hated Adam, his own people. And they *really* hated her.

Occasionally, a human would engage a vampire in conversation. The vampire would dissolve into an effortless charm for a few moments until the human drifted away, then resume their stoic pose. It made Lucy wonder how much of Adam's easy way with her was a mannered performance. Was everything?

'Adam,' said a smooth voice, and out of nowhere, Marcus was there, a glass of what Lucy thought was red wine in his hand. He shifted slightly, and she saw it was actually blood. Her stomach turned.

'Marcus,' Adam said.

'And your friend. You are quite the resilient one, aren't you?'

She shrugged, trying to look nonchalant but actually trying to shake the crawling sensation working its way up her spine. 'I try my best.'

Marcus laughed a hollow laugh, the epitome of forced politeness. 'I have to say, we weren't expecting either of you, but this is perfect. It's about time you came back on board, Adam.'

'I've never been *on board*, Marcus,' Adam growled in response, his tone sufficiently pointed to make several nearby revellers glance round with a smidge of terror on their faces.

'Well,' Marcus said, pointedly. 'None of that matters.' He took a sip from his glass. Lucy thought she detected the vaguest smidge of regret in his voice, but before she could follow up, the sound of clinking glass brought a hush over everyone.

A small man in a tuxedo appeared at the far end of the drawing room. He held a glass aloft and peered imperiously out across the revellers until he received the absolute silence he demanded. The band stopped the music mid-note. Once satisfied, he offered an insincere smile, reminding Lucy of a greasy man in a shop trying to upsell a mobile phone package.

'Ladies and gentlemen,' he began ostentatiously, allowing another beat for his majesty to sink in. 'Welcome to this most auspicious centenary celebration. Tonight we feast on the honour of the highest among us, and bear witness to a magical becoming.'

If anyone had a clue what the hell he was talking about, they did not show it on their faces. Even the assembled vampires seemed as interested in his words as everyone else.

'Lords and lay-folk, vampires and witches, humans and other assorted good people, may I please ask you to join us in the central hallway for the great unveiling?'

The wide double doors at the end of the room opened, and murmuring ran through the room. The humans in the crowd took it in with a joviality, while the vampires looked wary. Whatever Elle had planned for this evening; it was as much news to them as it was to anyone else.

Tricksters; liars — that was what Adam had said. The churning in her stomach told her that was probably right.

Slowly, they shuffled into the main hall. The grand staircase was bedecked in candles up and down the bannisters, and the ornate curtains were daubed in strange symbols with what looked a lot like blood. Not a great look, but it got everyone's attention.

'Isn't this fun?' a blond woman said next to them. She pulled awkwardly at the hem of the cocktail dress that hadn't fit her for years and looked up at her partner for reassurance. 'It's like that murder mystery evening we went to, isn't it?'

Her husband stared up at the staircase, mouth agape, there but not there. Whatever magic Elle had worked on her party guests, it seemed to affect each differently.

'Marcus,' Adam said. 'What the hell is going on here?'

Marcus shrugged. 'It's Missy's party,' he said. 'We've been working on her present.'

'Why?' Adam asked, the word coming with a little more force.

'Honestly,' Marcus said, a look of confusion on his face. 'I'm not sure. She said we were working for a common cause. She told us the plan. I'm sure she did. I can't quite...'

'We should get out of here,' Adam said to Lucy in a low growl.

Before they could make a move, however, the little announcer appeared at the bottom of the stairs, four stairs up and barely visible above the others. He tapped his glass again, unnecessarily since he already had everyone's rapt attention. 'Thank you, everyone. And may I please introduce you to her Ladyship, the High Priestess, Baroness Elizabeth Grenier.'

To scattered applause and the sound of the band striking up a fresh note, Elle appeared at the top of the stairs. Her beauty radiated — there seemed to be an actual halo coming off her, although that could be the candlelight refracting off the sequins in her silver dress. Whatever the cause, it was positively dazzling.

Instead of cheering for the grand revelation of their hostess, most of the crowd murmured and chattered with an air of awe. The vampires stared forward with the same statuesque demeanour Adam wore next to her.

'Good evening, honoured guests,' Elle said, her voice amplified by some unseen microphone of possible witchy trickery. 'And thank you for being here on this most auspicious of evenings. I'm sure a lot of you are wondering what this gathering is about. Some of you may well be wondering how you got here. Some of you may wonder how to duck out before the speeches.'

Polite laughter rippled across the gathering, but there was unease in there, too. There was something about Elle's manner that, for her obvious excitement, was far from welcoming.

'Shit,' Adam whispered, beside her.

'What?'

'Whatever happens, play along.'

'Well,' Elle said, clasping her hands together. 'Don't worry, there's no need to leave, and I promise you it will be far from dull. For many of you…' — she held her palms out, where a ball of blue light danced in an almost perfect sphere — 'it'll be the night of your lives.'

36

THE HUNGRY GHOST

Murmurs and whimpers rumbled through the crowd. Some turned to the doors behind Adam and Lucy, but these were already barred. They were trapped.

'Silence!' roared Elle, and the noise cut dead as though a switch had been flicked. The humans in the crowd pressed into each other like startled lemmings, their mouths moving up and down in empty voiced horror. The vampires in the crowd flashed each other looks, but made no move.

'Be still,' Elle continued, and everyone stopped, their attention back on the witch. She turned to the small man who'd led them in here. 'Go fetch the remains,' she barked, and the little man disappeared off.

'What is this, Elle?' Marcus called out, drifting through the crowd. 'What are you planning?'

Elle gave a wry smile, and the blue light shot out across the distance between them. Marcus tried to duck out of the way, but it caught him square in the chest. It clamped into him, spreading round him like liquid electricity, binding him, forcing him to his knees. Several of the other vamps made to move toward their fallen comrade, but thought better of it as Elle summoned another ball to her hands.

'Marcus has the right idea,' she said. 'I want every one of you on your knees.'

The humans sank as one, compelled by her voice. Lucy felt the power tug at her, but not so strong she couldn't fight it off if she so desired. But she played along, falling to her knees so quick she had to stop herself from crying out in pain. What did it mean that she was less susceptible than these others? That she hadn't drunk the punch, or that she was slowly shifting toward a new life as undead? The other humans were too silent in their painful descents, rendered mute by the witch's power.

The vampires followed suit slowly, their eyes fixed on the witch, varying degrees of loathing on their faces.

'Okay,' Elle said, ignoring their ire somewhat theatrically. 'We have gathered together here in celebration. Missy, my dear Missy, is having a birthday. A big one. One hundred years. It's not been easy for her. The call to the Wicca is like taking a stamp in time. For Missy, that calling came early, and it's left her frozen as someone who has forever been treated as a child. She is the most powerful witch I have ever known, and I have been glad to have her with me all these years.'

She smiled out at the crowd, glimpsed her audience's abject horror at their capture, and the smile fell.

'Well,' she continued. 'Let's bring her out, shall we? A round of applause, please.'

The humans in the room started clapping, a frenzied, uneven sound. Lucy did the same, clapping as hard as she could without breaking the skin, unlike the blonde woman next to her; she clapped so hard tiny flecks of red sprayed up in her face to join the tears streaming into the rictus grin her mouth was forced into.

Missy appeared at the top of the stairs, a child in appearance, dressed in her oversized gowns. She beamed, taking the stairs carefully as one would as a child, her smile seemingly oblivious to the state of the people below her.

'Thank you for coming,' she said, joining Elle halfway down the enormous staircase.

Elle waved her hand, and the applause cut out like a record scratch.

'Where's Adam?' Elle asked. She scanned the room until her gaze fell on him. He made no move to make himself visible, but didn't hide, either. 'Ah, there you are. I knew you wouldn't be able to resist coming.'

'You know I never miss a party,' he replied with a mouth full of disgust. 'Though I don't recall an invitation.'

Elle acted coy. 'Come, Adam. We both know you don't need an invitation to this house. Besides, I wanted to see if she would call to you as I knew she would. And here you are. Where's my box?'

The officious little man came back through, carrying what looked to be an old slab of solid stone, almost twice the size of himself. Carrying wasn't really the term for it, though. It floated on his outstretched hand as though lighter than a feather.

The crowd moved out of his way until he set the box down on the ground at the base of the stair. Not a stone, Lucy realised. A coffin, recently exhumed by the looks of it. Clumps of mud and dirt clung to its edges and corners; tattered roots dangled from the underside.

'Adam,' Elle said. 'Come to me, my darling.' Lucy tried to force down the heat rising up her neck at the way she addressed him, with limited success.

Adam got to his feet slowly and walked through the crowd. Lucy kept her head bowed, trying not to be seen.

'And of course, Lucy is here, too,' Elle added. 'Darling, come up here as well. I had wondered if the brothers Bloom might take care of you so as not to distract my ex-lover here, but you seem to be quite the resilient little thing. Bravo to you. But you might wish they had, by the end of tonight.'

Lucy stood, following Adam. Her fellow humans on the floor stared at her — she was no longer one of them. She was part of the bad thing they wanted nothing more than to escape from.

'Adam, be a dear and tell me where this coffin is from,' Elle said, gesturing to the stone box.

'How would I know, Ellie?'

Her hand whipped across his face like a pistol shot, the sound of it reverberating around the room. If it made any impact on him, he didn't show it, but it was enough to raise a red bloom to his pale skin. 'Don't be obtuse,' she spat.

'Ecsed,' he said. 'You found her.'

'You don't sound suitably impressed, Adam.'

'I gave up looking a long time ago.'

She sneered at him. 'One step away from greatness, and you walked away because you got bored. Well, we found her. The one who will unite our tribes. The source.'

'You don't believe that, do you?' Adam asked. 'How can you be sure that's even her? Everything I ever saw pointed to one conclusion — the villagers dug up her corpse and burned it.'

Elle gave a haughty, mirthless laugh. 'Oh Adam, you fool. As if someone that powerful could be brought to such an end.'

'It's an end that awaits us all,' Adam said. 'Once it comes, our power is irrelevant.'

'You'd like that, wouldn't you?' Missy said, stepping forward, tiny fists clenched at her side. 'Snivelling, whimpering excuse for a vampire. You are a creature of death, of power. Yet you spend your days sat on your tight little derriere, thinking about how unfair life is. Pathetic.'

Adam ignored her. 'Say that is her in there. What does it matter?'

'You forget. Today is Missy's centenary. It is the time when her power comes into being.'

'So?'

'A centenary heralds a ritual that can transform her, but we must do it tonight. It requires a fresh host. We will combine the ritual with the rites of rebirth, and transform Missy into a new body, twinning her essence with the Countess, who will be reborn, in her.' She held her arms aloft in triumph.

A shiver ran down Lucy's spine. She didn't have a clue what the hell was going on, but figured this development was not good.

'The Countess?' Adam said, a change in his tone. 'Reborn?' He stepped forward toward Elle, who met him with outstretched arms.

'Yes,' she said, taking his head in her hands and looking deep into his eyes. 'It's true. This is why I had to have you here. This is for you, Adam. For you, and for me, and for Missy.'

Lucy's heart sank like a depth charge into her stomach, spreading nausea throughout her body. If she weren't already on her knees, she'd have been there soon enough. Adam looked back at her, his face troubled, as though checking one last time what he was going to cast aside.

'The vessel?' he asked.

'You did your best to trample over that part of my plan,' Elle chuckled. 'You and your little new whore. But she will come to regret that.'

'Cain?'

'We can still proceed. Cain was... a dry run, a way to test our methods.'

'Elle,' Marcus called out, the crackling blue binding him even tighter as he struggled. 'Whatever you've gotten us mixed up in here, this was not our agreement.'

'Our agreement,' Elle snapped back, 'was to usher in a new age for your kind, to allow your precious darkness to spread. This will achieve that.'

'With a witch at its head,' Marcus spat back. 'We agreed to work with you, Elle, not be ruled by you.'

Beside Elle, Missy hissed, and for a second Lucy thought she saw some mask slip, as the little girl's skin seemed to age and sag for a second. It passed, and the same little girl stood before them. Muttering something under her breath, she fixed Marcus with a hard stare.

The binds holding him in place crackled, surging with power. Marcus screamed, smoke rising from the binds as they burned into him. Flames licked up, catching the vampire's clothes, and before anyone could react, he was aflame.

Lucy felt the heat from across the room, but for the humans stuck in silent sentry around him, there was no escape. The flames burned at them too, their mouths open in silent screams, their eyes casting about wildly.

'Stop!' Lucy screamed.

Elle waved her hands, and the fires dissipated.

A smouldering husk of burned flesh sat where Marcus had. In the immediate circle of people around him, raw burns and smoking clothes were the sole evidence of the pain of the people held in place by Elle's magic. The blonde woman who'd stood next to Lucy earlier was missing half her face, her right eye running down her face like jelly, her head sagging to reveal her burned scalp. Next to her, her partner wept in motionless agony. The stench of burned hair and seared flesh filled the room, even as the smoke dissipated.

'Does anyone else wish to argue against us?' Elle asked.

Lucy wanted to scream, to run at them, to rage against the wanton cruelty, but she couldn't. She was too busy staring at Adam, who'd taken his place by Elle's side.

37

STAY DOWN

'What happens now?' Adam said, unable to keep the excitement out of his voice. Lucy had seen him angry, had seen him happy, had seen him covered by a single sheet and shimmering with sexual intensity — but she'd never seen him like this; a schoolboy hanging off the arm of the prettiest girl in school, wondering how he got so lucky. It turned her stomach.

'We need a new vessel,' Elle said in hushed tones. 'The ceremony is in three parts. First, you will ingest the spirit of Lakesh, which will allow your blood to be a conduit. Then you must turn the body that will be the vessel. They will be reborn as vampire. Once reborn, we will summon the Countess and join her with the spirit of Missy, binding both to the new vessel. A trinity of darkness.'

'Cain was to be the vessel?' Adam asked. 'You did this for me?'

Elle smiled. 'You belong by our side, Adam. You are closer to the mystic than these other animals. At least, you were. Once. I believed you the one to ally our two branches, but you turned your back on both. It is time you turned back to who you are once more.' Whispering, pleading, leaning on her considerable wily charms, her mouth inches from Adam's ear. 'Rejoin us. As Missy will be a trinity in herself, so too will we be a trinity that will usher in a new age of darkness.'

Adam stared at his feet, taking this in. Lucy wanted to scream at him, to pummel him, to tear him away and bolt from the doors and beg him to come to his senses.

'There's no time to turn someone,' Adam said. 'They will be in the early stages. What if we cannot bring the vessel back under control?'

'You should have thought of that before you and your bitch girlfriend ruined everything,' Missy spat.

Lucy had heard enough. She might be risking everything, but there wasn't much chance of anyone getting out of that room alive anyway and she had no intention of going quietly. 'Excuse me,' she said, feeling so awkward that her hand involuntarily went up.

All eyes turned to her.

'What?' Elle replied coolly.

'This whole thing was a ploy, right? You wanted to guilt Adam into re-joining you by pouring Missy into his friend, right? And stuffing some legendary mojo queen in there for good measure? Is that about right?'

'You know nothing about...' Elle started, but Lucy cut her off.

'You conned the vamps into thinking you were going to bring back their legendary goddess, out of the goodness of your heart? So why the ruse to make me think you were dead?'

'To keep Adam interested,' Elle said, her pretty face twisted in an ugly sneer. 'Oh, I'm sorry, did you think you were special?' She let that hang there as though it was some kind of grave insult, but Lucy didn't feel remotely put out. 'No,' Elle continued, dramatically. 'It was for Adam. There was no way a simple invitation would bring him to my door. But as soon as he showed the slightest interest in you, I knew all we had to do to get him here tonight was to keep you in trouble. You think it was a coincidence the police showing up the moment you got here last night? Or that they let you leave? My boy Adam may be a lover for the ages, but he's also a sap.'

'Hey,' Adam interjected.

'Oh, darling, you know it's true. How many lovers does this make? Tragic, lonely human girls who you can save?' She turned back to Lucy. 'He has a type, my dear, and you are it. Red hair. Pretty, but not too pretty if you get my drift. Grateful.'

That stung. Lucy tried not to let the tears welling up spill down her cheek, to no avail. She felt hollow, empty, and even though she was almost certainly about to die at the hands of a man she'd shared a bed with, the shame felt like the worst betrayal.

'Of course,' Missy said, stepping forward and reaching out almost close enough to touch Lucy's cheek. 'Now you are more than a distraction.'

Elle grinned beside her.

'No,' Adam butted in. 'Absolutely no way.'

It took Lucy a half step to catch up. Her. They wanted her for the vessel. Lucy thought about darting for the door, but knew there wasn't the remotest chance she'd make it.

'Think about it, Adam,' Elle said. 'There is only one candidate for this. She's already ingested enough to make her ripe for the turn. You have a connection. You can keep her alive for eternity with you. And the Countess. Everything you've ever wanted.'

'I... can't,' he said.

Heat crept up Lucy's neck. How dare they discuss her like a cheap suit? Balling her fists at her side, she readied herself to swing at whoever came at her first. There might be no way out of here, but it didn't mean she had to go down without a fight.

'I want her,' Missy said, staring at Lucy like she was a hot dinner. 'Make me her.'

'You come near me,' Lucy said, fingernails digging into her palms, 'and I'll break your fucking spine.'

Elle laughed. 'She's a feisty one. Just wait until she's part of the trinity. She will be unstoppable.'

Lucy glanced around the room. There was no way out. The last exit from the room not currently barred and locked was up the stairs, through the two witches and the vampire she'd been idiot enough to sleep with.

With a wave of Elle's hand, green vines appeared on each of Lucy's wrists, pulling her hands round in front of her, binding them tightly together.

Lucy pulled, but every tug strengthened them more, her hands turning blue at the effort. 'Adam,' she said. 'Please. You can't let them do this to me. Cain didn't want this, and you couldn't protect him. You couldn't save him. But you can still save me.'

Adam stepped down the few steps, so he stood directly in front of her. For a moment Lucy thought her entreaties might have worked, that he might sever the binds, sweep her up and rush her to safety. Instead, he looked into her eyes, reached up with his cold dead hand and wiped a tear from her cheek.

'I'm sorry, Lucy. One day we'll look back on this and see it as a new beginning, I promise. She's too important not to bring back.'

'You said she was a myth,' Lucy replied, astounded.

He smiled; a smug grin. 'I convinced myself, but I'm so happy to be wrong.'

With all the rage and fury she could muster, Lucy spat in his face. He didn't look remotely surprised, or disgusted, or angry. That made her even angrier. She swung her leg out wildly, aiming for his kneecap. If the last tool left to her was feral rage, so be it.

Adam saw the leg coming, shifting his body with effortless grace to let it sail past him. What he didn't see coming was her following head-butt. Her forehead connected with the bridge of his nose, and there was a satisfying crunch of breaking bone before both tumbled to the ground.

Adam was up first, teeth out. 'Don't do this,' he said.

'Worried you'll have to break your precious vessel?' she replied, scrambling to her feet in an ungainly manner. The binding on her wrist had cut into her skin on one wrist during the fall, but it had snapped on the other wrist. She might be able to work her hand loose, but didn't want to give herself away yet. 'Because I'd rather die than that fate. I won't drink from you again, you arrogant prick.'

'You might not have to,' Elle said disdainfully. 'I believe you've consumed enough to turn on your own.' She shrugged. 'But we'll make sure, of course.'

Around Lucy, her fellow humans stared forward in terrified silence, statues frozen in place, wide eyes the sole sign of their terror. Amongst them, casting glances at each other, stood the vampires. The brothers Bloom were there, as was Marcus's partner, Lidia. That she hadn't reacted to Marcus's immolation spoke to the fear they had of the two witches on the stairs. She watched Lucy struggle to her feet with something approaching disdain, but there was a seething rage there, too. If there was a way out of here, it was using the other vamps.

'She's not that graceful,' Elle said to Missy.

'The Countess and I will have grace enough for both of us,' Missy said. 'I like her hair.'

Her mother always joked that red hair of hers would get her in trouble, Lucy thought, and here she was. In trouble.

Adam moved like a flash, positioning himself behind Lucy, his hands moving through her arms, pinning her to him. She pressed against his hip, the pair of them locked in an intimate clinch she for one had no desire to be part of.

'Lidia,' she called out, and Marcus's partner stirred from whatever sombre or violent thoughts she was having, back to attention. 'Are you going to let them get away with this? Adam told me you were people of honour, of a code. How does this stack up to you? How well do you like the idea of a witch leading your people? What's that going to do for your fucking purity?'

Every vampire's eye locked onto her, hackles raised, the glow of hate in their eyes.

'Oh, foolish child,' Elle said haughtily. 'Do not pretend you know the complexities of our world.'

Lucy may not know the complexities of the netherworld of mystical beings, but she knew about body language. You walk into a pub where an injury's the only thing keeping a fragile peace between warring revellers and you learned to read that as easily as you would a recipe for toast. It was instinct to her, and that instinct screamed at her that these vampires were pissed. If she had the read of the room, it was fear holding them back, and anger could override fear. If she and the other humans in this room were going to escape, their last hope was for the vampires to turn on the witches, giving them the room to get free.

'Listen to her,' Lucy continued, addressing the brothers Bloom. 'She thinks she owns you. Thinks the power is hers, not yours.'

'What are you doing?' Adam hissed in her ear.

She wriggled, easing one hand from its bondage. 'I thought vampires were the most powerful creatures on earth? I thought you wanted to rid the world of the pestilence of humanity? How are you going to do that if you can't even stand up to a pair of solitary witches and one turncoat bastard?'

A roar went up from the other side of the room. Boris was on the march, ambling forward with the grace of a lopsided barrel, knocking static bodies out of the way like bowling pins, an unintelligent burst of noise coming from his mouth.

Lidia hissed, crouched, and sprung forward to join him, her actions breaking the spell for the other vampires in the room. Lucy barely had enough time to take in the horrified panic on Elle's face before she had to make her own move. Stamping as hard as she could on Adam's foot, she brought her free arm round and slammed her elbow into his ribs. For good measure, she lashed out with a backward head-butt.

Adam staggered back, pulling her with him, but she shook herself free. 'No,' he said, somewhat pathetically, as he fell back to the floor, taking a frozen woman in a little black dress with him. The woman hit the ground hard; something cracked, but she remained static.

Lucy had to free these people.

On the stairs, Elle and Missy gingerly took steps back up while muttering under their breaths, summoning balls of energy and hurling them at the approaching vampires. But Boris and the others knew better than that, and dodged them with relative ease. One ball slammed into the far wall, setting an expensive-looking oil painting aflame, while another hit a man who looked like his last act before being frozen in place was doing a cheeky bump of cocaine off the back of his hand. He burned up in seconds before Elle could bring the fire under control. They were outgunned, and as the vampires approached them, they looked terrified.

Lucy sprang forward to a fireplace in the room's corner, its shelf full of the little urns. She didn't know how they worked, but it didn't matter. Grabbing urns in each hand, she threw the small clay pots against the walls. Each one shattered in a shower of clay and coloured powder. Purple, grey, green, yellow, red. She ignored the howl of pain from the staircase behind her and kept going until the shelf was empty, until she felt a hand on her shoulder pulling her around.

The hand grabbed a handful of Lucy's top, and a fair pinch of skin, and threw her against the wall. Lucy's head smacked against the hard brick and she slid down in time to see a tiny old lady — her skin stretched over a balding scalp — looming over her.

Missy. The truth of her. She sneered, pulling ancient skin so taut it looked like it might split.

'You'll pay for that, you bitch.'

38

WHAT YOU ARE

The effect of the witch's magic on the people in the room was wearing off, fast. Screams erupted from those nursing serious burns, while people scurried out of the way of the vampires and Elle, huddling into corners of the room. One man followed Lucy's lead and began smashing clay pots. Not a one looked anything like the ones Lucy had smashed, but he looked happy to be helping, at least.

'You sure you should be worried about me?' Lucy asked as Missy approached, catching movement out of the corner of her eye. The question gave Missy the moment's pause needed to stop her from getting out of the way of Boris, who charged into her from the side, sending her flying against the far wall. Given the witch's frail new state, Lucy half expected her to shatter into pieces, but she landed on her feet like a tossed cat, alert and ready to charge.

Before Lucy could brace herself against the tiny old woman's retaliation, she was blindsided. Adam appeared next to her, scooping her up in his arms, kicking out at Boris as he went. The burly vampire brother went sprawling to the ground.

'Through here,' Elle said, appearing by Adam's side, the huge casket with the Duchess's remains inside in her arms, carried as though it was nothing. Lucy tried to struggle, but the vampire's grip was too firm.

'Let me go,' she said, struggling to breathe against Adam's tight embrace, but he set his jaw in silent determination and followed in Elle's wake.

A wall of murky air cut the other vampires off from them, their movements as though moving through treacle. Mercy's wizened figure stood between them, moving her arms about as though conducting rag dolls to dance on strings. The air thickened further, turning to what looked like pudding around them, leaving two witches, a vampire, and a Lucy at its heart in a solitary bubble of air.

Elle waved at a wall, which dissolved to reveal a secret door. Another flick of the witch's wrist flung the door open, revealing an entirely impossible room beyond. There was no space for it, and yet there it was. Lucy gave up struggling — it was to no avail, and her strength was better conserved for whatever came next.

The new room was unlike the rest of the house. Green and white tiles covered floor and wall, with peeling white paint taking over halfway up and carrying on up to the ceiling. It was as though they'd teleported into some kind of Victorian sanatorium. Given how little Lucy knew about the power these witches commanded, she realised it was possible they'd done exactly that.

Old lady Missy sealed the door back up with a wave of her hand and turned to Lucy, striding forward as Adam set her gently down on the floor, bringing her tiny frail arm up in a wild slap, which connected with enough force to send Lucy stumbling, her cheek stinging and flushing red with pain.

'You're going to pay for breaking those spells,' she hissed, squaring up as though to come back with a second swing, but Adam got between them.

'Think, Missy. You want a nice new vessel? Or do you want one with half its teeth missing and a scar on its face? Those restoration spells of yours return to a baseline, and you know that.'

'I don't need restoration if I've got a vampire body,' she hissed in return.

'I don't know if we've got time,' Elle said, from across the room. She stood by an old wooden dresser, its doors spread open to reveal hundreds of tiny jars and old notepads with browning paper bound by string. It would have looked shabby chic if the jars didn't have eyeballs in them. She turned to Adam, her hands full of jars. 'If you turn her, how quick can she resurrect?'

'it could be a few hours.'

'Um, I don't want to be a vampire,' Lucy said. 'In case anyone's interested.'

'You don't get a say,' the Missy said in a singsong voice as childlike as she no longer looked.

'Oh yeah?' Lucy said. 'So I understand — I'll be a vampire, but I'll also have two people living in my head with me? A hundred-year-old child witch, and a half-millennia dead serial killer? Trust me, I'll be heading for a sunrise the first morning I get the chance.'

That stopped the other three in their tracks.

'That's... not how this will work,' Adam said.

'And you're sure about that, are you?' Lucy said. 'Done a lot of these rituals, have you? I vote we get to stay in the bodies we're in, or the casket, and everyone's a winner.'

'No,' Missy said, the sound coming out more pout than word, her bottom lip protruding like some kind of festering, bloated worm.

'Let's take this one step at a time,' Elle said, dumping urns onto a metal trolley and wheeling it into the centre of the room. 'Adam, kill her.'

Adam hesitated for a second.

'Don't do this,' Lucy said, as her lover approached uncertainly.

'Adam, you've known this girl for less than a week,' Elle said contemptuously, half her concentration on the pestle and mortar in front of her, the mix of ingredients at its core releasing a pungent smell that stung Lucy's throat. 'After searching for the Countess for half a century. This was more important to you than whatever nomadic life you've chosen to hide in. You don't have to be alone anymore. You can be a king, be part of a family.'

Adam stared forward past Lucy's shoulder, contemplating the far wall and what he wanted. In that moment, Lucy realised nothing she said would matter. She didn't enter into this. Every moment with Adam so far had been, to him, about him.

'Adam,' she said, but he didn't seem to hear her.

'I need her, Adam,' Missy cried. 'The age gaining on me — it hurts. I'm fading away.' She looked more frail, Lucy thought, with a minor note of satisfaction. 'Hurry, Ellie.'

Screams carried through the walls, anguished howls of panic and fear. The people. The vampires must have turned against the house guests when they couldn't find the witches, taking their violence out on the people who they were used to taking violence out on.

Lucy's stomach turned. To think she imagined she might do some good here. All she'd done was put herself forward for a pointless death, one that could usher untold pain and despair onto the world. Clinging to her earlier thought, she bit her bottom lip and tapped her heel on the floor in frustration. She would stay a part of herself, somehow, cling on enough to bring an end to the whole sorry affair.

Adam heard the screams, too. He stared forlornly at the door. Any trace of empathy she had toward him evaporated, and she realised there was no way out that didn't start and end with her. There was no help to come from him.

With Adam momentarily distracted, Lucy ran across the room toward Elle and grabbed the end of her trolley. Shoving it with all the violence she could muster, it clattered across the room, spilling Elle's magical concoction over the floor.

'No!' Missy and Elle cried in unison.

The powder, a strange rainbow blend with a muddy brown hue, splashed against the tiles, and promptly ate through them, releasing a steam that caught in the back of both Lucy and Elle's throat. Lucy hacked and coughed, trying to move away from it at the exact moment Missy moved toward it.

The tiny old child lady, beyond grief at the loss of her rebirth, stumbled forward, bending down to scoop up the powder. She scooped up green-brown murk even as it ate through the wrinkled old skin of her hands.

With the smell of burning flesh filling the room, Lucy stumbled backward, pressing herself against the tiles at the far end of the room. Missy screamed, shaking the powder out of what remained of her hands, heavy droplets of acidic goo shaking the burning flesh from her fingers. The howling and shaking intensified, sending toxic mess everywhere.

Stumbling, Missy placed what remained of her hands on the casket of the old dead vampire, as Elle hovered a few feet behind her, weeping, wanting to console her friend but not daring to touch her. By shaking her hands like she had, Missy had sealed her own fate. Burns pitted her gown, aged flesh burning underneath, each marking another nail in her resurrection.

'Quick, Adam,' Elle said. 'Turn her. We still have time.'

'No,' Adam said, watching the spectacle unfold in horror. 'I can't. I won't. It's over.' He turned to Lucy as though he was about to offer some kind of apology, but stopped himself.

Elle stepped forward, holding her hand out to her companion but falling short of contact. Missy moaned, sliding down the stone casket, leaving a groove within the thick stone that bubbled away even after her touch. She fell to the floor beneath it, moaning, weeping.

'Elle,' she said, the word barely making it past her sobs. 'I didn't want it to go like this.'

'I know,' Elle said, crouching before her, tenderness in her voice. 'I'm sorry. It's my fault. I never should have trusted a vampire.' She shot Adam a look of pure hatred, and Lucy realised they were far from clear of this thing.

'I love you, Elle,' Missy said, even as the flesh of her lips fell away. She was so small, so frail, dying what looked a horrible death; but Lucy couldn't quite bring herself to empathy, nor did she feel the normal compulsion to intervene, to save the old witch.

Within the stone coffin, something thudded.

Where Missy's acidic freakout had burned rivets in the stone, tiny cracks and gaps appearing along their surface. Lucy looked at the coffin anew. All this time they'd been talking about the Countess's remains, but this box, this was no ordinary coffin. Nearly seven centuries into its life, it looked more like...

A prison.

Fingers appeared at one crack, or at least, what may once have been fingers. Now more like pure white leather stretched over bone. They scratched and clawed at the hole, making it bigger, fussing and worrying until the hole was the size of an orange. Whatever was in there, it didn't lack for strength.

Thudding sounds came from inside, not that Elle paid attention to them. She was too busy weeping at the body of her friend.

The coffin above her shattered, which finally drew her attention. Too late. Out rose a figure, a horrific vision of wasted flesh and bone, eyes like sunken pits, hair dank and limp black plastered over what remained of the face. It moved with raw power and speed, gripping Elle by the throat and lifting her up in a fluid movement so graceful and powerful it took the witch entirely by surprise. Before Elle could react, the creature's mouth closed onto her throat, tearing it open and drinking deep, tearing the artery so severely the body expelled blood faster than the mouth of the newly released Countess could keep up.

Lucy looked behind her, wondering if the witch's death might undo her magic, bring back the door that would allow her to flee into whatever alternate hell was happening behind them. But no door came, even as the witch's eyes turned glassy with death and her body dropped to the floor.

Countess Bathory transformed before her eyes, flesh filling out, eyes sparking with red fire, skin flushing with colour. The nose turned from a thin outcropping of bone to a full Roman hook. She turned to Lucy and smiled.

'Éhező,' she said, the voice like sand moving over concrete.

39

CATHEDRALS

Before the grinning ancient vampire could launch at Lucy, Adam stepped between them.

'Your worship,' he said, keeping his head bowed.

The Countess stopped, looking at Adam as though a bug had stepped in front of her.

'Ki vagy te?' the countess replied.

'English, Countess,' Adam replied. 'Remember?'

The puzzled look on her face intensified. She looked almost human, the witch's blood restoring her to something she'd not been for hundreds of years. The tattered funeral clothes they had buried her in barely concealed the curves of her body as it grew back to normality.

'English?' she said, her voice heavily accented.

'Yes, Countess,' Adam replied. 'Do you remember? You learned while your husband Ferenc was in Vienna.'

'Ferenc?' she replied, as though the word filled her mouth for the first time. She looked around her. 'How long has been?' she asked, the words coming in halting, broken sounds.

'Four hundred years,' Adam said. 'Since your final capture and imprisonment.'

She stared at her hands, and at Adam. 'You have saved me?'

'You have saved yourself, Countess.'

'Hungry.'

'I know.'

Bathory looked up at Lucy. 'Eat.'

'No, Countess,' Adam said. 'She is mine. Remember the countenance. These are the rules you set for us, or so legend has it.'

Bathory hissed, but made no further move, looking again at her hands in wonder.

'I searched for you,' Adam said, moving closer to the Countess. 'For half a century I looked. Your legend amongst our kind is unparalleled. Your writings, your deeds — infamous. Since you have gone, we have lurked in the shadows, without leadership, without your wisdom.'

'The council?' she asked.

'It did not survive you. All that did was fairy tale and myth. Folklore. Ghosts in the shadows the humans used to entertain themselves.'

'Who is this... vitch?' she said, gesturing to the ground.

'She tried to bring you back. You must forgive us. The legends of your passing were quite clear — you were killed, and the body burned. They thought resurrection the only way. We looked for remains, anything we might use to bring you back. Witchcraft. Elle had an idea to bring back your essence, join it with that of a witch, and place it in the body of a newly born vampire.'

The Countess spat on the body by her feet, turned and spat at the other dead witch.

'It matters not,' she said dismissively. 'I am finally free.' She looked Adam up and down like a slab of meat. 'It has been five hundred years, and people still know of me?'

If Lucy weren't so utterly terrified she might have had to stifle a laugh. Fame was the universal desire, then? Go back five hundred years to Hungarian nobility and deep down, everyone wanted to be famous.

'Mostly people know you because of a film that tied you to a fictional character,' Lucy said, forgetting for a second the danger she was in. The look that Bathory flashed her reminded her soon enough.

'What is she talking about?'

'A writer, English,' Adam replied, almost apologetically. 'A few hundred years ago, he wrote a novel about our kind, Dracula. It outed us to the world. There was talk you were the inspiration, and you were sometimes called Countess Dracula.'

'It's not even a brilliant film,' Lucy couldn't help but add.

'It's a brilliant film,' Adam replied.

'This one is yours?' she said, voice dripping with disdain.

'She is.'

Before Lucy could react, Bathory crossed the gap between them, her thin bony hand around Lucy's throat, pushing her against the wall.

'Let me have her,' Bathory said.

'She is mine,' Adam said.

'But I wish to drink of her,' she pouted.

'She is mine,' Adam replied, a little more steel in her voice.

Bathory shrugged and put her down. Lucy dropped to the floor.

'Come,' Bathory said, and walked to the far wall, where the door should have been, but wasn't. She cast her eye over it, reached out, and pulled on the handle of the door that actually was there. Lucy's brain skipped over it for a second — there was no reveal, no smoke clearing. There wasn't a door there, but there was, at the same time. Bathory opened Schrödinger's door and stepped through.

Adam followed. Lucy thought for a second she might stay there, wait for this insanity to die down and go home. She'd had enough. She was done.

Except an incredibly powerful, centuries old psychopathic vampire had returned from the grave. In her city. In a room building full of people. She had to do something. And she wasn't sure the door wouldn't disappear the minute it closed and trap her in there forever.

She followed the two vampires back out into the hallway, which had been redecorated with arterial blood splatter. The candles burned down to their wicks and the surrounding corridor was full of bodies.

Lucy's heart sank. Dozens were dead at the hands of Lidia, Boris, Benjamin, and the others. Once it became clear they weren't getting out, and they weren't getting their hands on the witches, they turned to what they knew to do. There was no obvious sign of them still here, but they must be, unless they'd punched a hole through Elle's magic. Maybe it was the most fitting end to this — for these vampires to be trapped for eternity in a York townhouse by two witches who died before their magic did.

Sure, she'd be the only remaining food source, and would die an insanely unpleasant death, but there'd be some satisfaction in that.

How long would Adam protect her? And how much did she want the protection of a man willing to decant two other women into her body without so much as a please or thank you?

'There are others here?' Bathory asked. She felt the air like it had signals. Perhaps she had some of her own magic, or maybe she was batshit crazy. Then again, the floor was full of corpses with torn necks — it wasn't the hardest intellectual leap to make.

Walking back through to the main atrium, the doors were still barred, although their defenders lay dead next to them. The heavy wood showed signs of damage from where the vampires had attempted escape, but they'd held firm. There were more bodies piled up in a heap. Some charred, some bitten, all dead.

There was nobody in the room left alive or undead, but from around the house they heard shattering sounds, as though the place were being turned over by robbers with little in the way of subtlety.

'In here!' someone shouted from upstairs. The Countess and Adam headed up the stairs, while Lucy hung back. If they were smashing vases up there, they might hit upon the right one and free her, and if that happened, a few seconds' head-start might be enough for her to make it out of this alive.

Halfway up the stairs, the Countess stopped, turning back to Lucy. 'Come, human.' She turned away. 'Never know when might need a good human.'

Adam didn't protest, so Lucy made her way up slowly, hoping to hang back far enough to be forgotten.

At the top of the stairs, the extent of the destruction became apparent. Broken husks of every form of pottery lay about the place. Some were the tiny magical vials she was familiar with, others huge heavy vases and ceramics destroyed for good measure.

Boris came charging out of a bedroom, two tiny vases in his hands. Throwing them to the ground, he watched them shatter with a look of utter frustration on his face, disgust that a vampire of his standing was reduced to this. He looked up and saw the woman in tattered rags moving toward him.

'Who the fuck?' he asked.

Grinning, Countess Bathory ran toward him, sliding a foot out to his chin as she came close, before pivoting and bringing the other leg up to meet Boris's face. The sudden force of it felled Boris like a dead weight, his head slamming against the bannister, shattering it. The burly vampire came within inches of tumbling through the broken wood to the staircase below, where he would have missed Lucy by inches, but he came to with scarcely a second to spare. Face red with anger, he clambered — with little grace — to his feet, and turned to face the woman, who watched him with an amused glance.

'I'm going to rip your...'

'Wait!' came a voice behind him. Lidia emerged from the shadows of another bedroom, hands held out in front of her. Her eyes were fixed on the Countess, but flicked to Adam, who wore a stupid grin. 'Is this?'

Adam's grin matched Lidia's. 'No witchcraft required. She was in there the whole time, waiting to be freed.'

Boris's rage evaporated in a second. 'Countess?' he asked.

'I am your Countess,' Bathory replied, a rictus grin stretching over that not-yet-quite-human maw. 'Oh, but you are all children.'

Boris got to one knee, and Lidia did the same. Adam hung back, not getting to his knees but maintaining the correct height at the top of the stairs. Lucy hung back further, not about to get down on one knee.

Vampires wandered out of the other bedrooms, five more, each taking their place kneeling at the Countess's feet. Bathory drank in the adulation with a wry smile and beckoned them to stand.

'My descendants,' she said, gesturing around at each, looking somewhat less than majestic in her ruined burial rags, but not letting that stop her. 'Half a century ago, I embraced immortality for the same reason we all do. The desire for eternal life is one mortals cling to, through their religions and their quests for infamy. We are the only ones who get to enjoy the fruits of that desire... even locked inside a coffin.'

This brought about some chuckles from the assembled vampires. Lucy was not moved to join them; they might remember her existence. She'd be dead before she reached the bottom of the stairs. She doubted Adam's claim over her would wash with Borisand the others.

The Countess continued. 'I have returned. Not my full strength, but it's amazing vhat vitch blood will do. I have magic coursing through my veins, and I will bring down the barriers holding us here.'

She soaked in the cheers of approval from her audience, and stepped forward to speak to them in more hushed tones. 'I slept.

Long years broken only by pain, thirst, hunger. Wishing an end to my life. Desperate, pathetic. I heard whispers, thought long about what needed to be done, if I ever knew freedom again. Too long have we lived in the darkness of the mortal world. It is time to take our rightful place at the head of this new world.' Her voice rose to a crescendo, and the cheers of the vampires she addressed grew louder. All, that was, except Adam.

'Countess,' Adam said, behind her. 'For half a century, I searched for you, believing you to be the source of our power. You, more than most, know the folly of living beyond the power we can cast over the mortal world.'

She scoffed and turned to the others. 'This one,' she said, 'is a hound who thinks himself a bear. I asked him to share his human with his Countess. He refused.'

Boris scoffed. 'Not for the first time.'

Bathory shook her head, and walked back toward Adam, who bristled but made no move away from her. 'He is weak. If this is what we have become, no wonder you hide in witch's houses, pining for the power you've always had inside.'

'You know nothing of this world,' Adam said. 'Five hundred years has given them advances and weapons you could not dream of.'

'It has also made them soft and lazy,' Lidia chimed in. 'You know what she says is true, Adam. You used to believe it, too. Join us.'

'This one is weak, too,' Boris said, pointing to Lidia. 'She let a witch burn her partner to ashes in front of her eyes.'

Lidia's jaw tensed. 'I did it for her,' she said. 'We need her more than we needed him. He sacrificed himself for the cause.'

'Bull...'

'Enough,' Bathory barked. 'You,' she said, pointing to one vampire who had yet to speak, or even look up. 'Go to the vitch's chamber. Find me clothes.'

He scurried off.

'You,' she said to Boris. 'You are strong. I like you. You will serve me.'

Boris beamed, as the other vampire returned with a pair of jeans and a sweater, both entirely too pedestrian to house an un-living legend. Bathory cast off her rags in a fluid movement, revealing her figure to be stocky but firm. She was around the same height as Elle, but stared at the witch's jeans as though handed a cup of butter to wear.

'You...' Lidia said, miming pulling on jeans. Bathory managed to get them on, but they were too small. Her minion rushed back into the room, and came back with a flowing dress, flowery and utterly at odds with Bathory's personality. She took it with better grace than the jeans, however, and pulled it over her head, finding it a better fit.

During this whole spectacle, Adam tried to catch Lucy's eye a few times, but she didn't much feel like catching his back. She was still too angry with him, the man more than willing to sacrifice her for some ancient psychopath. No, not a man, she remembered. A vampire. One who might not share his kind's insane blood lust, but a vampire nonetheless. No amount of him being good in bed could make up for that.

'Better,' Bathory said, admiring herself in a mirror at the end of the hallway. 'Adam, you have but one chance to prove yourself to me. Give me your pet, let me drink from her. I want to bathe in her blood.'

'No,' Adam growled, and Lucy finally understood the message of his searching eyes. They were telling her to run.

'Too bad,' Bathory said. 'You could have been interesting.' She turned to Boris. 'Kill him and bring me the girl.'

40

THE LAST TIME

Violence erupted behind Lucy, even as she turned to run back down the stairs. Adam screamed, a howl of pain that tore at the part of her that still held the tiniest flicker for him, but there was no time for that. The main hallway was locked up, she knew, and there was the entrance to the magic room, but she didn't want to go in there, not if she didn't have to. Bathory had already showed her ability to move through those walls, so when they got past Adam to get to her, she should be somewhere else entirely. The corridor leading off from the hallway deeper into the house was still open, so she went for that. It led into a library room, one where magical pots lined the shelves in front of books that looked as old as the Countess herself.

Adam's scream filled the air. Full of rage, but pain, too. There was no way he could stand his ground for long against all of them. It hit her that he'd sacrificed himself for her. An immortal, turning his back on eternal life. For her.

Fuck him.

Eyeing up the shelf, she wondered whether one of these might be the magical key to pick the lock left in place by the dead witches. It occurred to her there were other ways in and out of a building.

Through into the next room, the splendour and majesty of the rest of the house gave way to a drab utility room, home to washing machines and tumble dryers older than Lucy herself.

And — crucially — a window of frosted glass. Under the glass sat a small table and a single chair. A dog-eared paperback, along with an ashtray filled with cigarette butts. This was someone's little bolt hole — whoever came in to clean up after a pair of century-old witches.

Somewhere, perhaps, they'd never think to protect.

Lucy closed the door behind her, sliding the bolt across. The chair tucked under the table was plastic and uncomfort-able-looking, but with a thick, round, metal base. Behind her, the wooden door rattled as someone tried to make their way through it. Whatever efforts Adam had made to hold the Countess and her minions off, it hadn't worked. Grabbing the plastic end of the chair, Lucy picked it up, swinging the base at the frosted glass.

The window shattered as the hammering at the door behind her intensified. Using the metal base to clear as much of the glass as she could, she climbed up onto the table, levered herself carefully across the remaining jagged shards, and out onto the terrace.

Fresh air.

The door to the utility room burst open in a shower of splinters. Boris bolted through the door at pace — his hand out, grabbing Lucy by the wrist even as she pulled it through. Panicking, she jerked back, slamming the protruding arm against the jagged glass lining the bottom of the pane.

Boris roared as blood spurted from an ugly wound in his forearm, gushing down the brickwork. He let go of Lucy's arm, sending her sprawling down to the ground. She landed in the broken glass of the window with a painful, spiked thump. As she tried to get back to her feet, Boris's thick head came through the window, hissing, fangs out. Without thinking, and before he could get his already healing arm out to reach for her once more, she grabbed his hair and slammed his head hard against the frame.

Ragged glass cut deep into the side of Boris's neck, tearing at the skin and gushing yet more vampire blood over Lucy. Paying the blood and the howls of pain coming from the head she still held in her hand no mind even as Boris tried to pull himself back inside, she tightened her grip on his hair and pulled downward, impaling the vampire's throat on more ragged glass.

The body shuddered violently before going limp. Thick black poured from the wound as though propelled from Boris's body. Adrenaline coursing through Lucy's heart, she couldn't quite bring herself to let go of the tuft of hair until she heard voices coming down the corridor in the house.

Letting go, the body slid back inside, falling to the floor with a thud. Lucy picked herself back up and ran out into the back garden. She glanced at the back fence, wondering if she should attempt to climb it once more — her hands hurt at the thought of it. Running across the terrace, she rounded the house, through the back gate, and out onto the street.

Fishing in her pocket, she pulled out her phone. No signal. Damn.

The street looked deserted. It was closer to morning than to midnight, but far enough away she couldn't rely on the cover of sunlight anytime soon.

Once again, she was covered in blood. At this time of night, she should be able to pass through town relatively unnoticed, but where the hell to go?

The police. It was the last road left open to her. No matter what happened, this ended with her sat across from a detective, trying to explain the unexplainable. Why not get it over with and get herself in a nice secure building full of weapons and trained policemen and women?

With one last look around to check the coast was clear, she set off. But no sooner was one foot in front of the other than a hand landed on her shoulder, pulling her around.

Bathory. The ancient vampire stood before her, eyes glowing red. A long gouge ran down her face, healing before Lucy's eyes, leaving a long smear the colour of her lips.

'Where do you think you're going?' Bathory asked. Picking Lucy up as effortlessly as if she were a can of beans, she threw her at a parked car.

Lucy crashed onto the bonnet of a Fiat Punto, sending a howl of pain through her back that spread through the rest of her like a wave. She screamed, hoping the sound might draw someone's attention long enough to call the police, until she remembered the magical cloak drawn around the house.

'Peasant,' Bathory hissed, hauling Lucy back to her feet and pushing her into the road. 'Looking for your protector? Gone. I ripped his throat out, traitorous little sore that he was. But you know what was most disappointing?' She pushed Lucy back on her arse, shoving her further into the centre of the street. 'Seeing one of us snivelling after you. This is not how it is, Lucy of York.'

She stopped, admiring the car next to her. She looked around, as though seeing the world for the first time, her hand going up to shield herself from the streetlight. Of course, Lucy thought. The witch's house had candlelight, and this woman went into a coffin hundreds of years before electricity was even a thing.

Bathory smiled. 'Much has changed,' she said, leaning over Lucy as she scrabbled backward to the kerb.

Across the road, the other vampires assembled, hanging back and watching their new leader. Lidia stood nominally in charge, while Benjamin was conspicuous by his absence. That was something, Lucy thought. She doubted he'd take the time to have a chat with her over the death of his brother — he'd kill her in a heartbeat. Maybe Adam had taken care of the problem for her. Not that it mattered, of course — once Bathory finished toying with her, she'd be dead either way.

Unless...

Movement caught the corner of her eye, and having clocked its source, Lucy tried desperately not to look in its direction.

'You know,' Lucy said, moving herself up onto the kerb, 'many things have happened since you went away.'

'I can imagine,' Bathory said, grinning at Lucy.

'There's one thing in particular I'm a big fan of.'

'Oh?' Bathory asked, playfully. 'What's that?'

'Trucks.'

In the approaching ambulance, its lights off as it crawled up the street, Adrian hit the accelerator, the lights, and the horn at the same time.

Startled, Bathory turned, hissing at the approaching hulk of green metal, light, and sound.

When it hit, it wasn't with the typical bounce that happened with most traffic collisions. That happened when the driver slows down, tries to minimise the impact, that human instinct of slamming on the brakes. Inside the cab, Adrian had no such compassion in mind, speeding up as Bathory hit the front corner of the ambulance, going under the wheel in a crunch of bones, sinew, metal and rubber.

By the time he finally hit the brakes, twenty or thirty metres later, Bathory's body had been dragged the whole way under the wheels, leaving an ugly dark smear along the road.

Lucy was left at the kerbside, staring down the road, when she remembered there was more than one vampire to worry about. Lidia and the others could take their vengeance out on her and Adrian for mowing down their new leader. But when she looked back across the road, they were gone. Getting awkwardly to her feet, she ran down the street to the ambulance, fearing a sudden ambush.

The doors to the ambulance opened, and out jumped Pawel. Adrian followed a moment later. 'Please tell me that was a vampire, not a person,' he shouted to her, breathlessly.

She nodded, sobbing, picking herself up and running to her friend, taking him into an enormous hug that highlighted the various cuts and bruises she'd picked up. She barely indulged a second, however, before checking under the wheels. Bathory was under there, alright, or what remained of her. There was a formless lump of flesh and dress, but it no longer represented anything close to life.

It was over.

'How did you find me?' she asked her two rescuers, who stood looking around them with some dawning mix of horror and fear.

'You mean, at the house I've already had to rescue you from once before?' Adrian laughed. 'Pawel told me he'd spoken to you at the start of our shift, and I knew you'd get yourself in more trouble. Figured it'd be good to be on hand. You want to tell me what the hell's just happened?'

She stared back at the house. 'I'll tell you everything, I promise. But first I need to go back in there.'

'What?'

'It's okay,' she said. 'The bad guys have gone.' Somehow, Lucy could... feel... that Lidia and the other vampires were no longer anywhere nearby. She suspected they wanted no more part of this shambles. She knew how they felt. 'Grab the kit bags,' she said. 'There may be people alive in there.'

41

WHERE I END AND YOU BEGIN

Crossing the threshold of the house was almost impossible — every nerve ending in Lucy's body screamed to turn and run. The kitchen area leading from the back garden was still clear of the violence beyond — this detritus was of the party, before it moved deeper inside. The doors through to the main atrium were still closed, but whatever magics had bolted them closed were long gone. She pushed them open, revealing the carnage beyond. Bodies lay everywhere — dozens of them. Behind her, Pawel and Adrian stood in open-mouthed horror while she scanned the area. No vampires, not even Marcus's carcass. She bet if she checked the rear exit where she'd killed Boris, she'd find his body gone. Lidia and the others hadn't skulked away in defeat; they'd gone into clean up mode. If that was the case, they'd have to tread carefully.

Adrian and Pawel went straight into work mode, moving slowly and methodically through the room, checking pulses. Lucy had her own task — she looked around desperately for a sign of the man who'd saved her life.

'Lucy,' Adrian called, as she turned over a man of a similar build to Adam, but not the same face. 'Over here.'

She picked her way over to him and found her friend kneeling over Adam. His face was badly broken, his skull fractured, at least. Blood covered his top, and next to him was a slick pool of dark blood, presumably from whichever other vampire was on the other side of this fight.

'I'm sorry,' Adam said, the world foaming out of his mouth in a bubble of blood. 'Lucy, I'm so sorry.'

'Shhh,' Lucy said, leaning over him. Twin impulses fired inside her. She wanted to drive a stake through his heart, watch the light die from his eyes, to burn the body after, to be sure. But she also wanted to carry him out to the ambulance, take him home, curl up in bed with him and nurse him back to health.

He held a shard of wood in his hand, a broken-off chair leg stained red in whatever previous attack he'd used it in. She prised it out, staring at it in her hand.

'Do it,' he said. The words were a struggle.

She held the stake in front of her and closed her eyes. He'd wronged her — more than wronged her.

She let the stake fall from her hands. Her eyes locked with Adam's. 'Adrian, bring me your bag,' she said.

'What are you...' Adam started, but the pain overwhelmed him, and he lay grimacing.

Adrian handed the jump-bag over, and she fished out a scalpel. 'Hold still,' Lucy said, and sliced into the flesh of her palm.

'Lucy,' Adrian protested, but she ignored him.

She held the dripping palm over Adam's mouth, the droplets spilling into his mouth. He gargled as he tried to swallow, but the blood hit his system and he reached up, pulling down her wrist and taking the flesh of her palm in his mouth.

The pain was excruciating, but she had to marvel at how quick the effect was. The cracked skull so visible under his skin filled out, reforming before her eyes.

He took more and more blood, enough to set her heart pounding. His teeth sunk deeper into the flesh above her wrist, and panic filled her as she realised could hit a major artery, that he could drain her completely.

'Stop,' she said, ready to raise up the stake again.

He pulled away immediately, gasping, teeth out. Her palm looked wrecked, flesh and tendons ripped and torn. Adam sat up, collected a drop of his own blood from his cheek, and smeared it on the wound like a balm. The flesh healed almost immediately.

'The balance of vampire blood within you is already too high,' he said, his voice calm. 'You should get a blood transfusion. I can assist with that.'

'Thanks,' she said, awkwardly.

'Thank you,' Adam said, staring deep into her eyes. 'I did not deserve it, but I'll do my best to earn it.'

'Doesn't mean I forgive you,' Lucy said, getting back to her feet. 'But it's a start.'

'There's nobody left alive,' Adrian said. 'What do we do now?'

'We phone the police,' Lucy said.

'But...' Adrian said.

'No,' Lucy countered. She wasn't in the mood to discuss it. 'This has always ended up with me trying to explain this to a room full of detectives. Might as well get it over and done. Otherwise, this will never be over and done. You came here looking for me, and that's all you have to say. Call it in.'

Pawel took a deep breath. 'Unit fifteen calling in, we have a code two...'

'Let's go wait outside,' Lucy said, helping Adam to his feet. They walked out of the house, into the chilly night air. Neither of them said a word, nor looked at each other. A numbness crept over her. She knew saving Adam was the right decision, somehow, but she wasn't sure she'd ever want to see him again.

Outside, they stepped out into the street. All was calm and normal, save for the huge green ambulance in the street, blocking the road. She doubted anyone would much care at this time in the morning. Especially when most of the neighbours were probably piled up amongst the dead in the house behind her.

She peered underneath — as she suspected, the mass of ex-vampire under the wheels was gone, too.

'I have to go,' Adam said, making no move to do so. 'Thank you,' he said once more, but there was a sadness there, too.

She sat down on the kerb. When she looked to her left, he'd gone, leaving her alone in the street, the approaching blue lights in the distance heralding the last obstacle to being done with this.

42

AFTERMATH

The cell was cold and the lighting stark. They'd turned the lights out when Lucy got here, which allowed her a few hours of fitful and restless sleep. The lights came back an hour ago, rousing her from whatever hell her mind had running through it. Ever since, she'd been staring at the walls.

A clanking sound reverberated around the cell. A small hole appeared in the door. 'Breakfast?' asked a guard.

'No thanks,' she said. She didn't think she could keep anything down.

The hole closed back up.

In the next few hours, she would have to sit opposite a police officer and try to explain the last few days to them. Or, she'd have to lie, weave some kind of web so intricate they were bound to catch her in it.

They'd taken her clothes, so she was in a kind of smock, much too big for her. It was like lying in a billowing paper tent, and she felt practically naked. At least there was nobody to watch her discomfort, aside from the CCTV eye in the room's corner, no doubt being scrutinised as she lay there for signs of guilt.

Another hour passed, enough time for her back to hurt from hunching over on the thin mattress. She'd been in these cells a few times, usually patching up someone who'd had a fight, or tending to someone who'd passed out and couldn't be revived.

They scared her a little, and being inside one with the door locked wasn't any better than she'd imagined.

The clink of the lock rang out, and the door opened, revealing a duty sergeant who looked tremendously bored. 'Interview,' he said, barely looking up at her.

She slipped on the slippers they'd provided, trying not to think how many feet had been in them before hers, and trudged after him. It always surprised her they let suspects walk behind them, but they never seemed concerned. She sure as hell never let a drunk patient get behind her, but she supposed this place was a lot different than the streets. You pull some shit in here and you were going down hard.

They ushered her into an interview room and showed her to the other side of the desk. She sat down, looking at the tape recorder, trying to control the shaking in her knee.

The door opened again, a man came in. He didn't look much like a cop — he wore an ill-fitting suit, had a bald head and a wicked smile.

'Lucy, right?' he said, but before she could confirm, he was already talking again. 'Okay, here's the deal. Say nothing other than no comment to any question that isn't your name. I've looked over what they've given me and you're going to be out of here in a few hours. Okay?'

'I...'

'Don't worry, it's going to be fine.'

'Who are you?'

'Alex,' he replied, with the air of someone who expected her to know it already. 'Your friend, Adam, he arranged for me to come help you.'

She chuckled. Of course he did. He wouldn't want her blabbing about his existence to the police.'Oh,' she said.

He joined her across the table, barely looking at her. 'You work for him much?' she asked, more to break the silence than anything else.

He shrugged. 'Occasionally. I see you have a habit of filling uncomfortable silences. Don't do that. No comment, and only when addressed, okay?'

She looked him over again. It wasn't the suit that was ill-fitting; it was the frame. The no doubt expensive tailor had done their best with what they were working with. But it was expensive. As was the watch that dangled off the man's wrist. Not ostentatious, but lovely.

'Okay.'

The door opened again, and lawyer Alex straightened his his seat. Suddenly the suit no longer seemed ill-fitting. Two officers came through the door, both looking perplexed at the sudden company she had. Neither of them said a word, but Alex smiled at their discomfort.

'DI Turner and Detective Laghari, interviewing Lucy Knowles in relation to events on December 13th,' the younger one said. Asian, her dark hair tied back into a bun framing a pretty, oval face. Turner was overweight and balding, sweat beading on his forehead already, his breath heavy and laboured. 'And you are?'

'Alex Temple, QC,' he said, handing over a card that seemed to come from inside his sleeve. 'I've looked at your discovery, Detectives, and I'm not hugely impressed. What exactly is it you intend to charge my client with?'

'We'll get to that,' Laghari said, opening her notes. 'But first, Lucy, if you could run us through the events of last night, that'd be a big help.'

Lucy looked at Alex, who raised his eyebrow. 'No comment,' she said.

A weary look passed between the detectives.

Their questions came thick and fast for a good two hours, each one met with a firm No Comment from her or an objecting word from lawyer Alex. He was good, and she realised after a while that they had no evidence tying her to the events of the last few days, save from knowing she'd been there. There was no evidence at her flat, thanks to the magics still in place. The hospital CCTV had been wiped on the day Cain was taken, and there was no trace of her at the witch's house. All rather miraculously. Vampires sure were efficient. It clearly put the DI out that she'd embarrassed him, but without her engagement, all he could do was scowl.

'Interview terminated at 08.30,' Laghari said, finally, pressing stop on the recorder.

'A moment with my client, if you don't mind,' Alex said.

'Sure,' Laghari said.

'Good job,' Alex said, putting his notes back in his briefcase. 'Say nothing more to them, even in passing. They've got...' — he checked his expensive watch — 'ten hours before they can charge you, but they won't. Adam's already put me up in a hotel for the rest of the day, so you rest up and I'll be here to get you out in a few hours. If they do it while I'm not here, say nothing. No questions. No chit chat. Don't agree to remand or bail if they offer. If they do, tell them to call me first. Okay?'

She felt grubby at the whole affair. She'd come here to unburden, but she guessed it wasn't on the cards. What was worst about it was how relieved she was.

Alex left her, and they guided her back to her cell, where she stayed for ten minutes before Detective Laghari came back.

'We're releasing you without charge,' she said, sounding half disappointed, half resigned.

Lucy bit back the urge to ask why, and got up from her bed.

'Your clothes are still being tested,' Laghari continued. 'Take these.'

She handed over a pair of the cheapest jogging bottoms Lucy had ever seen, and a black vest top, which Lucy took gingerly. It would be better than leaving in the tent, she supposed.

'You can wash them and return them,' Laghari said.

'Thanks.'

With no further chat between them, Lucy dressed, and they walked through to the front desk, where there were surprisingly few formalities. No caution. No licence to be bailed. She had to hand it to Alex. He was thorough.

There was no sign of the snake-oil salesman, however, she as she stumbled out the door into the bright light of a cool winter morning.

'That's a new look on you,' a voice called out, as her eyes adjusted to the bright. Adrian. He was waiting at the bottom of the stairs, no longer in his uniform, leaning against his battered Nissan Micra.

'I'm going incognito,' she said. 'What are you doing here?'

He laughed. 'Waiting for you. Adam told me you'd be out sooner rather than later. Come on, I'll take you home.'

She rushed down the steps and gave her friend a hug. He hugged her back; the relief pouring out of each of them. Lucy had to wipe away tears as she pulled away and gave a little laugh. Neither of them said anything about it, but in that moment were a million unsaid words of relief, gratitude, and joy to be through the entire ordeal, alive.

Once inside the car, Adrian looked at her. 'There's something I need to explain,' he said. 'For the last few weeks I've been driving around with this in my pocket.' He pulled out an envelope, folded many times over. She had to stifle a laugh. It was even the same sort of envelope as the one she'd been carrying around. 'I've been thinking of leaving,' he said.

She smiled. 'Would it surprise you to know that I've been feeling the exact same way?' she asked.

He raised an eyebrow. 'Seriously?'

'Seriously.'

'Wow. Well, I figured I'd tell you, not least because that's why me and Dan haven't been, um, getting along, recently.'

'He wants you to quit?'

Adrian laughed. 'God no. After everything we went through while I was doing my exams and training? Besides, he's under threat of redundancy from the theatre, so we can't really afford for me to... anyway. I wanted to tell you, because I've decided to stay, after all.'

She frowned. 'Me too.'

'Oh thank God. I was going to say that you were what's keeping me in the job, or one of the things, anyway. I don't know what I'd have done if you quit, after all that.' He gave a little chuckle, and stared down at the envelope in his hand. He tucked it back into his pocket, and started the car.

They said little more on the drive from the police station, Lucy preferring to stare out at the city as it crawled by, bathed in sunlight and free of monsters. She thought at first they were heading to Adrian's. She daydreamed about cuddling up with Jones on their spare bed and sleeping for a thousand years, until she realised they were heading back to her flat — somewhere she didn't want to go, but she guessed she didn't have a choice.

Adrian pulled up outside alongside a battered white van. Three burly men stood outside it, smoking against the wall of her building. All three looked vaguely familiar, but Lucy was too tired to place them. They got out; Adrian waving to them as they passed, so she offered a weak smile and followed Adrian into the building.

'Are you okay?' Adrian asked, as they trudged up the stairs.

'I'm tired,' she said.

'Don't worry,' he said. 'I've spoken to the shift commander, and he's agreed to switch your shifts around for a few days. And Adam's got you a doctor's note for the last few days. He's pretty resourceful.'

She said nothing in return, not sure she was pleased with how indebted to the vampire who'd tried to kill her she was becoming.

Once they reached her floor, she looked at Mrs Patel's door with longing. The sounds of a child playing came from within, and her eyes welled up.

'Come on,' Adrian said, leading her into her own flat, still cloaked in what may well be the last vestiges of the magic of two dead witches.

Inside, Pawel and Adam stood, along with Dan, who gave Adrian a warm enough smile that it warmed Lucy's heart a little. Pawel held Jones, who purred amiably as the big Polish man stroked her. As soon as the big tabby saw her, however, he escaped and ran to her, fussing around her feet until she picked him up, not even protesting as she gave him a little squeeze. He didn't even seem perturbed by the presence of Adam.

'Hello, shithead,' she said, as the cat purred in her arms. 'Hey, Pawel,' she added, as he gave her a warm smile. 'Are those your housemates downstairs?'

'Yes. We might need them in a minute. Up to you.'

'Gentlemen,' Adam said, his low voice like butter on a warm bagel. 'Could you give me a minute?'

Pawel shot her a look. She nodded. Whatever else, she didn't feel under threat from Adam. Not anymore. The three men moved back out into the hall, pulling the door closed behind them, leaving Adam and Lucy alone, standing in uncomfortable silence.

'I would say I owe you an apology,' he said. 'But I don't think it would cover it.'

'It'd be a start,' she said.

'I'm sorry,' he said, and there was genuine sorrow in it. 'I would like to believe I wouldn't have let Elle go through with it. That I would have stopped her. But I am no longer so sure in myself.'

She frowned, stroking Jones. 'I went into that house thinking that, if nothing else, I could trust you. When you turned on me, it was like the entire world fell away. I'm an ordinary person, and

I was up against mystical forces I could scarcely have dreamed of a week ago. I trusted that you would support me, protect me.'

She sighed. 'And in the end, you did. I can't forget that moment of weakness, Adam, but I also remember what happened after.'

He crossed to her and took her hand. She surprised herself by letting him.

'Do not dare to call yourself ordinary,' he said. 'You brought down the most powerful coven in England. Killed vampires with a hundred times your physical strength. You have inner strength, Lucy. You are a beacon of light against the darkness in this world, and... I have not felt... connection with another being for a long time. I wasn't sure if that part of me had passed until I met you.'

She pulled her hand away, but looking into his eyes, she wanted nothing more than for him to lean and kiss her, no matter how angry she was.

'Adam...' she said.

'I know I have no chance of being with you,' he said. 'I understand the violation I have made against you. But you will always have my friendship, and my respect.'

She stepped back. 'Thank you,' she said.

Her step backward seemed to break the spell. He straightened up and gave her a half smile. 'We should bring the others in,' he said.

Adam opened the door. Both Adrian and Pawel gave her looks of curiosity, wanting no doubt to know what happened in here. She said nothing. She was so tired, and, frankly, a huge part of her wanted to go into the bedroom, lie down on the bed, and go to sleep.

Once they were inside, Adam picked up the small urn and held it out to Lucy. 'This spell,' he said, 'offers something you might not have realised. It is a spell designed to bring everything back to a fixed point, from before this happened. If you leave it here, it will extend to you. Over time, you will forget, and you will be able to put this away. It will not bring your neighbours back, but in time you'll forget they ever left. You will forget anything related to these magics. You will forget me.'

She took the urn, turning it over in her hands. It occurred to her how much she'd lost her fear of it. The last fear she had left was of walking out of her door and hearing the fake laughter of a dead child. She did not know whether the Patels could find peace while this existed. Nor if she could, either. What peace was there in ignorance? She knew things about the world, and about herself, she never knew possible.

She threw the pot against the floor, where it shattered in a puff of blue smoke. Immediately, the façade of normality disappeared, flickering away into reality. The broken door. The smeared blood in the corridor beyond. The dents in her wall, and the smashed mirror. Echoes of violence that already seemed like a distant memory.

Adrian stepped forward and took her hand, squeezing it. Dan stared around at the change, slack jawed. It was one thing hearing about magic, she guessed, and another entirely in seeing it for yourself.

Pawel took out his mobile and hit a number. 'Up you come, lads,' he said.

A sense of relief washed over Lucy, helped by Jones nuzzling into her, and Adrian continuing to squeeze her hand.

A minute later, the lift pinged, and out came Pawel's housemates, carrying pots of paint, tools, and cleaning equipment.

Lucy looked around at her friends, all ready to chip in and help her. 'Thank you,' she said.

Pawel smiled. 'Right,' he said. 'Lot's to do. Let's start with that door.'

She smiled back at her friends, this odd assortment of men and one creature of the night. Her hand went to her pocket and found the folded note that had been among her possessions back at the police station. The note that had been in her pocket for days now, the one to her boss, handing in her resignation. She wouldn't be needing that, either. Without opening it, she ripped it into pieces, letting them fall like confetti onto the floor. Adrian gave her a smile and took out his own note, tearing it up in the same fashion.

'Right then,' Lucy said. 'Let's get to work.'

LEAVE A REVIEW

I really hope you've enjoyed reading *Darkness Come Alive*.

If you did, the nicest thing you could do for me right now is to leave a review, on this or any of the books you've enjoyed. Reviews are absolutely crucial to discoverability, and social proof. If you could take a second to rate and review this at the store of your choice, I'd hugely appreciate it.

Thanks,

Paul

AUTHOR'S NOTE

I've always been drawn to the vampire. Of all the creatures of legend and lore, the vampire has always fascinated me, because what they represent is so unerringly, unforgivably human. They are the manifestations of our id, the promise of a world without consequence, without end. As a wise person once wrote: *'Sleep all day. Party all night. Never grow old. Never die. It's fun to be a vampire.'*

Throughout my life, there has always been a vampire mythos to suit my life at that time. As a child, I had the Count from *Sesame Street*, and the legend of *Dracula*. As I moved into reading more grown-up fare, *'Salem's Lot* was my true, brutal introduction to their kind. Then *The Lost Boys* made vampirism cooler than anything else on the planet. Anne Rice added the sexiness. As I got ready to leave home, *Buffy* was there, growing up alongside me.

As I started fussing around the idea that I wanted to be a writer, the first idea that came to me was a vampire story. I started writing it at the age of 19, and it was my first foray into something more than the short stories and abandoned screenplays that I had written to that point. It was about a vampire called Adam, a daywalker born in the midst of his mother's turning, a story that opened in the hospital with his birth.

I was maybe three chapters into writing it when I heard about a cool new vampire comic book movie coming out at the cinema.

It even had Wesley Snipes in it (at that point undeniably the coolest of the action megastars of the age) and so I popped along to the flea pit in Sunderland along with some friends to see *Blade* and watched in horror as the first three chapters of my nascent introduction to the world of novel writing were played out on the big screen. Possibly the worst example of cosmic coincidence I ever experienced.

The idea got shelved, and more ideas came and went over the years. It would be well over a decade before a story would really grab me and refuse to let go — my first book, Blood on the Motorway. But I always knew I'd circle back around to the vampire again, one day. When I did, it seemed only fair for the creature of my night to retain the name, Adam.

I've dedicated this to my Dad, who left us nearly two years ago, as I write this. He would have probably hated it, as someone who never really liked anything with beasts or creatures, spaceships or dragons. But he would have been immensely proud of me nonetheless. I miss him every day.

There are so many people I'd want to thank for this story, not least the creators of all this wonderful lore, from Bram Stoker on down: King, Rice, Schumacher, Newman, Harris, Whedon, Bigelow, Lindqvist. One of the great joys of playing in this sandbox is choosing which lore you're getting to use. I also want to say that I wouldn't have been able to make this story what it is now without the book *The Vampire: A New History* by Nick Groom. If you're interested in the facts and the fiction behind this lore, it's an indispensable read.

As always, all the love in the world to Ellen, Rose, and Jacob. Thanks for continuing to put up with all my nonsense.

GOT BLOOD?

An apocalyptic storm. A killer on the loose.
The battle for humanity's survival starts here.

START THE CHRONICLES

Plague. Murder. Unrest. Humanity's future looks far from bright.
The year is 2115, and Earth is dying. For Wyn, Lois, and Judd,
that's the least of their problems.

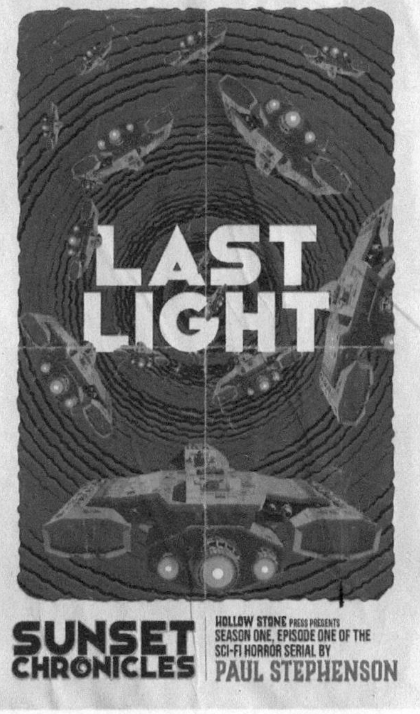

Get the first episode in the monthly sci-fi horror
serial that's guaranteed to knock your socks off...

SCAN ME

DARE YOU VENTURE INTO BLEAKWOOD?

WHAT TORE A HOLE IN THE WORLD?
CAN WE EVER GET IT BACK?

Find out in Bleakwood, the new horror podcast from the creator of Blood on the Motorway and The Sunset Chronicles

Created and narrated by Paul Stephenson and with stories by some of the most exciting voices in British modern Horror, subscribe to Bleakwood for a fresh story every month.

SCAN ME

About the Author

Paul Stephenson writes pulp fiction for the digital age. His first novel series – the apocalyptic *Blood on the Motorway* trilogy – has been an Amazon bestseller on both sides of the Atlantic. A former journalist, he has a diploma in Creative Writing from Oxford University.

His stories have been featured on the chart-topping horror podcasts, *The Other Stories* and *The Night's End*. His newest project, the ebook serial *The Sunset Chronicles*, is a dystopian sci-fi thriller that will delight and terrify fans of science fiction and horror alike. He is also the creator of the podcast *Bleakwood*, tales of terror from a mysterious English town, and one half of the *All Creatives Now* team, with fellow horror author, Kev Harrison.

He lives in England with his wife, two children, and one hellhound.

To keep up to date with his books, please visit his website PaulStephensonBooks.com

Also by Paul Stephenson

Blood on the Motorway

Blood on the Motorway

An apocalyptic storm. A killer on the loose. The battle for humanity's survival starts here.

Sleepwalk City

The fight for control has begun. Who will prevail in the battle for humanity's future in the pulse-quickening sequel to Blood on the Motorway?

A Final Storm

The sky is full of lights once more, and the survivors will need more than luck to get them through the coming storm. Who will survive, and who will thrive, in this heart-pounding finale to the Blood on the Motorway saga?

SUNSET CHRONICLES

Plague. Murder. Unrest. Humanity's future looks far from bright.

The year is 2107, and Earth is dying. For Wyn, Lois, and Judd, that's the least of their problems. Each holds a key to Earth's cure and humanity's survival in The Sunset Chronicles, the new sci-fi horror thrill-ride from Paul Stephenson, author of the bestselling British horror saga, Blood on the Motorway.

BLEAKWOOD

Introducing Bleakwood, a horror podcast from the creator of Blood on the Motorway and the Sunset Chronicles.

In the years since the fall, many of us have tried to find out why. To find what lead us here. But with so much of the old world gone, there are more questions than answers. What tore a hole in the world? Can we ever get it back?

But I think I've found something. A binder in the rubble. Don't ask me where. Full of stories about a little town called Bleakwood, stories that seem to show a way that....

They're not in any order, really. And I might be wrong. They might not have the answer. But I think it's in here.

A way back. To the before.

Listen, I'm just going to read them out, and you judge for yourself.